D0344399

GRAVEYARD FIELDS

GRAVEYARD FIELDS

A NOVEL

Steven Tingle

CROOKED
LANE

NEW YORK

Copyright © 2021 by Steven Tingle

Published in the United States by Crooked Lane Books, an imprint of The Quick Brown Fox & Company LLC.

Crooked Lane Books and its logo are trademarks of The Quick Brown Fox & Company LLC.

Library of Congress Catalog-in-Publication data available upon request.

ISBN (hardcover): 978-1-64385-686-5
ISBN (ebook): 978-1-64385-687-2

Cover design by Nicole Lecht

Printed in the United States.

www.crookedlanebooks.com

Crooked Lane Books
34 West 27th St., 10th Floor
New York, NY 10001

First Edition: August 2021

10 9 8 7 6 5 4 3 2 1

For Julian and Emily

Prologue

When my phone buzzed, I was sitting on a barstool at Claudia's on James Island. It was Laura. She said Greg had gotten another call, then jumped in his Yukon and taken off. My sister had been suspicious for a while, and I know suspicions are like herpes—once they show up, they never go away.

It was hard to hear what she was saying. The bar was busy with the regular low-rent crowd. James Island has a redneck tinge to it, and the place was full of big men with ball caps, goatees, and those jeans with elaborate white stitching on the pockets. But Claudia's had forty-five good beers on tap, so I was willing to ignore the alpha-male vibe.

I was drinking my second Dogfish Head 60 Minute IPA. Claudia had drawn the first one as soon as I walked in and it was on the bar waiting for me before my ass hit the stool. Being a regular has its benefits.

I set a cardboard coaster on top of my pint glass and stepped outside. There was a guy vaping just past the entrance. At first glance I thought he was trying to swallow a flashlight. I walked over to my Mercedes SUV, leaned against the bumper, and asked Laura for details.

"Greg just left," she said. "Where are you?"

It was a redundant question. I was at Claudia's almost every night.

"What's going on?"

"Greg should be passing by there any minute. Follow him. I want to know who she is."

Greg was a sergeant with the Charleston PD, my former employer. I'd told Laura sergeants are always on duty. Which means that now and

1

then they get called and have to go in and take care of shit. I told her this again, but she wasn't having it.

"Just follow him, Davis. Please do this for me."

Laura was convinced Greg was cheating on her. That his late-night calls weren't from work but from some woman who was probably younger, better built, and better in bed. The kind of woman who tore up the sheets in a silk teddy rather than snored and farted in a thread-bare T-shirt from the 2009 Cooper River Bridge run. I told Laura she was paranoid. Greg adored her. The idea of him having a side piece was ridiculous. But then again, ridiculous and true aren't mutually exclusive.

As Laura ranted, I watched the traffic flow on Folly Road, a busy four-lane that runs from Folly Beach through James Island and on to downtown Charleston. As if on cue, Greg's white GMC Yukon roared past, headed north toward downtown. I told Laura I had to go, then hopped in my Mercedes and pulled out into traffic. I felt bad about taking off without paying. But I felt worse about leaving half a pint of good beer sitting on the bar.

Traffic was unusually light but enough to give me cover. Not that I needed it. I knew Greg was headed to the police department on Lockwood Drive. It wasn't necessary to follow him. I could just roll up on my own, spot the Yukon in the station's lot, then call Laura to tell her I was right. But if I wasn't . . .

I was about a hundred yards behind Greg when he crossed the Ashley River and turned onto Lockwood without bothering to use his signal. By the time I closed the gap between our vehicles, Greg was just a few hundred feet from the police station's main entrance. He cruised right past it.

Five minutes later I'd given up trying to guess where Greg was headed and followed him across the Ravenel Bridge into Mount Pleasant. We were almost to Sullivan's Island when the Yukon turned left into a residential community. I caught the light, and it was a good minute before I made the turn. I couldn't see the Yukon and wondered if Greg had disappeared into one of the driveways that fringed both sides of the road.

After about a mile the residential area turned industrial and I saw a sign for a twenty-four-hour storage complex. It was one of those places where people store stuff they don't need but can't bring themselves to get rid of: old furniture, VHS players, great-grandpa's collection of antique back scratchers. Shit like that.

I pulled up to the gate blocking the entrance and counted five rows of blue buildings, each containing about ten storage units with white metal garage doors. Greg's Yukon was parked next to one of the doors at the far end of the center building.

The complex was surrounded by a chain-link fence topped with razor wire. I called Laura and asked if she and Greg rented a storage unit. She had no idea what I was talking about, and I hung up before she could ask any questions. When she immediately called back, I turned off the phone.

I drove past the complex and parked in an abandoned lot next to a convenience store. I was about to start walking toward the fence to get a better look when a gray Audi sedan pulled up in front of the entrance. A second later the gate started moving and its chain clanked against the gears like a roller coaster being tugged up a hill.

When the car pulled through, I took off in a sprint. Fifteen seconds later I was inside the fence and the gate was closed. I put my hands on my knees and tried to catch my breath. When I looked up at the razor wire, I realized I hadn't really thought this plan through.

I walked toward the side of the middle row of units and peered around the corner. The Audi was parked behind Greg's Yukon. I leaned against the building and listened for voices but didn't catch anything more than the occasional sound of Greg's high-pitched laugh. A few minutes passed before I heard the rattle of a metal garage door followed by two car doors slamming shut. I ran down the adjacent row and pressed my back against the building. When I looked around the corner, the Yukon and Audi were pulling through the gate. A moment later they were gone. The gate began to close, and I knew there was no way to reach it in time. I was trapped, at least until someone came through the gate, which might not be until morning.

I walked over to the unit where Greg had been parked. A four-digit padlock hung from a latch on the metal door. I grabbed the lock and entered the month and year of Laura's birthday. No dice. I tried Greg's birthday, then his and Laura's anniversary, but the lock didn't budge. I tried to think of other four-digit combinations that might be significant to Greg. When I entered *0715* and pulled down on the shackle, the lock opened with a loud click. That was the birthday of Cantrell, Greg and Laura's asshole of a Boston terrier. I knew the date because just a few weeks earlier I'd watched them sing happy birthday to the dog while he gobbled up a cupcake Laura had made out of garbanzo flour and Greek yogurt.

I opened the storage unit door, stepped inside, and found a light switch on the wall to the right. The unit was about fifteen feet square and filled with big-boy toys: a Jet Ski, a set of golf clubs, a chromed-out Triumph Bonneville. Along the back wall sat several stacks of black Pelican cases, the kind professional photographers use to store their cameras and lenses. I pulled down one of the cases and opened it. It was packed with plastic gallon bags filled with marijuana. I stared at the bags for a long moment, wishing Greg had just been screwing around. An occasional piece of ass would've been easier to swallow than a felony-size stash of pot.

Each case I opened inched my temper closer to its red line. More bags of pot, bags of pills, rolls of cash, and a Glock 9mm handgun wrapped in a dish towel. By the time I'd opened all the cases, my veins were ready to burst. Greg was screwing around with my sister's life, and I wanted to hurt him for it. The devils on my shoulder had some ideas about how to make that happen. They also suggested pocketing a few bags of pills before making any rash decisions.

I was considering my options when I heard the rattle of the entrance gate. A few seconds later Greg pulled up in front of the open storage unit door. He was glaring at me through the window of his Yukon while speaking to someone on his phone. He ended the call, stepped inside the unit, and pulled down the door.

Greg said he'd spotted my car and figured Laura had asked me to follow him. He told me he really wished I hadn't done that.

I'd had a pretty good idea of what Greg was up to as soon as I'd seen what was in the cases. He was either shaking down small-time dealers for drugs and guns or he was slipping evidence out of the station. The former was more likely than the latter. It would be pretty easy, especially in some areas of North Charleston, for Greg to flash his badge and squeeze young wannabe gangstas for a few ounces of pot or a baggie of pills. Drugs he could redistribute to other dealers for quick cash. Getting guns would be a little more complicated, and traceable, and I figured that's why there was only one.

I told Greg my theory.

"Well done, Sherlock," he said. "So what are you going to do now?"

I pulled out my phone and turned it back on.

"Seriously?" Greg said. "You're going to call this in?"

I ignored him and scrolled through my contacts.

Greg laughed. "You better hope the right person answers, 'cause there are people in the department way deeper into this shit than I am."

I knew Greg was right. Even though I'd been with the force for only what seemed like a long weekend, I'd heard the rumors. Some said it was widespread throughout the department; others said it was just one or two bad apples. Either way, the bunch was spoiled.

Greg strolled over and grabbed a roll of cash from one of the cases. "Here. Take it. I know you need it."

I focused on my phone. I knew exactly who to call. Someone in the department I could trust. Someone who could set this straight.

Greg reached over and snatched the phone out of my hand.

"Davis, just take the money and forget all this, okay? I'll be out of it soon, I promise."

Greg's bullshit was stretching my temper like a rubber band. I didn't want it to snap, for my sake and his.

I took a deep breath. "Give me my phone."

Greg threw the cash back into the case, reached into another one, and pulled out a small baggie of white pills. He held it out like a peace offering.

"Take 'em. I've got all you need right here."

The devils started whispering again: *One bag wouldn't hurt. Put it in your pocket. Go back to Claudia's.* The lone angel on my other shoulder repeated a single word: *Laura.*

I shook my head and held out my hand.

"Give me my phone."

Greg smirked. "Davis, you really are a worthless piece of shit, you know that? Between the beer and the pills, I don't know how you function. I've begged Laura to kick you out, but she says you need a babysitter. What you really need is a rope and a rafter."

We stared at each other for a long moment. The devils were primed to have a go at Greg's throat. The angel was busy humming John Lennon's "Imagine."

Finally Greg snickered and tossed the phone in my direction.

"Go ahead, call whoever you want," he said. "Nobody in the department will believe a word you say anyway. You think they still don't talk shit about you? The ex-cop with the short fuse. Raging Reed, that's what they call you. It's a good thing Laura feels sorry for you; otherwise you'd be living under a bridge picking fights with the other bums."

The other bums. The comment stung because it was true. For the past two years I'd been living off the good graces of my sister. Sleeping in her and Greg's guest room, eating their food, cluttering their kitchen with my brewing equipment. Taking the occasional assignment in order to prolong my slow-motion suicide of alcohol and pills.

I wanted to hurt Greg, but doing so would hurt Laura. I just needed to stay calm and call Perry. He would know what to do.

While searching for Perry's number, I glanced up and saw a wicked grin cross Greg's face. He threw the bag of pills aside and bent back down in front of the cases.

"Actually, I might have something else you need," he said.

I didn't like the sound of that.

As Greg rummaged through the cases, I pulled a seven iron out of the golf bag and held it over my shoulder. Greg stood up and slowly turned to face me. He was holding a gun. I guessed it was the gun I'd seen earlier wrapped in a dish towel. At the time I hadn't bothered to check to see if it was loaded; it didn't seem to matter then. But then wasn't now.

When Greg saw the golf club, he raised the gun and started to speak. By that point I didn't care what he had to say: the rubber band had snapped, and I swung the club like a lumberjack trying to split a knotty piece of oak. The head of the iron connected with the side of Greg's neck. He fell over onto his back, and I straddled his chest. I punched Greg in the face. Then I punched him again. Raging Reed was firing on all cylinders.

When Greg stopped moving, I pushed myself up and tried to shake some feeling back into my hand. The room was spinning. The motorcycle, the Jet Ski, the Pelican cases were blurry streaks of blue, silver, and black. I dropped back down to my knees and closed my eyes. Nausea was building, and I could feel the burn of stomach acid on the back of my throat. I took a few deep breaths and finally worked up the nerve to open my eyes. Greg's face was starting to swell. I choked back some vomit and tried to think. I needed to call an ambulance and I needed to disappear. But I knew better than to call 911 from my phone—I didn't want any record of having been in that storage unit. I'd use Greg's phone to make the call, leave the line open, then take my chances climbing over the razor wire.

I was searching through Greg's pockets when I heard a noise outside. A moment later the door rose and the unit was illuminated with blinding light streaming in from the headlights of a car. I stood up and saw a figure standing in the doorway, silhouetted against the glow, its arm raised as if the person were offering to shake my hand. The shot sounded like the crack of a whip. My left leg went out from under me and I fell onto the concrete floor beside Greg. Suddenly my rage and fear evaporated. All I wanted to do was go to sleep.

1

Waking up is the worst part of my day. In those first moments after I regain consciousness and try to shake the spider webs off my brain, I make an assessment of exactly how shitty I'm going to feel for the next few hours. On a scale of one to ten, with one being full speed ahead and ten being don't even bother rolling over, this morning was a seven. Which wasn't too bad, considering recent history.

I grabbed my phone off the nightstand and checked the time—10:17 AM. My cell phone company promises service throughout 99 percent of the Southeast, but apparently the cabin I'd rented constituted the 1 percent dead zone. The company should have a map on their website with an arrow pointing to a tiny black dot in the middle of western North Carolina alongside a note that reads EVERYWHERE BUT HERE. Since moving into the cabin, my phone had become little more than an eighty-dollar-a-month digital clock.

I put the phone back on the nightstand and picked up a bottle of Xanax. I popped one pill in my mouth and washed it down with what little saliva I could muster, which wasn't much. My tongue was dry and chalky, and I was convinced that one night I'd wake up and catch the cat that kept shitting in my mouth.

I walked into the kitchen and put some water on to boil, then opened the laptop on the kitchen table and checked my email. It was all spam. Offers to reduce my mortgage and cure my erectile dysfunction. Fortunately, I didn't have either.

I was hoping to find an email from Laura. It had been almost a month since I'd heard from her. I checked the sent-mail folder, just in case I'd emailed something to her in those late hours when my body was still awake but my self-control had already turned in for the night. Thankfully, the folder was empty.

I put a teaspoon of instant coffee in a mug and filled it full of water from the kettle. I've never climbed aboard the fancy-coffee bandwagon; even those pod coffeemakers seem extravagant to me. I'd calculated that instant coffee cost me a little under seven cents per cup. That left more money for other things, like good beer, anxiety medication, and intermittent cell phone coverage.

I carried the mug across the living room and out through a sliding glass door that opened onto a large deck. It was unseasonably warm for mid-November. The thermometer with the Cheerwine logo nailed to one of the deck posts read sixty-five degrees, and I was comfortable in a sweat shirt and jogging pants. Not that I had any intention of jogging—those days were long gone. A bullet through the leg will do that to you.

In the distance a small scattering of fog drifted through the trees like coal smoke trailing from the chimney of an old train engine. They call this area the Great Smoky Mountains, and on most mornings, if you didn't know any better, you'd swear fires were burning out of control all through these hills.

I sipped my coffee and fought the urge to go back inside and check my email again. The cabin didn't have Wi-Fi, so the laptop was connected to a DSL modem on a counter next to the sink, and the cable wasn't long enough to stretch farther than the kitchen table. Maybe that was a good thing.

The cabin was nestled into a steep hill in the Pisgah National Forest in a little town called Cruso. Cruso isn't really a town, by definition. It doesn't have a main street or a post office or even a bar; the closest alcohol is twelve miles away in Waynesville. But it does have a volunteer fire department, a Mexican restaurant, a golf course, and a gas station filled with cigarettes, beef jerky, and scratch tickets. It also offers what I was looking for most—solitude.

I'd discovered the cabin on Craigslist. A man named Dale Johnson was advertising it for $575 a month; I'd called from Charleston and asked if he'd take $500 if I'd pay six months in advance. I told him it would be just me, no pets, no drama, no trouble, just one guy who wanted some peace and quiet in order to write a book. Dale said he was a deputy with the local sheriff's department and knew how to handle trouble. We went back and forth for a bit until he finally accepted my terms. I packed up the Mercedes that same day and headed out, leaving behind what I was trying to escape and wondering if it would still be there when I got back.

Four hours after leaving Laura's house in Charleston, I drove across the North Carolina border and through a small town called Canton, where a paper mill enveloped the streets in a sour-smelling haze. A few minutes later I was headed east on U.S. 276 when I passed a sign that read WELCOME TO CRUSO: 9 MILES OF FRIENDLY PEOPLE PLUS ONE OLD CRAB. I figured if I stayed here long enough, I might be in the running for that title, or at least Old Crab Pro Tem.

Just past the golf course, the road curved to the south. The houses began to spread out the farther I drove, and by the time I reached the campground where Dale said he'd meet me, I thought I'd literally entered that storied location known as East Bumfuck.

I'd called Dale from Canton to tell him I was about twenty minutes away, and he was waiting in his patrol car when I pulled into the campground. When he stepped out, I couldn't help but wonder just how out of shape a person would have to be to fail the physical fitness requirements for a law enforcement job in the area. He was at least 275 pounds, and not an ounce of that was ass. His back was flat as a board, but his belly hung over his belt like a sack of fertilizer about to fall off a tailgate.

I got out of the Mercedes and shook his hand.

"Davis Reed," I said.

"Dale Johnson, nice to meet ya."

I reached in my pocket and handed him a check for $3,500. He stared at it for a moment, then finally seemed to accept that it was legit. He grinned and said, "Follow me."

We got back on 276 and continued south along the east fork of the Pigeon River to a dirt road marked by a black mailbox with the word JOHNSON spelled out in gold stick-on letters. We turned right and followed the road up a steep incline, doubling back several times. It was like tracing the path of an erratic EKG. The road was surrounded by forest and barely wide enough for one vehicle. I wondered what we would do if we met someone coming in the opposite direction, but Dale didn't seem to be worried about that possibility—his patrol car slung gravel and whipped from side to side like he was responding to a break-in in progress. It was all I could do to keep up.

Eventually the road straightened out and we entered a clearing with a modest wooden cabin built into a steep bank. There was a rusted-out Jeep parked off to one side of the clearing next to a few pieces of firewood peeking out from under a ragged gray tarp. The cabin looked tired and worn, and I wasn't sure if it had been wise to pay six months in advance for a place sight unseen.

The inside of the cabin was sparse. There was one bedroom, a tiny bathroom, and a wood-paneled living room with a stone fireplace along one wall. The kitchen was painted pale yellow, and a small wooden table sat in the center of a stained linoleum floor. A door next to the refrigerator revealed a set of wooden steps that led down into darkness. "There ain't nothing down there," Dale said when I opened the door and peered into the black expanse. "But look at this." He grabbed my arm, and I followed him through the living room and out onto the deck. The view was breathtaking.

"You said you's writing a book about Cold Mountain, right? Well, there it is. That's it."

The deck sat above the tree line like the top floor of an observation tower at a national park. In the distance a few small hills in different shades of blue and gray rose up from a valley of trees. Behind them, perfectly framed in the center of the vista, was the tall, rounded peak of

Cold Mountain. It was a view that could never get old. If I'd had 3,500 extra dollars in my bank account, I would've written Dale another check right then and there.

"Incredible," I said. "How long have you owned this place?"

"It's belonged to my family for years. Me and my ex lived here a while before things turned bad. When she moved out last spring, I figured I could move in with Daddy and rent this place out. Weren't no reason for me to stay up here. Daddy's got plenty of room, and his place is closer to town anyways. I started doing weekly rentals, but that shit got old quick. Folks would come up here with a bunch of kids and they'd bitch about the internet and cell phone service and this and that, like I was running a motel. So in October I started advertising it by the month. You were the first person to call. Most people ain't interested in coming up here in the winter."

Dale sat on the deck while I brought in my stuff from the Mercedes. With my leg injury, it was a pretty slow process, but Dale never offered to help. When he saw me unload my brewing equipment, he told me he'd recently started brewing beer himself. That began a long conversation about recipes and brewing techniques. As the sun dipped below the hills, I poured him a glass from one of the sixty-four-ounce growlers I'd brought with me from Charleston, an American pale ale that I'd been tweaking for months.

"Damn, brother, you know what you're doing," he said, after taking a swig that drained half the glass. "This is some good shit."

We kept drinking through the evening and on into the night. When the moon appeared above the tree line, Dale pulled out his phone and scrolled through his music selection.

"Now this is the kind of shit I like," he said.

Seconds later Ozzy Osbourne's "Bark at the Moon" was blaring out of the tiny speaker in Dale's phone. I'd grown up listening to eighties heavy metal and had since moved on to hip-hop, electronica, and jazz. But Dale was committed to what he'd listened to back in high school, what many consider to be the most embarrassing of hard-rock eras, the hair metal period. That evening he played tracks from Dokken, Poison,

Mötley Crüe, Def Leppard, Cinderella, and Ratt. It was nice to hear songs I'd thought I'd long outgrown. And I was surprised to find those ridiculous lyrics still occupied some dusty cabinet in my brain.

As the music played and the beer flowed, Dale and I swapped stories. I told him about my short time on the Charleston police force and my half-ass career as a private detective. About the cheating husbands and insurance frauds I'd been hired to photograph doing things they shouldn't be doing. About my parents dying in a car accident a week shy of their forty-ninth wedding anniversary, and a heavily redacted version of what had happened to me in that storage unit. I told him about my plans for the book and how I hoped to be finished with it by the time I left Cruso in the spring.

In return Dale told me how he'd grown up in the area and played football in high school. How he'd spent one year on a football scholarship at the University of Tennessee before drinking himself into an expulsion. How he'd come back home and started taking criminal justice classes at a technical school while watching his mom slowly die of lung cancer. He told me about joining the sheriff's department and about the young man he'd shot and killed during a drug raid at an apartment complex over in the nearby town of Clyde. He told me a little about his ex, Carla, and a lot more about the women he had dated since his divorce, most of whom he described as "chunky."

"I don't like them women that's all skin and bones," he said. "It's like fucking a pile of paper clips."

By the time Dale eased his mass out the deck chair and said goodnight, we'd finished off almost six growlers of beer, the equivalent of over twenty pints.

I hadn't come to Cruso to make friends, but Dale and I seemed to have a few things in common. We were both in our midforties, we both loved good beer, and we both suffered from early-onset grumpiness.

* * *

That was twenty-seven days ago, and since then I'd spent many evenings on the deck with Dale, talking about the things we agreed on (beer and music) and arguing about the things we didn't (just about everything else).

In fact, most of my days were spent on the deck as well: drinking beer, popping pills, and not writing a book. This morning was starting out no different from the rest—me, hungover, taking turns staring at Cold Mountain and at a blank legal pad where I kept hoping a book outline would magically appear.

Hope was about all I could do. I had no idea how to write a book. It had seemed like a good idea when I was in the hospital and wondering what to do during my recuperation. I'd thought working on a book might force me to focus. And if I could focus long enough to finish it, I might earn a little respect from all the people who'd watched me fail time and time again.

I finished my coffee and opened a beer. Then another. Then another. By midafternoon I was four beers deep and the legal pad was still blank. I was about to get a fifth beer when the angel on my shoulder suggested that a change of scenery might stir up my creative juices. The devils laughed at the idea, but I silenced them with a Xanax and a promise to ignore the angel for the rest of the day.

I went to the laptop and pulled up a trail map of the surrounding area. After clicking around for a few minutes, I settled on what looked to be an easily accessible and fairly flat trail at a place called Black Balsam. I knew I wouldn't be able to walk very far, but at the least I would appease the angel for a while and feel like I was being productive. I changed into some old jeans and hiking boots, then hopped in the Mercedes and headed toward Cold Mountain.

2

After my hundred-yard hike on the Black Balsam trail, I drove to Dale's father's house, which was a few miles west of the cabin. The house sat at the end of a gravel driveway that snaked along the edge of a small family graveyard where four generations of Johnsons presumably rested in peace.

As I approached, I noticed Dale's patrol car out front and caught a glimpse of his pudgy face looking out through one of the kitchen windows.

"I hope that trunk's full of beer," Dale yelled as he waddled down the steps toward my Mercedes.

"The IPA's not ready yet," I said. "It's got a few more days of conditioning."

"A few days? Shit, I might wither away before then."

I had a better chance of staying sober than Dale had of withering away.

Dale loaded his mouth with chewing tobacco and said, "So what brings you around?"

I tossed him a large silver key ring holding numerous keys.

"Did you rob a janitor?" he said.

"I was up at Black Balsam today and found them on the trail."

Dale stared at the mass of metal. "That's a shitload of keys."

"Is that your official opinion, Deputy?"

"What do I want with 'em?"

"I didn't see anyone else in the area, and there were no other cars in the parking lot. I thought they might belong to a ranger. I didn't know where else to take them."

Dale shot me a suspicious look. "What the fuck were you doing up at Black Balsam?"

"Book research."

Dale scoffed, then started to examine the keys closely. "What is all this shit?" he said.

"I don't know—usual stuff, house keys, car keys, some padlock keys."

Dale's eyes grew wide as he held up the ring by a long silver key etched with black markings.

"Holy shit! Do you know what this is?"

"No."

"Me neither." He laughed and threw the key ring back to me. "People lose shit up on the parkway all the time. Keys, cameras, phones. Take 'em up to the ranger station at Pisgah, somebody'll claim 'em."

I heard a couple of grunts and turned to see Dale's father standing just outside the home's front door.

"How are you, Junebug?" I yelled.

"I ain't for shit," he said.

I should have known better than to ask. It hadn't taken me long to come to know Junebug as a quarter ton of grumpy hillbilly poured into the largest pair of overalls I'd ever seen.

Junebug spit a long stream of brown fluid into an empty flowerpot, then asked, "Did you bring some beer?"

"It's not quite ready yet," I said. "Give it a few more days."

"Well, hurry up. Dale's beer tastes like skunk piss."

"That don't stop you from drinking it all," Dale yelled.

"I'll bring you some as soon as it's ready," I said, as Junebug turned around and squeezed himself back through the doorway.

I looked at Dale, who seemed a little dejected. "My beer ain't that bad," he said.

"Well, I don't know. I've never tasted skunk piss."

After Dale and I traded insults for a few minutes, he looked at his watch. "Since you drive about as slow as you walk, the ranger station will be closed by the time you get up there."

I didn't bother telling Dale that I had no intention of going to the ranger station immediately. There were impatient devils to tend to first.

"I'll come by and get you in the morning," he said. "We'll ride up together."

It was unusual for Dale to offer assistance, and I figured there was an ulterior motive for his generosity. But in the end I just nodded and climbed into my Mercedes. By that time the devils were screaming so loud I could hardly think.

3

The next morning I was sitting on the deck, basking in the warmth of cheap coffee and pricey benzodiazepines, when I heard the sound of gravel crunching under tires. It was soon followed by the siren squawk of a patrol car. Dale loved to announce his arrival.

When he pulled into the clearing, I leaned over the railing and raised my mug.

Dale rolled down his window and held up a bottle of Mountain Dew.

"I got my caffeine right here. Now grab them keys and get your ass down here. It's a nice day for a ride on the parkway."

I went into the bathroom and swallowed another pill. If I was going to ride with Dale, I needed to be as numb as possible. No matter where he was headed, Dale drove his patrol car like he'd just stolen it. When I slid into the passenger seat, Dale was on his phone. He used a different carrier and had service all through the area.

"I understand, sir," he said. "But I ain't gotten that impression."

He looked over at me and mouthed the words *Sheriff Byrd*.

"Yessir, he's writing a book on Cold Mountain, 'bout that airplane that crashed up there."

Dale started the car, gunned it out of the clearing, and raced down the dirt road. When we skidded onto 276, Dale punched the accelerator for the ten-minute drive up to the Blue Ridge Parkway. Although with Dale behind the wheel, it would probably take less than five.

"Yessir, I'll be sure to tell him," Dale said into his cell.

He pressed a button and wedged the phone into a holster on his belt.

"Sheriff Byrd's pretty curious about you. He seems to think a private detective from Charleston, showing up out of nowhere and sniffing 'round the department, is probably up to no good."

"I'm not sniffing around the sheriff's department," I said. "Where did he get that idea?"

"Byrd knows you and I hang out, drink beer, talk shit. He's got a buddy with the Charleston PD and they've probably been talking about that storage unit mess."

So the local sheriff and the Charleston PD were talking about me. I didn't like that one bit. I was supposed to be recuperating and trying to get my shit together enough to write a book. I was also hiding, albeit in plain sight. Whoever had shot me was almost certainly with the Charleston PD, someone in cahoots with Greg who drove a gray Audi. I worried that if that person knew my exact location, they might come and try to finish the job.

I wondered who Sheriff Byrd's friend in the department might be. I remembered several of the guys on the force talking about vacationing in the mountains around Asheville. It wouldn't be strange for one or more of them to make friends with a local sheriff.

"He wants to have lunch with you," Dale said. "Tomorrow at twelve thirty down at the Mexican place, El Bacteria."

"Is it a request or a demand?"

Dale finished his Mountain Dew and tossed the empty bottle onto the back seat.

"Well, that all depends on how you look at it. But I'd go if I was you. You don't want on Byrd's bad side. Just tell him about your book. How's it coming along, anyway?"

I looked out the window at the blur of trees.

"I'm just about ready to start chapter one."

* * *

The Blue Ridge Parkway runs for almost five hundred miles along the spine of the Blue Ridge Mountains, connecting the Great Smoky

Mountains National Park in North Carolina to the Shenandoah National Park in Virginia. The land adjacent to the parkway is owned by the National Park Service, which means the two-lane road is surrounded by forests and waterfalls rather than homes and businesses. The parkway is one of America's best escapes. It's also a time machine, revealing the scenic landscape early settlers in this area enjoyed before the days of junkyards and dollar stores.

The scenic overlooks that adjoin the parkway are small parking areas with picnic tables and hundred-mile views. Some are the starting points of trails that range in difficulty from "no problem" to "you might break your ankle." The overlook near where 276 meets the parkway offers a view of Cold Mountain, but from the overlook's elevation the mountain is nothing more than a rolling hill. The view from the cabin deck is much more awe-inspiring.

Dale and I headed north on the parkway toward Mount Pisgah, a 5,700-foot peak topped with a red-and-white TV transmission tower owned by the local ABC affiliate. At night the tower was a glowing beacon rising from a dark, imposing mountaintop. During the day, it looked like a swizzle stick poking out of the top of a bran muffin.

We pulled into the parking lot of a ranger station that sat next to the Mount Pisgah trailhead. When we walked inside, a ranger dressed in green pants and a brown button-up shirt stood behind a glass-topped counter covered with maps, pamphlets, and brochures. The station looked more like a gift shop than an official Park Service office. There were racks of postcards and a display of stuffed black bears alongside shelves of caps, stickers, and T-shirts. HIKERS DO IT OUTDOORS, one read.

"Hello, Terry," Dale said to the ranger.

"Deputy Johnson," the ranger replied. It was more of a statement than a greeting.

"This here's Davis Reed. He's renting my cabin and found these keys yesterday over at Black Balsam."

I said hello and put the keys on the counter.

"He thought they might belong to one of you'ns," Dale said.

Terry picked up the keys and studied them. "I don't recognize these," he said. "Joanne, could you come out here?"

A door behind the counter opened and a female ranger appeared. I guessed her to be in her late thirties. She couldn't have been over five feet tall and was dressed in the same uniform as Terry. She was a bit on the heavy side, and the buttons of her shirt strained against her breasts. I now understood why Dale had offered to be my chauffeur.

Terry held up the keys.

"Have you seen these before?" he said.

Joanne took the keys and weighed them in her palm. "Now that's a handful."

"That's what she said," Dale muttered.

Joanne rolled her eyes and sifted through the keys. She picked one out and held it up. It was flat and stubby, with the letters BMW stamped on the head.

"I don't know who they belong to, but I do know what this key is," she said. "It's for a BMW 2002."

"How do you know that?" I asked.

"My ex-boyfriend had one and I drove it for a few weeks when my 4Runner broke down. I hated that car; it was as slow as Christmas."

Dale walked over to a beverage cooler with a sign taped to the door that read *Cold drinks, $2.*

"I didn't know Travis had a BMW," he said.

"This was before Travis," Joanne said. "And it's none of your business anyway."

Dale smirked and popped open a fresh Mountain Dew.

"But that's what the key looked like?" I asked.

"Yeah, it looked just like this. There's a 2002 over in the Graveyard Fields parking lot. At least it was there yesterday morning."

Terry cleared his throat. "We'll keep these here in case someone comes looking for them."

Dale strolled back to the counter.

"That's all right," he said. "We wouldn't want to put you out none. We'll see if that car's still parked over there. Find the owner. Hell, maybe there's a reward."

Dale threw an open palm toward Joanne. She let the keys dangle for a moment, then dropped them into his hand.

"You ever get lonely up here, you give me a call," Dale said with a sleazy wink.

Joanne shook her head. "You're a pig, Dale."

"Literally and figuratively," I said.

We were almost to the door when Dale suddenly turned around. "By the way, how's Terry Junior getting along? He keeping in line?"

Terry straightened some of the papers on the counter. "He's fine."

Dale pointed a finger at Terry. "Well, you be sure to let him know I was asking after him."

* * *

When we were back in the car, I looked over at Dale.

"Did I sense a little static between you and Ranger Terry?"

"Shit, Terry's just wound too tight," Dale said. "Last summer I picked up his son doing forty-five in a thirty. Now, the sheriff's department don't normally worry about speeders. We leave that shit for town police and highway patrol, but this little sumbitch had been warned before. He back-talked when I pulled him, which pissed me off royally, so I dragged him out of the car and searched it. Found a little bag of weed under the driver's seat. I gave him a talking to, then wrote him a ticket for speeding and put the weed in my pocket. I heard later that the dumb fuck told his daddy about the ticket and about the weed. Now Terry can't figure out if I was doing his kid a favor by not reporting the weed or if I'm the kind of guy you can't trust to work by the book."

"What did you do with the pot?" I asked.

"I gave it to daddy. It keeps him from drinking all my beer."

"The life of a rural deputy."

Dale raised his Mountain Dew. "It has its benefits."

4

There were two cars in the Graveyard Fields parking lot when we arrived: a blue Land Rover Discovery with a large cargo box bolted to the roof and a red BMW 2002.

"Thins out this time a year," Dale said. "During the summer they's cars lined two hundred yards up the road on either side of this lot."

We got out of the patrol car, and Dale walked over to the BMW while I took in the view. I'd driven past Graveyard Fields a few times since coming to Cruso but had never stopped. There was a sign at the edge of the parking lot:

A natural disaster occurred here 500 to 1000 years ago. A tremendous "wind-blow" uprooted the spruce forest. Through the years the old root stumps and trees rotted, leaving only dirt mounds. These odd mounds gave the appearance of a graveyard, and the area became known as Graveyard Fields.

The sign went on to say that the forest had eventually regrown but was destroyed again, this time by fire, in 1925. The area didn't look like a graveyard to me, just a wide rolling meadow spotted with spindly gray trees and the outlines of a few walking trails. I'd read online that one of the trails eventually led to the peak of Cold Mountain and that it was a long and strenuous hike. The Black Balsam trailhead, where I'd found the keys, was a half mile west of Graveyard Fields. That trail also led to Cold Mountain, and although it started out flat and well marked, I'd read that the last few miles were steep and difficult to follow.

Because of the book I was trying to write, I felt compelled to stand on top of Cold Mountain. But with my leg injury, I wasn't able to walk more than a couple hundred yards without stopping in pain. Unless I was lowered from a helicopter, I doubted I would ever step foot on the peak of that mountain.

* * *

"Now that kind of shit really pisses me off," Dale said.

He was standing behind the BMW, and I walked over to take a look. The car was beat to hell. The quarter panels were beginning to rust, and the doors and hood were full of dings and dents. The rear of the car was covered with bumper stickers: COEXIST (the letters written out in the symbols of various religions), BERNIE 2016, WE ARE ALL IMMIGRANTS, SCIENCE IS NOT A LIBERAL AGENDA, HATE IS NOT A FAMILY VALUE.

"Why would somebody ride around with all that shit on the back of their vehicle?" Dale said.

"Joanne told us the car was here yesterday," I said. "Do people camp out here overnight?"

"Yeah. And this is the best time of year to do it. Too cold for bears and snakes but not cold enough to stop you from getting it on in a sleeping bag."

I couldn't imagine a sleeping bag large enough to hold Dale, much less him and the size of woman he was partial to getting it on with.

Dale pointed to the car's Florida license plate. "It don't look like this piece of shit could make it all the way up here from Florida."

"Is that place around here?" I asked, pointing out several stickers on the back of the car that read LONG BRANCH BREWERY.

"It's over in Waynesville," Dale said. "Down in Frog Level."

"Have you been there?" I asked.

"Yeah, a couple of times," Dale said. "Good beer; they got a restaurant with some decent food. And the girl that owns it's hot as shit. I think her name's Beth."

I walked over to the end of the parking lot, where a set of stone steps led down to the trailhead.

"I ain't going down there, if that's what you're thinking," Dale yelled. "I ain't chasing no tree hugger across the mountains just to ask him if he lost his keys."

I went back to the patrol car and took the key ring off the dash. I found the key Joanne had shown us and put it in the lock in the BMW's driver's side door.

"Ten bucks says it don't work," Dale said.

I turned the key clockwise, and the lock clicked open with a thump.

"Shit," Dale said.

"Mind if I look inside, Deputy? Maybe find the name of the owner?"

"Do you think I give a rat's ass?"

I opened the door and slid into the driver's seat. The car's inside was just as ragged as its exterior. The seats were torn and marked with what looked like cigarette burns. The floorboards were full of discarded food wrappers, mostly Chick-fil-A and Hardee's. The odometer on the dash read 96,452, but I assumed it had already rolled over at least once. I popped the glove box open to reveal a few trail maps and a digital tire pressure gauge but no insurance or registration information. I reached under both seats and found a few empty Ziploc bags and a bottle of something called kombucha. I got out of the car and folded down the driver's seat. There were two receipts crumpled on the back floorboard. One was from a Home Depot store in Asheville for a shovel, ax, pick, tarpaulin, and spade—someone must have been planning on doing some heavy-duty yard work. The other was for two growlers of beer called Dark Secret IPA from Long Branch Brewery.

I turned to Dale and held up the BMW's key. "Mind if I pop the trunk?" I said.

"Be my guest. It's probably full of tofu and bongo drums."

I tried to put the key in the trunk lock, but it wouldn't fit. I turned the key over and tried again—same result. The trunk lock wasn't centered properly, and I figured maybe it had been replaced. I shuffled through the keys, looking for one that might open the lock. I tried a couple but they didn't work. I gave up and turned to Dale, who was shaking his head.

"Are you done?" he asked. " 'Cause I got shit to do."

I held up the key ring. "So what do we do with these?"

"Hell, leave 'em on the seat."

"I'm not going to leave them here; someone could steal the car."

Dale laughed. "You seriously think someone's gonna steal this thing?"

"Just take me home. I'll come back up later and give the keys to Terry. I should probably talk to him about Cold Mountain anyway, get some background for the book."

Dale raised his eyebrows.

"You just wanna talk to Joanne, don't ya? Get yerself another look at them Smothers Brothers she's lugging around."

"You really are a pig," I said.

Dale beamed at the compliment.

* * *

Dale dropped me back at the cabin a little before eleven. I took a pill, poured a beer, and spent some time on the laptop researching BMW 2002s. I learned they had been produced between 1966 and 1977. While they had always been popular with BMW aficionados, they had recently become a favorite of the hipster set—those twentysomethings who liked beards, vinyl records, and for some reason Pabst Blue Ribbon. I also researched the long silver key etched with black markings. After about half an hour of going down multiple Google rabbit holes, I felt pretty sure the key belonged to a brand of gun safe manufactured by a company called Steel Freedom. The company's website was plastered with images of eagles, American flags, and rattlesnakes with DON'T TREAD ON ME printed underneath. The gun safes the company offered ranged in price from $1,500 to over $3,000. *We sell serious safes to serious people*, the website noted at the top of the home page. It seemed that whoever owned the beat-up red BMW was more "serious" than the car's liberal bumper stickers suggested.

As I sat behind the laptop, it was hard not to not check my email in hopes that Laura had decided to reach out. I'd promised myself I wouldn't check it until tomorrow morning.

I kept that promise until the fifth beer kicked in, which was just a little past noon. The fifth beer is the one I can count on to finally break its way into my prefrontal cortex, the part of the brain that controls decision making and willpower. The prefrontal cortex is where beer goggles live.

I clicked the GET MAIL icon, then deleted all the spam, including an email from a Nigerian prince who needed my help getting $12 million into the United States. He would give me half the money if I would be so kind as to send him my bank account number and credit card information. My beer goggles weren't that hazy.

There was one email from my friend Perry, a senior detective with the Charleston PD and the man I'd been trying to call right before I took a seven iron to Greg's neck. Perry had been my field training officer during my short-lived law enforcement career and was now in charge of the investigation into who shot me. It was also a robbery investigation, since no cases of drugs or cash had been found at the storage unit. When I'd given Perry my statement at the hospital, he'd promised to get to the bottom of what Greg was into. He'd also suggested, since whoever shot me was still at large, that I find a secluded place off the radar to go to recuperate. I figured I had Perry to thank for being in Cruso.

Perry's email said Greg was still in a coma and the investigation was ongoing. I was confused about Greg's condition. I'd beaten the shit out of him, but it was hard to believe I'd put him in a coma. I felt proud for standing up for Laura but ashamed that I'd lost my temper. Pride was a new feeling for me. Ashamed was one I had plenty of experience with.

* * *

I had every intention of driving back up to the ranger station to hand over the key ring and talk to Terry or Joanne about Cold Mountain, but in the end I spent the rest of the day on the deck, riding a nice pill-and-beer buzz until the sun dropped behind the trees, dragging the temperature down with it. It was only eight PM when I limped into the bedroom and crawled under the covers. I didn't normally go to bed at that hour, but to be honest it had been a long time since I'd done anything normally.

I closed my eyes and thought about Laura sitting at Greg's bedside at the hospital. I imagined her staring at the tubes snaking across his body, the mazes of plastic feeding air into his lungs and fluids into his veins. I wondered if he would make it, and wondered more what would happen if he didn't.

Before I left Charleston, Perry had told me everything would be okay. Along with his promise to get to the bottom of the situation, he'd promised to keep the fact that I'd beaten Greg a secret. The story he was going with was that whoever had shot me was the most likely person to have injured Greg.

But it was a secret I couldn't keep from Laura. I'd told her what I'd done in that storage unit. But I didn't tell her why. Perry had ordered me not to, and I trusted him. So Laura didn't know Greg was dirty. She didn't know he'd pulled a gun on me. All she knew was that her rage-filled brother had beaten her husband into a coma because of an alleged affair.

If I was a praying man, I would have begged God's forgiveness and asked for Greg's health to be restored. I would have prayed for clarity. I would have prayed for insight. I would have prayed for the comfort of knowing everything would be okay.

Instead I took two more pills and let a nice heavy fog roll over my brain.

5

The next morning, sunlight streamed through the bedroom window and I could hear birds chirping in the trees behind the cabin. Some squirrels scampered across the roof, their feet clicking frantically as if winter might set in any second. As far as I was concerned, winter could hold off indefinitely. My Charleston blood was pretty thin, and I could use all the time on the deck I could get.

I stayed in bed for a while, trying to calculate how hungover I was. My head felt like a sponge soaked in motor oil and my stomach rolled and gurgled. This was nothing new. I was always a little queasy, sometimes a little more little, sometimes a little less little. It was what my mother used to call a nervous stomach. My beer consumption certainly didn't help the condition, but the pills seemed to even things out. They didn't necessarily settle my stomach, but they sure helped me forget that it hurt.

When I finally summoned the energy to get up, I walked to the bathroom and took the Xanax bottle from the back of the sink. I poured the contents into my palm and counted twenty pills—they would get me through the next three, maybe four days if I was careful. I put the bottle in my pocket and made a mental note to call Dr. Landry's office for a refill when I was somewhere with cell service. I could always count on the good doctor to keep me numb, and numb was what I was after. Not stoned, not bombed, just agreeably numb.

I went through the coffee-making ritual and opened the laptop. There were a few new emails, including one from Perry, checking on me—"Stay focused and finish that book," he'd written. I'd rather he'd said he'd found the man in the gray Audi and that Greg was out of his coma and on the way to a full recovery. I hoped that news would come soon.

I closed the laptop, threw on a jacket, and took my coffee out to the deck. I fished one of the pills out of the bottle and placed it under my tongue, the fastest way to get it into the bloodstream. Nineteen left, I thought—not nearly enough.

With Cold Mountain looming in the distance, I sat back and thought of how I would spend the day. I could ride into Waynesville and pick up a Wi-Fi router at a big-box store. That would allow me to bring the laptop out to the deck, but I was still debating whether or not that was a good idea. While in town I could swing by Long Branch Brewery, grab a couple of growlers, and try to catch a glimpse of the "hot as shit" owner. Then I could pick up the parkway on the west side of town and follow it east back toward the cabin. That would take me past Graveyard Fields and give me a chance to see if the BMW was still there. From there I could continue on to the ranger station at Mount Pisgah and drop off the keys and talk to Terry about my book.

In the end I decided my head and stomach hurt too much to venture out into society, so I closed my eyes and let the first pill of the day do its work.

A few moments later my phone vibrated in my pocket. For a second I thought the stars had aligned and sent a beam of cell service down to the deck. But it wasn't a call or text; it was the calendar reminder I'd set up the previous day: 12:30 – SHERIFF BYRD LUNCH.

"Shit," I said, although no one was around to hear it but the squirrels.

I had one hour to clear the cobwebs and become human again.

*   *   *

El Bacaratos was less than ten minutes down 276 toward Waynesville. I pulled into the parking lot at 12:40 and slid the Mercedes in next to a large black SUV with tinted windows.

I'd never been to the restaurant, but when I walked in, an older woman with a tight white perm nodded at me and said, "He's waiting for you back here."

She led me toward a booth tucked away in a back corner. Above the booth was a giant sombrero attached to the wall. It was one of many Mexican stereotypes that passed for decor: maracas, bandannas, serapes, piñatas. The restaurant was a virtual fiesta, but from what I could see, not a single person in the place was Hispanic.

"Here he is," the tight-permed woman said as we walked up to the booth. I wasn't sure if she was speaking to me or the man I assumed was Sheriff Byrd.

"Guacamole," the man said, dipping a tortilla chip into a small bowl of green mush. "I'd never had it until this place opened up. It looks like cat puke, but damn if it's not tasty. Royce Byrd; nice to meet you, son. Sit down."

I slid into the booth with a craving for a cold Mexican beer. But El Bacaratos was outside the city limits, which meant the restaurant was dry—no alcohol. I grabbed a menu off the table and looked at the beverage choices: sweet tea, coffee, or Pepsi products. I opted for a root beer, hoping it would settle my stomach.

"Eating this makes me think of all the things I might like that I've never tried," Byrd said. "I guess it's natural when you get to my age to start wondering about all the things you might have missed. Although I did try sushi a couple of weeks ago at some place in Asheville my granddaughter took me to. And let me tell you, they can keep that."

The tight-perm lady returned and set my drink down in front of me.

"Doris," Byrd said, "how about another bowl of this delicious guacamole?"

"Some more chips too?"

"Well, of course."

I guessed Byrd to be in his early seventies. He had short white hair and the droopy eyes of an old basset hound. His face was worn and tired and his jowls hung down just above the top of his shirt collar. Unlike Dale's uniform, which always looked as if he'd slept in it, Byrd's was crisp and neat. He looked like a man who had seen a lot in his lifetime but still woke up every morning, put on his perfectly pressed uniform, and went out the door willing to see more.

"I've been wanting to meet you for some time," Byrd said. "Dale tells me you used to be with the Charleston PD. And that now you're a private detective, come up to our neck of the woods for a little R and R. Is that correct?"

"Close enough," I said.

"I always like welcoming new people to our area, especially those in the investigative field. It's stimulating to talk shop with those who understand the business. What kind of detective work do you do?"

"Surveillance, mostly," I said. "But I'm taking a break from that to give writing a shot. That's actually why I'm here. I'm working on a book."

"Yes, Dale mentioned that. About that B-25 that crashed on Cold Mountain, right?"

I nodded.

Byrd shook his head, then used a chip to transport the last glob of guacamole into his mouth.

"That's a tragic story. The men on that plane fought dozens of air battles against the Japanese and came away unscathed. Then after the war they crash into the side of a North Carolina mountain. Just goes to show you how something can appear out of nowhere and take you down."

"Just when you least expect it, just what you least expect."

Byrd nodded.

"Yessir. You never know what's out there waiting for you. So what made you decide to write a book about it?"

That was a good question and one I'd often pondered. I'd seen a documentary about the plane crash a couple of years earlier, and the story had stuck with me. The idea that you could outwit and outmaneuver highly trained enemies determined to kill you only to fly straight into the side of a mountain somehow resonated with me. Maybe I identified with those men. It wasn't the things I was aware of and tried to avoid that hurt me; it was the shit I didn't see coming that slapped me in the face and took me down a few notches. I'd flown into the side of a mountain many times, so to speak. The only difference between those airmen and me was that I survived each crash, then crawled back in the cockpit and took off again, completely unaware, or in complete denial, that another mountain was out there waiting for me.

"Like you, Sheriff, I guess I started thinking about all the things I might have missed. Writing a book has always been on my bucket list. That plane crash seemed like as good a subject as any."

Byrd nodded thoughtfully, as if he understood some deep meaning to my response. The way he'd talked about something coming out of nowhere to take you down made me think he just might.

Doris waited for us to pause our conversation, then placed a fresh bowl of guacamole and towering basket of tortilla chips on the table. "You fellers ready to order?"

"Doris, I'll have a plate of those delicious enchiladas," Byrd said. "One chicken, one beef, one shrimp."

He handed Doris his menu and looked at me.

"Now the shrimp here certainly aren't as good as what you're used to down in Charleston, but once they're mixed in with all those beans and sauce, you hardly notice them. Here they're more of a texture than a flavor."

"Nothing for me, thanks."

"Suit yourself," Doris said. "Hey, are you going to write about the gold that was on that plane when it crashed?"

I studied Doris's face for a second, then turned to Byrd just in time to see him roll his eyes.

"Now, Doris, don't go filling his head with that nonsense."

Doris shrugged and walked off toward the kitchen. I tried the guacamole and decided it was a lot better than it had any right to be. Hopefully my stomach could handle it.

"What was she talking about?" I asked.

Byrd shook his head and laughed.

"Some rumors never die. Years after that plane crashed, people started talking about bricks of gold bullion being found near the wreckage. Of course it wasn't true, but you know how people talk. I was just a teenager back then. One summer my friends and I scoured the mountainside looking for that treasure. But by time the crash site had been picked nearly clean. All we ever found were a couple pieces of burnt metal."

For someone planning to write a book on the subject, I'd actually done very little research on the Cold Mountain plane crash. It was my usual MO, narcissism mixed with laziness. I'd always found it easier to fantasize about something than to actually do it. Why write a book when you could just dream about writing a book? Plus, I'd been pretty busy. Moving to Cruso, recuperating from my leg injury, and spending evenings arguing with Dale.

"How did the rumor get started?" I asked.

"Aw, an old bear hunter started carrying on about finding a chest full of gold on that mountain somewhere near the crash site. According to him, it was too heavy to carry down the mountain by himself, but when he went back up there the next day with some help, the chest was gone. Now, some people believe he buried the gold as soon as he found it, then couldn't remember where it was. Others believe he actually did get the gold down off the mountain and just made up the story about it disappearing so no one would come after him looking for it."

"And what do you believe?"

Byrd laughed again.

"Ol' Gerald Johnson told more lies than truths. And every lie was the same: missed opportunity. The prize bear that got away, the UFO sighting when he didn't have his camera, the sweepstakes check that got lost in the mail. That chest of gold was just another one of his tall tales."

Doris brought Byrd's food and refilled his sweet tea. As the sheriff dug in, I had a couple more chips topped with guacamole. So far my stomach was cooperating, but I didn't want to push it.

"So how long will you be staying with us?" Byrd asked.

"I've rented the cabin through March. I hope to be finished with the book by then."

"So how does one go from private detective to author? I guess we all have to change gears at one time or another. Although I never have."

I didn't get the chance to answer. For the next half hour, Byrd talked about himself. About how he'd been elected sheriff in the mideighties and had been reelected unopposed ever since. How he'd handled differ-ent drug problems over the years. Pot in the eighties, coke and speed in the nineties, meth in the early 2000s.

"These days it's prescription drugs," Byrd said. "A man gets hurt down at the paper mill or gets himself in a car crash and some doctor goes and prescribes him six weeks of painkillers. The man can't do noth-ing but sit in a La-Z-Boy and try to manage his pain. After a while he becomes a lazy boy himself. He's no longer managing pain, he's chasing a high. Now, I don't mind somebody having a little fun or trying to escape their worries. These days I figure if you want to smoke a little marijuana every now and then, well that's your business, safer than drinking that 'shine that used to flow around these parts when I was young. But I have a no-tolerance policy when it comes to abusing pharmaceuticals. I will not let that get out of hand here like it has in so many other rural areas. It may happen here one day. But it won't happen on my watch."

I wasn't impressed by Byrd's speech, but it did remind me to call Dr. Landry.

After Byrd's plate was clean, I walked with him to the counter by the front door. As Doris rang up the check, Byrd said, "Your root beer was a dollar fifty. The guacamole is on me."

I pulled out two singles and handed them over. Byrd didn't bother giving me my change.

Out in the parking lot Byrd stood next to his SUV and used a tooth-pick to pluck the remnants of his lunch from his teeth. I told him it was nice to meet him and thanked him for the five bites of guacamole. I was reaching for the door handle of the Mercedes when the sheriff said, "About that business down in Charleston."

Finally, I thought.

"You know, son, I have a good friend with the Charleston PD—Jack Emory. Do you know him?"

"Can't say I do. I wasn't with the department very long."

"Jack and I go back a long way. He told me there's something not quite right about that robbery you and that other man were involved in. His advice to me was that I'd be wise to keep an eye on you."

That statement didn't do much for my queasiness. I didn't care for the fact that someone with the Charleston PD thought I needed to be watched closely.

"From what I hear, Sheriff, you keep your eyes on everyone in this county."

Byrd flicked his toothpick across the hood of his vehicle.

"Well, son, that's my job."

At that, Byrd climbed in his SUV and drove away. I hopped in the Mercedes, pulled out my cell phone, and noticed two bars illuminated on the signal-strength indicator. I called Dale.

"How was El Bacteria?" he said. "I hope you've got plenty of toilet paper at the cabin."

"I had the guacamole, and it was actually pretty good."

"What did Byrd have to say?"

"He just wants to know what I'm doing here."

"Listen, Byrd's been sheriff going on thirty-five years. He's a good one too. He stays in control by knowing everybody's business. So I ain't surprised he wants to know yours."

"He told me a story about a chest of gold being found near where that plane crashed on Cold Mountain."

Dale laughed. "Ah, that's an ole wives' tale; they ain't no truth to it. Don't stop people believing it, though."

"And what do you believe?"

"I believe in getting my drink on. I picked up a couple a growlers of IPA from that new BearWaters place in Canton. I'll come over later and let you have a sip."

I heard a squishing sound and assumed Dale was loading his mouth with tobacco.

"D'you take them keys back up to Terry?" he said.

"No, I haven't gotten around to it yet."

Dale snorted. "You don't get around to much, do ya?"

"Not if I can help it. Hey, why don't you run the tag on that BMW?"

There was a pause, and I figured Dale was trying to find a place to spit.

"Now why the fuck would I do that?"

"I'm just curious."

"Daddy says being curious is a good way to get your ass handed to you."

I rubbed my leg. "He's right about that."

* * *

I drove back up the river to the cabin, swallowed a pill, and took a beer out to the deck. A storm was brewing off to the west, and the peak of Cold Mountain was hidden under a cover of gray clouds. I closed my eyes and imagined an old man and his dog tracking a black bear across the side of a mountain. He stumbles over a tree root and falls face first into the moss and damp leaves that cover the forest floor. As he's pushing himself up, he catches a glint of something shiny in the distance. He investigates and discovers it's a metal chest sitting on its side. He rights the chest, then bends over to lift the buckle securing the lid. He stands up straight and looks around to make sure he's alone. When he's satisfied, he bends back down and raises the lid. He can't believe what he sees. He thinks his eyes must be playing tricks on him. Just like when he saw that UFO.

6

"**W**ake up, brother!"

When I opened my eyes, Dale was sitting next to me on the deck with a brown growler of beer balanced on his formidable stomach.

"This shit's pretty good," he said, taking a swig right out of the jug. "There's another one in the fridge, if you want a taste."

"Did you run the plate on that BMW?" I said.

Dale sneered, then pulled a folded piece of paper out of his shirt pocket. He jerked the paper open with a flick of his wrist and read from it.

"Lester Cordell, thirty-five years old. Address is in someplace called Deerfield Beach, Florida. Got a list of priors as long as my dick. Mostly petty shit. B and Es, bounced checks, simple possession."

Dale handed me the paper, and I stared at the mug shot in the top right corner. Cordell looked like a man trapped in the wrong era—thick black moustache, curly black hair, white V-neck T-shirt revealing a thick gold chain. It was like a time machine had coughed him up from a seventies porn set.

I handed the paper back to Dale.

"Where do you think he is?" I said.

Dale shoved the paper into his pocket.

"I don't give a shit," he said. "Why the fuck do you?"

I shook my head.

"I don't know. I just feel something's off."

"Listen, when Cordell comes out of the woods after a few days of beating his bongo drum, he'll realize his keys are missing and call the ranger station. End of story."

I nodded while Dale hoisted the growler off his stomach and took another giant swig.

"Don't you want a glass?" I asked.

"That would involve getting up. So what did Byrd say about that shit that happened down in Charleston?"

I shrugged. "He said he'd been told to keep an eye on me."

"Yeah, I figured that. I think his buddy down there's filling his ear with a bunch of shit."

"What's Byrd's deal, anyway? How's he been sheriff so long?"

"Byrd can be a hard-ass, but he's a good man. He grew up in this county and he's got his fingers in a bunch of pies. Owns a few rental properties and a couple of mini storage places. Was part owner of that Ford dealership over by the interstate until a couple of years ago. And he does an ass load of charity work. He knows everybody in this county, and everybody respects him. But like I said, you don't want on his bad side."

"I really don't care what side of Byrd I'm on. I'm just here to write a book."

Dale fiddled with his phone, and soon "Walk in The Shadows" by Queensrÿche echoed through the trees.

"Well, if you ask me, you're off to a slow fucking start," he said.

"You know, I read somewhere that there is nothing easier to do than not writing. So far I've found that to be pretty accurate."

Dale laughed.

"You should write about the gold. Even though it ain't true, it would make for a helluva story. Private detective searches for lost gold from an old plane crash. Hell, even I might read that book."

"Really?" I asked.

Dale took another swig from the growler and nodded his head along to the beat.

"Nah, probably not."

* * *

As the sun dipped and the shadows grew long, Dale and I finished off the growlers while listening to songs by Tesla, Helix, and Kix. After Dale left, I took my spot at the kitchen table and logged in to Facebook. I pulled up Laura's account. She'd unfriended me and all of her posts were hidden. All I could see was her profile picture. The image showed her standing next to Greg. They were on their patio by their backyard pool, holding red cups filled with rum and pineapple juice. I knew what was in the cups because I'd made the drinks. I'd also taken the picture. It had only been last summer, but it seemed like a lifetime ago.

I dug out a beer from the back of the fridge and then just for the hell of it searched Facebook for Dale Johnson. Several accounts came up, but I recognized Dale's face immediately. I clicked on the picture and was surprised to find his account wasn't private. Most people in law enforcement are very careful when it comes to social media, but Dale's account was an open book. He obviously didn't care what anyone thought about him.

I scrolled through Dale's timeline. Most of his posts were about the Carolina Panthers and Tennessee Volunteers. A few were short rants about the Second Amendment and stand-your-ground laws. There were several links to Fox News stories and some unflattering reviews of local breweries. I clicked on the PHOTOS tab. One picture showed Dale standing on the deck of what looked to be a pontoon boat floating in the middle of a lake. Dale held a fishing pole in one hand and a can of Boojum Hop Fiend IPA in the other. His face was sunburned, and I guessed the flesh underneath his wraparound sunglasses was pale as the belly of a catfish.

The next picture was similar to the first, but in this one a woman stood next to Dale. She was small and thin, although anyone standing next to Dale would appear that way. She had short blonde hair and wore cutoff denim shorts and a bikini top. She was less bosomy than I would have expected, and she was beautiful in an innocent, Applebee's-waitress kind of way.

I looked at the date of the photo—July 2016. Carla, I thought. Dale's ex-wife. In the time I'd known Dale, he'd loved bragging about his success with women, but when it came to Carla he would say, "It just didn't work out." As if that could reasonably explain the end of a marriage. I wondered how they'd met and how they'd fallen in love. I was more curious about how they'd fallen out of it. Was he unfaithful? Was she? Did he miss her? Did she miss him? Did she ever consider giving it another shot? Or was she content to say, "It just didn't work out"?

7

The next morning I shook off the cobwebs, made some coffee, and checked my email. I deleted the usual spam, comforted by the knowledge that I didn't need erectile dysfunction pills from some fly-by-night pharmacy in India. Getting an erection had never been my problem. Getting someone else interested in it was the real dilemma.

I clicked open a new email from Perry, hoping he had some news on Greg's condition and how the investigation was proceeding. I'd done my best not to obsess over the identity of who'd shot me and what I'd do to them once I did find out. I was certain it was someone in the department, another dirty cop working in tandem with Greg who'd cleaned all the drugs and cash out of that storage unit before calling in the good cops and EMTs. I just hoped whoever it was didn't feel the need to hunt me down and put another bullet in me.

Davis,

I stopped by MUSC yesterday afternoon, Greg is stable but unresponsive. Laura is with him. She's strong, she'll be okay. But don't contact her until I give the word.

IA's on the investigation now. I'll let you know how things proceed. We'll get through this. Now keep your head down and finish that book.

Perry

Stable but unresponsive. My condition had always been the opposite of that: unstable but responsive. I wondered if that was an official medical term.

I was glad to know Internal Affairs was now on the case. Perry had said he'd get to the bottom of what Greg was involved with, and I wondered how deep down or high up the trail would lead. As long as the police were convinced I had nothing to do with Greg's side hustle, I didn't have much to worry about. Now, if Greg died, things might change. Perry would then face a moral decision: arrest the man he knew had beaten Greg in that storage unit or continue to keep quiet and protect his friend. I hoped it wouldn't come to that.

I also hoped the IA investigation would speed things up. It had been weeks since the shooting, and I was starting to feel like a sitting duck. The last thing I needed was to look over the deck and see a gray Audi pulling up the driveway. If that happened, I wouldn't even be able to call for help. I'd just have to email Dale and hope he'd see it before the cabin became a murder scene.

I shook off that thought and sent Perry an email saying that if he needed to get away and clear his head for a couple of days, I knew the perfect spot. I included directions to the cabin and said the invitation was open and to show up whenever. I didn't fill him in on the book's progress, mainly because there was no progress to report. Hopefully I would at least have an outline when and if he did come up for a visit.

I closed the laptop, took a pill, and drove up to the parkway. When I pulled into the Graveyard Fields parking area, I saw the BMW. It was the only vehicle in the lot. I stopped behind it and read all the bumper stickers again, reminding myself that I needed to visit Long Branch Brewery.

I pulled out and drove over to Mount Pisgah. There were a few cars in the ranger station parking lot, including a blue Land Rover Discovery. It was the same vehicle I'd seen parked at Graveyard Fields a couple of days earlier. I got out of the Mercedes and stared at the Land Rover for a moment. The cargo box on its roof was made of thick black plastic, rounded in the back and sloped in the front like a wedge. It looked like an aerodynamic coffin.

When I walked into the station, Ranger Terry was standing behind the counter. He was talking to a young couple and didn't notice me when I entered and limped over to the beverage cooler. The couple looked to be in their mid to late twenties. The man was dressed in skinny black jeans and a red-and-green-checked flannel shirt. The woman had shoulder-length black hair and wore an oversized gray sweat shirt over leggings, or maybe they were yoga pants—I'm not sure I know the difference. I watched them for a moment. I couldn't hear the conversation, but it was pretty obvious by the couple's body language that they weren't very happy with what Terry was saying. After another minute the couple turned and stormed out.

I ran over to the counter and threw two dollar bills in front of Terry. He noticed the Diet Coke and said, "Hey, there's tax." I barely heard him because I was already halfway out the door.

I limped out to the parking lot and saw the couple climbing into the Land Rover. They stared at me through the windshield as I approached their vehicle. When I stopped by the driver's side door, the man started the engine and rolled down the window.

"Excuse me," I said. "I noticed your vehicle parked at Graveyard Fields a couple days ago. I'm wondering if you happened to see anyone camped out along the trails."

The man stared at me for a few seconds before speaking. "That wasn't us."

His answer took me by surprise. Of course, the beer and pills had frayed the edges of my memory, but how many blue Land Rovers topped with cargo boxes could there be?

"That's strange," I said. "I could swear this is the same vehicle."

The man shook his head, and the window rolled up with a soft purr.

I felt a bit of my temper come to life and gave the window a few raps with my knuckles.

The man swallowed hard and lowered the window.

"So, do you come up to the parkway often?" I asked. "I'm looking for some trails to hike. Especially around Cold Mountain."

The man glanced down toward my bad leg. He'd obviously noticed me limping across the parking lot and was probably wondering why someone in my condition was interested in hiking.

"We're not familiar with this area," he said.

The woman leaned over the vehicle's center console toward the open window.

"We're just riding through," she said. "We're going to have a picnic."

The man shot her a look, then turned to me and said, "Why are you interested in Cold Mountain?"

"I'm actually writing a book about it. I'm up here doing some research."

"There's already a book about Cold Mountain," the woman said.

"Yeah, I've heard of that one. But this is nonfiction. It's about the plane that crashed there in the forties."

The man straightened up. I looked over his shoulder and noticed a large Yeti cooler sitting on the back seat.

"You don't happen to have any beer in that cooler, do you?"

The woman's eyes lit up, and she turned and reached back over her seat. She opened the cooler's lid and pulled out a dripping-wet bottle.

"We sure do," she said. "We make this ourselves." The woman handed me the bottle, and I studied the three letters written in bold type across the label.

"P.U.B.," I said. "What does that stand for?

"Pucker Up Brewery," the woman said. "We brew sour beers."

I thanked them for the beer and watched as they pulled out of the parking lot and turned east toward Asheville. I didn't think they were going to enjoy their picnic very much—their beer was already warm.

I walked back into the ranger station to give Terry what I owed him in tax. When I approached the counter, he looked up, and I noticed a hint of recognition on his face.

"Hey," he said. "I wish I had known that was you. That young couple was asking if anyone had turned in a set of keys."

8

I climbed in the Mercedes and headed back toward the cabin. I passed the turnoff and drove another few minutes to El Bacaratos, my sweet spot for cell phone coverage.

"Hey," I said, when Dale picked up. "I was just at the ranger station, and . . ."

"Hold on," Dale said. "Don't get your panties in a wad. Terry's already called me."

"So you know they didn't leave a name or number, right? Told Terry they'd call the sheriff's office themselves."

"Yep."

"Well, have they?"

"What?"

"Called!"

Dale snorted.

"Beats the shit out of me—I'm out on patrol. Some of us work for a living, dickhead."

"They didn't tell me their names, but the woman said they brew beer at someplace called Pucker Up Brewery. Ever heard of it?"

"Nope. It ain't around here or I'd know it."

"What were they doing up there? Why did they ask Terry about the keys?"

Dale snorted again. "I know you don't want to hear this, but whatever they were doing is none of your fucking business."

I could hear Dale spit in the background and wondered if he kept a supply of empty Mountain Dew bottles in the trunk of his patrol car.

"But they lied to me about how long they'd been up on the parkway. They said they were just passing through, but we saw their car at Graveyard Fields two days ago."

"Look, Davis, they ain't under no obligation to tell you their shit. You're some weird, half-crippled, hungover dude who approached them in a parking lot. I'm surprised they talked to you at all."

"You don't think any of this is strange?"

"Yeah, I do. I think you're fucking strange. Why are you so bent out of shape about this? If you put this much energy into writing that book, you'd be finished in a week."

"I guess I'm just bored."

"Yeah, this is a good place to get bored. Carla used to say, if you have only one year left to live, move to Cruso, because every day there is like a fucking eternity."

I couldn't help but laugh. Carla was right. Cruso was like another dimension, unbound to the rules of time and space.

"Here's what I think about that couple," Dale said. "That's probably their buddy with the BMW. Maybe they was asking about the keys because he realized he'd lost them. They'd been camping together, they go to leave, and he tells them to stop by the ranger station to see if anybody's turned them in. Then you drag yourself over and start asking a bunch of questions and they tighten up. I don't blame 'em. I wouldn't tell you shit if I didn't know you and you wandered over to my vehicle wanting to know where I'd been."

I didn't want to say it, but I said it anyway.

"Yeah, you're probably right."

"Damn straight I'm right. And if you'd given Terry them keys when you's supposed to, then I wouldn't have to deal with this shit. But since Terry told them that I had the keys, and since you didn't correct him on that shit while you's up there, now I got another to-do on my list."

*　*　*

I pulled out of El Bacaratos and headed back up the river toward the cabin. I thought about my conversation with Dale. I hated it when Dale was right, and in this case he probably was. I was concerning myself with things that were none of my concern. Dale's dad Junebug was right too— doing that was a good way to get your ass handed to you. And I'd been handed my ass more times than I cared to remember.

I was a few miles from the cabin when I noticed a sheriff's department patrol car sitting out in front of Cruso's lone gas station. Out of instinct I checked my speedometer; I was doing forty-three in a forty-five-mile-per-hour zone. I had always driven fairly slow. My ex-girlfriend Sarah used to say I drove like a grandma on her way to a church social with a Crock-Pot full of collard greens on the passenger seat. The truth was, I was just safe. The Xanax slows down my reflexes, and when I'm behind the wheel, I take it nice and easy.

I looked in my rearview mirror and noticed the patrol car pull out behind me. The car accelerated, and in a few seconds it was so close behind me I thought it might touch my bumper. The lights flashed and the siren let out three quick squawks. Dale was such an asshole.

I pushed the Mercedes up to fifty-five, but the patrol car held its place as if I were towing it. I straightened up in my seat and placed my hands at ten and two on the wheel. If Dale wanted to screw around with me, I'd screw around with him in return. By the golf course the road stretched out into a half-mile passing zone. I took the Mercedes up to seventy-five and laughed at the thought of Dale cursing my name.

Halfway through the passing zone the patrol car swerved into the oncoming lane and pulled up next to me. I stared straight ahead and pressed a middle finger against the driver's side window. When the patrol car's horn blared, I looked over, ready to see Dale giving me the same one-finger salute. Instead I saw a deputy in aviator sunglasses staring at me with pure fury.

I slowed down and pulled over into a small parking area next to the river. The patrol car parked behind me, and I waited for the deputy to approach my vehicle. I guessed it would be a couple of minutes before he did. He would need to run my tag to identify the owner of the vehicle and check for any outstanding warrants. There's a big difference between pulling over an idiot who's speeding and an idiot who's just knocked over a jewelry store or abducted a toddler. Looking in the rearview mirror, I tried to see what the deputy was doing, but the glare was so bright that the patrol car's windshield looked like a sheet of ice. That was why I hadn't been able to see who was driving when the car was chasing me. I had just assumed it was Dale. Like many of my assumptions, it had turned out to be dead wrong.

I was digging around in the center console for my registration card when I heard a tap on my window. The deputy was young—I pegged him to be in his midtwenties. He sported a buzz cut and closely cropped goatee, and I was pretty certain his shirt sleeves covered biceps inked with tribal tattoos. Just based on his look, he struck me as the kind of guy who thought *Road House* was the pinnacle of American cinema.

I rolled down the window and immediately started in on my excuse.

"This is actually funny," I said. "I thought you were Deputy Johnson; he and I are friends. He gives me hell about my slow driving, and I thought he was just busting my balls. That's why I sped up instead of pulling over."

Deputy Road House let me finish, then asked for my license and registration. When I handed them over, he put them in his shirt pocket and took two steps back.

"Sir, I need you to step out of the vehicle," he said. His voice was so clipped and brusque, it was as if his jaw were wired shut.

"Look, man, this is just a misunderstanding. If you'll call Dale, he'll vouch for me. I'm actually renting his cabin for the winter—it's just up the road."

"I said step out of the vehicle."

I held up a finger to indicate I needed a moment, then grabbed my cell phone off the passenger seat. At this, the deputy took another step back and put his hand on his side arm. This guy was all business, and I felt my rubber band start to stretch. The last thing I needed was to get in a scuffle with a testosterone-fueled bully, but I'd ended up doing the last thing I needed to do more times than I could count.

I looked at my cell phone and wasn't surprised to see the NO SER-
VICE icon illuminated. Without being able to call Dale, I figured I had
no choice but to let Deputy Road House go through whatever motions he
saw fit. I just hoped he didn't stretch my rubber band too far.

I stepped out of the Mercedes and raised my hands to show I wasn't
a threat. The deputy wasn't convinced and told me to turn around and
face the vehicle. I didn't like that sound of that, and I stared at my
reflection in the lenses of his aviators as I considered whether or not to
comply. From behind the deputy, I could hear the river flowing toward
some unknown destination. It sounded like static coming from a far-
away speaker.

"Turn around and face the vehicle, asshole."

My hands were still in the air, and it took an enormous amount of
self-control not to step toward the guy and tempt a response. The asshole
remark stretched my rubber band to its limit.

"I was speeding, and you were right to pull me," I said. "But I figure
Dale has about twenty years' seniority on you, and if you haul me in on
some bullshit charge, he'll laugh in your face and I'll walk away smiling
from ear to ear."

The deputy seemed to consider that scenario for a minute, then said,
"You're that private detective, aren't you?"

I started to respond, but the deputy cut me off.

"I've heard the sheriff talk about you. He don't seem to trust you as
far as he can throw you. And I don't much trust you either."

The angel on my shoulder was in a lotus position taking deep,
measured breaths. The devils were grinning and rubbing their hands
together.

"Will you please call Dale?" I said.

The deputy kept one hand on his side arm and pulled out his phone
with the other. He touched the screen a couple of times, and soon I heard
a ring tone coming from the phone's speaker. I was looking forward to
listening to Dale ream out this shithead for pulling me over. Hell, Dale
would probably be impressed that I got the Mercedes up to seventy-five.
Then again, Dale could be a moody bastard. He might tell the deputy to

write me a ticket or even haul me in just for the fun of it. When the call connected, all of those thoughts immediately vanished.

"What do you need, Skeeter?"

I was so surprised to hear Byrd's voice that I almost didn't register that the deputy's name was Skeeter. I filed that bit of information in with all the other things I hated about him, including the sunglasses and the goatee.

"Sheriff, I'm up in Cruso with that man from Charleston, Mr. Reed. I clocked him going seventy-five on 276."

There was a long pause, and I imagined Byrd's jowls dangling on his collar.

"That's a mighty fast pace," Byrd said. "Did he give a reason?"

"It was a joke," I yelled toward the phone. "I thought Dale was chasing me."

Byrd laughed. "Skeeter, write Mr. Reed a warning and send him on his way."

Skeeter tapped the phone screen and put it to his ear. "But Sheriff, he was going thirty miles over the limit; we can take his license for that. He needs to be brought in. We can't allow this—he should be punished."

I couldn't hear Byrd's response, but whatever the sheriff was saying made Skeeter's jaw clench so tight I thought his teeth might shatter inside his mouth. A moment later Skeeter put his phone away and stared at me like I was a dog who'd just taken a shit in his living room.

"Wait here," he said.

I stood by the door of the Mercedes and watched Skeeter climb into his patrol car. I wondered what Byrd had said to him. I guessed it was probably something akin to "Let him go, but keep your eye on him."

My leg was starting to hurt, so I got inside the Mercedes and plugged my phone into the stereo. When Skeeter reappeared next to my window, I was blasting "Breaking the Law" by Judas Priest. It was a dick move, but it was satisfying.

Skeeter returned and threw my license, registration, and a blue warning ticket into my lap. He then walked slowly along the side of the Mercedes back to his patrol car. I let the stereo blare the entire time.

I drove up to the cabin never topping forty miles per hour. When I got out of the Mercedes, something compelled me to look at the side of the car. Skeeter had walked strangely close to my vehicle on the way back to his patrol car. I saw it almost instantly, a long white scratch that ran from the passenger door all the way back to the rear bumper. The son of a bitch had keyed my car.

9

I was fuming when I walked inside the cabin, so I distracted myself by going to the basement to check on my batch of IPA. I'd brought most of my brewing equipment up from Charleston, at least what I could fit in the back of the Mercedes: three 5-gallon stainless-steel brew kettles, several 6.5-gallon fermenting and bottling buckets, a copper immersion chiller, a hydrometer, a thermometer, a couple of siphons, and a dozen or so empty glass growlers along with bags of various malts and hops, yeasts, herbs, and spices. The IPA had been conditioning for almost a month, and it was just about ready to drink.

Dale hadn't been lying my first day in the cabin when I looked down the stairs into the dark basement and he said, "They ain't nothing down there." The basement was bare aside from a few load-bearing wood beams that ran from the ceiling down into the red dirt floor. I'd found a couple of plastic folding card tables behind the cabin and dragged them down the basement steps to serve as the base for my makeshift brewing operation. The basement was dark, damp, and smelled like a locker room. But some really good beer has been brewed in some really shitty places.

I started drinking beer during my senior year in high school, and for years I didn't care what brand it was or where it came from. If it was cheap and contained alcohol, it was good enough for me. Then one day a friend invited me to a tasting at the Palmetto Brewing Company in downtown Charleston. The first beer we tried was a double IPA served in a small goblet. "What a rip-off," I said to my friend. But once I tasted it, I was hooked. It was slightly bitter and full of flavors like pine, lime, grapefruit, and caramel. It was unlike anything I'd ever had. It made the beer I'd been used to drinking taste like bottled water.

"It's only a six-ounce pour because it's eleven percent alcohol," my friend said. "That's more than double the alcohol of the crap you've been drinking."

After that day I never looked at beer the same way again. I stopped buying twelve-packs at the Piggly Wiggly and started running up tabs at craft beer stores. I read beer magazines and bookmarked home-brewing websites. Instead of hanging out in dingy dive bars drinking Miller Lite, I downed double IPAs and stouts at authentic taprooms. I bought an entry-level beer-making kit and started brewing barely drinkable amber-colored liquid. But I read more, experimented more, and bugged the hell out of brewers for advice. My beer making slowly improved, and as it did, I upgraded my equipment. After years of trial and error I finally brewed a batch that would rival some of the best beers on the market. But I didn't have any intention of selling it—I just wanted to drink it. Lots of it.

But steady alcohol intake increases anxiety, which doesn't do much for my temper. The pills help regulate it to a certain extent, but even when loaded down in antianxiety medication, I can feel it bubbling just below the surface. My temper has cost me jobs, friendships, and romantic relationships. One of the more recent casualties had been Sarah, a woman I'd lived with for a little over a year. Sarah was a nurse at MUSC—the Medical University of South Carolina—in downtown Charleston. She worked long hours, which meant when I wasn't out photographing adulterers and insurance frauds, I was home alone, drinking beer and popping pills. That setup was actually fine with me; the less she was around, the less opportunity she had to judge my lifestyle. But one day when I woke up around noon and stumbled into the kitchen, I noticed a note taped to the refrigerator. It wasn't a Dear John letter; it was a Dear Davis letter. The long and short of it was that she wanted me out of the house by the end of the day. Apparently she'd had enough of my drinking, temper, and self-medicating. She ended the note with the phone number of a support group that she said helped people like me. As if she knew what kind of people I was. I threw the note in the garbage and got dressed. If Sarah didn't want me, I didn't want her either.

That was the day I called Laura. We'd once been incredibly close, up until the day I was a no-show for our parents' funeral. It had driven a wedge between us and we hadn't spoken in years. But she'd actually seemed happy to hear from me when I called, maybe even relieved. She said she was ready to start over, to be family again. We talked on the phone for an hour while I packed up my stuff: clothes, shoes, books, a laptop, a few cases of beer, and my beer-making equipment. I crammed it all in the Mercedes and drove from Mount Pleasant over the Ravenel Bridge into downtown Charleston. From there I went south past James Island to a residential development at Folly Beach and a three-bedroom, three-and-a-half-bath house with a pool and sauna. Laura was standing on the doorstep when I pulled in the driveway. When I got out of my car, she came over and held me tight. We made a pact right then and there to never speak about the past.

10

The following afternoon Dale asked me to come down to Junebug's to watch the Tennessee / Georgia game. Since Dale knew my IPA was ready to drink, I didn't know if he was interested in my company or my beer. Either way, I wasn't going to take it personally.

I turned off 276 onto the gravel driveway and drove past the small family graveyard, where a few concrete tombstones held firm against the encroaching weeds. Beyond the graveyard stood a vegetable garden that by this time of year was nothing more than a mess of dead plants and rotting squash. I parked in front of the house and honked the horn a couple of times. I got out of the Mercedes and was opening the back tailgate when Junebug appeared at the door.

"You gonna give me a hand?" I asked.

Junebug waddled over and grabbed two growlers of my IPA, then turned and waddled back into the house without saying a word. I grabbed two more growlers and followed him.

The house smelled like chewing tobacco and cheap aftershave— much like Dale's patrol car. Actually, much like Dale himself. I went into the kitchen and grabbed a pint glass from a drying rack next to the sink. I poured a beer from one growler and set it and the other in the refrigerator.

"Shit!" I heard Dale yell from somewhere in the back of the house. When I walked into the living room, Dale and Junebug were sitting in matching recliners, staring at an enormous TV that sat atop an old whiskey barrel. I moved a fleece blanket from the seat of a slat-back rocking chair, the only other chair in the room, and sat down. It was early in the first quarter and Georgia was already up by ten points.

"Them sumbitches couldn't defend against a Girl Scout troop," Dale said.

Dale and Junebug drank their beer right from the growlers, which they'd set on a side table between the two recliners. Every minute or so, almost like clockwork, they'd grab a growler by the handle and take a long swig. The scene reminded me of an attraction I'd seen at Disney World as a kid. It was called the Country Bear Jamboree. I remembered sitting in the audience and watching a group of animatronic bears pluck banjos, strum washboards, and blow into clay jugs. "Those are just stereotypes," my dad had told me when we left the theater. I didn't know what stereotypes were at that time. But the older I got, the more I realized they existed for a reason.

Every now and then Junebug would spit chewing tobacco into a Styrofoam coffee cup packed with paper towels. Dale spit his into an empty two-liter Mountain Dew bottle. I tried to imagine these two at a beer tasting: the brewer lecturing about subtle flavor notes and mouthfeel while two enormous men, one in overalls and the other in a stained deputy uniform, spat loudly in the background.

"Do you like it?" I asked Dale, after he took another swig.

"Hell yeah!" he said. "What's the ABV?"

"Probably around seven. What do you think, Junebug? Is it any good?"

Junebug grunted.

"Better than that piss Dale makes."

"Bullshit!" Dale yelled. He was staring at the TV. The Bulldogs had just scored again. "Where's a fuckin' flag?"

In his defense, Dale's beer wasn't all that bad. Dale's problem was that he wasn't patient. It takes time to brew good beer. You have to let it sit and ferment, then sit longer to condition. That's when the flavor takes hold. A good IPA can take more than a month to go from a sludge of water, grains, yeast, malt, and hops to something close to sublime. Dale just couldn't wait that long. Whether it was ready or not, the thought of a few gallons of beer sitting in the pantry was just too tempting.

At halftime the score was Georgia thirty-one, Tennessee seven. Dale was in a mood. He'd unbuttoned the front of his uniform shirt, and the white tank top underneath was stained brown with tobacco juice. When the halftime show started, he slammed down the leg rest of the recliner and got up and left the room. Junebug grabbed the remote and changed the channel over to a NASCAR race.

Dale's father wasn't much for conversation, but I thought I'd give it a try.

"Did Dale tell you I was writing a book?" I asked.

"Nope."

"Well, I am; that's why I'm up here for the winter. I'm writing about Cold Mountain."

"They's already a book about that."

"I know, but this is nonfiction, about the military plane that crashed up there."

"Uh-huh."

"Did you ever go up there as a kid?"

"Where?"

"Cold Mountain? Did you ever hike up there and explore?"

"Yup."

"Did you see any wreckage, any debris?"

"Yup. Birddog's got a piece a metal from that plane."

"Birddog?"

"The sheriff."

"Yeah, I talked to him a couple of days ago. He told me there were rumors about gold bullion being found near the crash site."

Junebug spat into his Styrofoam cup and wiped his mouth with the back of his hand. The race had gone to a commercial, and the screen showed a middle-aged couple riding horses on the beach, then hugging under a waterfall. I didn't pay close attention, but I figured the ad was for either a Caribbean resort or low-testosterone medication.

"Junebug? Was there gold on that plane? Was it ever found?"

Junebug watched the commercial as closely as he had been watching the race.

"Who's Gerald Johnson?" I asked. "Sheriff Byrd said he was the one who claimed to have found the gold. Is he any relation to you?"

"That's Floppy's granddaddy," Junebug said, his eyes never leaving the screen.

"Who's Floppy?"

Dale walked back into the room holding a bag of pork rinds.

"You stay away from Floppy," he said.

"Who's Floppy?" I asked again.

Dale plopped his mass into the recliner and tore open the bag of rinds.

"Here," he said, grabbing the remote from the arm of Junebug's chair.

"Who's Floppy?" I asked for the third time.

Dale jerked his head like he was trying to shake off a bad memory.

"Floppy Johnson," he finally said. "He's a mechanic. Got a shop up at Sunburst, near the lake."

"So it was his grandfather who found the gold?"

Dale leaned forward and gritted his teeth.

"There weren't no fucking gold," he said. "Gerald Johnson was batshit crazy. And his grandboy Floppy's just as crazy as he was."

"From what I'm learning, crazy and Johnson seems to go hand in hand."

Dale shot me a look. "I can make it so you're never found."

The third quarter started, and on the first play the Bulldogs ran back the kickoff eighty-five yards for a touchdown. Dale's face turned bright red, and I worried that he might spontaneously combust and wallpaper the living room with pork rinds, tobacco juice, and beer.

* * *

I left Junebug's house around five. Tennessee had lost by over forty points. A sport's analyst called it a blowout; Dale called it "fucking bullshit." On the way back to the cabin I stopped by El Bacaratos. Doris wasn't there, but a woman who could have been her twin took my to-go order for a large bowl of guacamole and bag of chips. The place was packed. Folks in Cruso seemed to eat their dinner early, generally between five and six.

I stood at the counter near the front door and surveyed the customers. Most were families, moms and dads with young kids in grass-stained football uniforms. An elderly couple sat at a table near the front of the restaurant. The man was wearing light-blue coveralls and the woman a green floral housedress. They could have been in a Norman Rockwell painting if not for the two large chimichangas sitting in front of them.

I looked toward the back of the restaurant and over to the booth where Sheriff Byrd had warned me of the evils of sushi and prescription pharmaceuticals. Now two women were sitting in the booth. The one facing me had wavy blonde hair and wore a black fleece jacket. The other woman, whose back was to me, had dark-red hair that jutted out in all directions from underneath a white knit cap. The redhead was obviously telling a story, because the blonde kept smiling and nodding. Occasionally she would lean back and laugh, revealing dimples in her cheeks the size of cashews.

The blonde glanced over and caught me staring, so I quickly turned my attention to the elderly couple, who were still working on the chimichangas. When I looked back at the booth, the two women were getting up leave. Just then Doris's twin appeared, holding a white plastic bag with the words THANK YOU printed on the sides in red.

"Large guacamole and chips?" she asked.

As I was reaching for my wallet, the blonde and the redhead walked by me on their way out.

The blonde nodded at the bag in my hand. "Best guacamole in the county," she said.

"Yeah, I had it here a couple of days ago, and—" But the women were already out the door.

* * *

In the parking lot I got in the Mercedes and placed the bag on the passenger seat. I started the car and pushed the button for the heated seats. The warmth felt good on my legs, especially the bad one, which most of the time felt as if it had been left in a freezer. I rooted around in my pants pocket and dug out my cell phone. I was hoping to find a text, a missed call, or a voice mail from Laura. But there was nothing. I'd not connected my email to my phone, so checking that would have to wait until I got back to the cabin. I really wanted to hear from her. I couldn't imagine what she was going through, and honestly she probably couldn't imagine what I was going through either. I wondered if she even cared.

But as I sat there warming my ass, I couldn't help but wonder if whoever opened that storage unit door and shot me had had their own go at Greg after I was unconscious. Maybe they'd done the real damage that had put him into a coma. Maybe I was only partly to blame. I doubted it, but the thought offered a small amount of comfort, and I needed comfort wherever I could find it.

As I was putting my phone back in my pocket, I heard laughing coming from the other side of the parking lot. I looked out the driver's side window and saw the blonde and the redhead standing next to a green Jeep Wrangler. They talked for a minute, then hugged. Then the redhead climbed in the Jeep and took off on 276 toward Waynesville. The blonde walked over to her vehicle, a brown, vintage Mercedes sedan. She got in the car, buckled her seat belt, and pulled out of the parking lot, turning in the same direction as her friend. On the back of her car, a LONG BRANCH BREWERY bumper sticker was barely legible in the fading light.

11

I awoke the next morning to the sound of a police siren. It was so loud, I thought it was coming from under my bed. I reached toward the nightstand for my phone and knocked over an empty beer glass in the process. The time on my phone read 8:49. I lay still for a few seconds, waiting for the siren to grow softer as it chased whatever trouble it was after. But the sound didn't relent. I crawled out of bed and walked through the house to the sliding door that led out to the deck. Looking through the glass, I could see rain coming down in sheets, billions of drops reflecting blue slivers of light. Wearing nothing but a pair of boxers, I opened the door and stepped out onto the deck. The rain felt like tiny little ice picks bouncing off my back and shoulders. I leaned over the railing and saw Dale's patrol car in the clearing below, lights flashing, siren going full steam. Suddenly the siren stopped and the driver's window lowered a few inches. Dale pressed his fat cheeks and mouth into the crack. It looked like a squid trying to squeeze through a mail slot.

"Get your ass down here," he yelled. "And bring those fucking keys."

I limped back into the house and pulled on a pair of jeans, a sweat shirt, and sneakers. I grabbed the keys from the kitchen table and went out the back door and down around to Dale's patrol car. By the time I hauled myself into the passenger seat, I was soaking wet. Dale didn't seem to notice—he was too busy playing air guitar to the song blasting on the stereo: "Wild Side" by Mötley Crüe.

"I saw them back in '87 in Knoxville," he yelled over the music. "Tommy Lee had that floating drum kit that came out over the crowd. That was badass."

Apparently there was no emergency.

"Why did you blare the siren instead of just coming up to get me?"

"What?" Dale said.

I reached over and turned down the volume.

"Why did you blare the siren instead of coming up to get me?"

Dale gave me a confused look. "Because it's raining."

I shook my head. "What do you want?"

"That couple called the station about them keys this morning," Dale said. "They's gonna stop in to claim 'em this afternoon. So hand 'em over."

"How do you know the keys even belong to them?"

"I don't know that they do, but it don't matter. I told you they're probably collecting 'em for their buddy. They're just fucking keys, for crying out loud."

For me those keys were a welcome distraction, and I was reluctant to give them up. They kept me from obsessing over all sorts of uncomfortable scenarios, such as comatose brothers-in-law, mystery gunmen, pissed-off sisters, and blank pages.

I clicked the stereo off and faced Dale.

"Don't give that couple these keys," I said.

"Why the hell not?"

"Because these keys don't belong to them. And because they lied to me about being at Graveyard Fields."

Dale laughed. "You've lost your fucking mind."

"I asked Terry if that couple mentioned Cordell's name when they came in asking if anyone had turned in a set of keys. They didn't."

Dale shrugged.

"So?"

"Doesn't that seem weird to you?"

"No. They don't need to give the man's name. Either someone turned in some keys or they didn't."

"Look," I said. "That old BMW is registered to Lester Cordell. Right?"
Dale didn't bother to respond.

"This," I said, holding up the key that unlocked the BMW, "opens his car. This is his property, so let him come get it."

"For fuck's sakes, Davis, you gotta let this shit go. That hippie's just up there camping. Let his buddies collect his keys for him. Man's probably too stoned to find his car, much less his fucking keys."

"You really think he's up there camping?"

"Hell, I don't know. Maybe the car's broke down. Did you think of that possibility? Wouldn't surprise me if that piece a shit just gave up the ghost and that hippie abandoned it up there. He's probably back at his house soaking in a tub full of patchouli."

"Let's drive up there right now and see if the car is still parked."

Dale looked at me like I'd just offered him a hand job.

"Are you out of your mind? It's pouring rain—that means it's gonna be foggy as shit up on the parkway. Drag your own ass up there if you want, but I ain't going."

"All right then, let's make a deal. Let me hold on to the keys for a couple more hours. I'll go up to Graveyard Fields and see if the BMW is still there. If it is, I'll bring the keys to the department and that couple can pick them up."

"And if the car is gone? Then what?"

I turned my head and watched the rain bounce off the hood of the patrol car. I didn't know what I'd do if the BMW was gone. It wouldn't prove anything other than that someone had been able to drive it away.

"I don't know," I said. "I guess I'll bring in the keys either way."

Dale shook his head. "You'd do just about anything to not write that book, wouldn't you?"

"Is it a deal?"

Dale looked toward the cabin, then back at me. "How many growlers of that IPA you got left?"

"Seven."

"Put three in the trunk. And drop off them keys before noon."

12

By the time I pulled into the Graveyard Fields parking lot, the fog was beginning to lift and I could just make out the gray, wiry trees that dotted the meadow. I sat there for about half an hour watching the sun slowly wipe away the haze like a washcloth over a fogged-up mirror. I wished there were something that could do that to my brain.

I looked over at the BMW, then to the key ring sitting in the cup holder between the seats. I wondered where Cordell was and why the hipster couple had lied to me. I thought for a minute but couldn't come up with a reasonable explanation. I wasn't surprised. I'd never been a good detective. Never a good cop, for that matter. Maybe I'd never had the chance. My police career had ended before it really ever got started, and my private detective business didn't involve intricate mysteries. People didn't hire me to solve murders or find their missing kids; they hired me to lurk in the shadows and watch cheaters. I was the guy you called if you thought your spouse was stepping out on you. For a hundred bucks an hour I'd follow some man to a cheap motel or apartment complex. Then I'd wait in my car and point my telephoto lens at whatever door the man happened to knock on. When a woman answered, I'd start shooting. I didn't need shots of the man and the woman in the throes of passion; I just needed a picture or two of them standing together in a doorway at a place the man couldn't reasonably explain being at. I would print out the photos and hand them over to my client, whose attorney would use them to negotiate a settlement.

Spurned women were my biggest clients. Right behind them were companies looking for insurance fraud. The HR department would get in touch with me and give me the information on an employee who had been injured at work and was collecting disability. My job was to make sure the employee wasn't milking the system. I would track them down and sit out in front of their house and monitor their comings and goings. Sometimes I'd see them hobble out on crutches and walk down their front path to the mailbox. I'd see people delivering covered casserole dishes to them and home health care workers arriving to help them with their physical therapy program. I'd watch for a couple of days and then call their employer and tell them I was satisfied that the person in question was legitimately injured.

But other times I would catch a fraud. I'd photographed one man who was collecting disability for a back injury riding a Jet Ski down the Ashley River. Another man, this one claiming shoulder pain, played golf for three days straight. I photographed him high-fiving his playing partners on the eighteenth green of the Coosaw Creek Country Club. My favorite was a woman who was collecting disability due to "blunt force trauma." A box had fallen on her in the warehouse where she worked, and she'd complained of whiplash and neck pain. One afternoon I followed her to the executive airport and photographed her climbing into a prop engine plane with a parachute strapped to her back. I didn't hang around to see whether or not she landed safely.

It was easy work and didn't require much cognitive power. It didn't require much physical power either. I rarely had to get out of my car. I'd just sit there with my camera, a couple of books, and an insulated growler of beer and wait for the right shot. A hundred-dollar-an-hour voyeur—not a bad gig.

But occasionally I would have to confront someone. That's when things could get dicey. Because of my quick temper, I've always tried my best to avoid confrontation. That's why I left the police department a little more than a month after my training ended. I was afraid one of those Charleston frat boys who wore pink shorts and popped-collared polos would give me some lip about a ticket and bait me into smacking the entitlement out of him.

When I left the force, my friend Perry had suggested I see a psychiatrist to try to wrap my head around the whole temper thing. I took his advice and left my one and only appointment with a prescription for a ninety-day supply of Xanax, no refills. The pills didn't abolish my temper, but they did lower its ceiling. Confrontations that could cause me to lose my shit and lash out at someone became merely uncomfortable situations. The psychiatrist had told me the pills were just a temporary tourniquet and that I could learn to control my temper through months or maybe years of cognitive behavioral therapy. That road didn't interest me. After that first prescription ran out, I called Dr. Landry. I'd been numb ever since.

But the pills weren't one hundred percent effective. Even with them I could still lose it if pushed hard enough, like with Greg. But most of the time I was cool. I knew the pills were a crutch, but they kept me where I needed to be. I'd rather be slow and foggy than locked and loaded. I was much safer that way. So were those around me.

* * *

When the sun had erased the last bit of fog, a Volvo station wagon pulled into the parking lot. I watched as an older couple got out of the vehicle and pulled two walking sticks from the back seat. They both wore large-brimmed hats and carried water bottles strapped to their waists. A leisurely morning hike, I thought. Must be nice to be able to walk some sort of distance. I rubbed my leg and considered the fact that I hadn't walked all that much when it worked properly. I've always been real good at taking things for granted.

The couple headed across the parking lot over to where the steps led down to the trail. They were walking slowly and holding hands, the same way my parents used to. I'd never liked holding hands with a woman. It always made me feel like I was in high school. But my parents held hands everywhere they went. I'd written a couple of lines about that in the eulogy I was to deliver at their funeral. *They held hands to show the world they were one.* It wasn't a very good line, but I remembered being proud of it at the time. I'd imagined standing behind the church altar and reciting those words while everyone wept.

But I never said them. The night before the funeral I chased four pills with eight pints of beer. I didn't wake up until three the next afternoon.

By that time my parents were already in the ground. Laura called me that evening to tell me that the funeral was beautiful. Then she told me to go away. After that call I swallowed four more pills and drank eight more pints. I'd hoped what made me an asshole would make me forget I was an asshole.

It was a fine morning to be sentimental. For a good hour I looked out over the spiny trees covering Graveyard Fields and thought about the past. I thought about Laura and Greg, wondering if I had hurt them both beyond repair. I thought about my parents and Sarah and how Perry had been so kind to me both during and after my time on the force. I thought about all the people I cared about and all the people I'd let down. The lists were almost identical.

I shook off the nostalgia, grabbed the keys from the center console, and cycled through them for what must have been the hundredth time. Good detectives connect dots—Perry had told me that years ago. Good detectives draw lines between what seem like unrelated and insignificant pieces of information, then step back and analyze the picture. Every clue is a dot, and once you connect the right dots in the right order, the solution appears. That's how good detectives solve a case. Perry would know; he was one of the best.

But what dots did I have? A couple dozen keys. A locked trunk. Two hipsters who'd lied about how long they'd been on the parkway. Were these clues? Not according to Dale, and he was the law enforcement officer. I was creating a mystery where there wasn't one. I needed to forget about the keys and find another distraction.

* * *

I pulled out of the parking lot and headed north toward Mount Pisgah and the ranger station. When I walked in, Joanne was standing behind the counter drinking a cup of coffee.

"Do you remember me?" I asked. "I was in here a couple days ago with Deputy Johnson."

Joanne chuckled. "Dale Johnson. How'd you get tangled up with him?"

"I'm renting his cabin for the winter, and he seems to think that makes us best friends."

Joanne rolled her eyes. "Lucky you."

I shrugged. "He's kinda like a hangnail. The more you pick at him, the longer he sticks around."

"So what can I do for you?"

"I'm curious about something," I said. "Have you ever heard about gold being found on Cold Mountain? I'm working on a book about the bomber crash, and a couple of people have mentioned gold being found near the crash site."

Joanne laughed.

"These mountains are full of stories," she said. "The ghost at Devil's Courthouse. The headless body found at Frying Pan Gap. The teenage lovers who threw themselves off Looking Glass Falls. I've heard them all, and none of them are true."

"So you don't believe there was gold on that plane when it crashed?"

Joanne laughed again, and I started to feel like a fool.

"Look, after that plane went down, the Army and a bunch of local volunteers scoured that crash site. I don't think there was any gold on that plane, but if there was, it was found a long time ago."

"Do people ever come in here and ask about it?"

"Once in a while, but it's really more of a local rumor the old-timers talk about. Heck, most people who come in here asking about Cold Mountain don't even know that a plane crashed up there. They're more interested in the book or the movie. They want to know if I met Jude Law or Nicole Kidman. It makes their heads spin when I tell them the movie was filmed in Romania."

* * *

I left the ranger station and drove down to El Bacaratos to call Dale. I wanted to get back to the deck as soon as possible and hoped I could convince him to save me a trip into town. As soon as he picked up, I knew the answer was going to be no.

"Where the fuck are you?"

"I'm at El Bacaratos. Drive up here and I'll give you the keys."

"Nice try, dumbass. You drive yourself down to the station and turn in those keys like you promised."

I really didn't want to drive all the way into town, but a deal was a deal.

"Perk up, little camper," Dale said. "Don't be all sore because you have to hand over them keys."

I didn't respond.

"I tell you what," Dale said. "Let's go to Long Branch tonight. I wanna talk to that sweet thing who owns the place. Pick me up at seven."

"When did I become your Uber?"

"What? I don't speak Spanish, dipshit. Now get them keys to the station."

13

The Haywood County Sheriff's Department was located just off Main Street in the middle of downtown Waynesville. The street was a half-mile-long strip flanked by restaurants, real estate offices, and a disturbingly high number of stores selling cinnamon brooms and enamel mugs. Waynesville was a tourist town, and proudly so. But it was mid-November and the sidewalks were practically empty. I guessed things would pick up closer to Thanksgiving, which was only a few days away. I didn't know how the stores stayed in business during these cold winter months. I would just have to add that to the long list of things I didn't know.

I pulled into the sheriff's department parking lot and found an empty spot marked VISITOR. I walked through the department's front door and entered a small lobby, where the top of a gray bouffant hovered near the far side of a tall counter.

"How can I help you?" the bouffant's owner said as I approached.

"I'm looking for Dale Johnson."

"He's on patrol at the moment. Is there something I can assist you with?"

"Can you give him this?" I put the key ring on the counter.

The woman—who, if her name tag could be trusted, was Barbara—grabbed a yellow Post-it note.

"And your name is?"

"Davis Reed."

She wrote my name on the note, saying the words out loud as she jotted them down. When she finished, she gave me a knowing look. "Wait a minute. You're the writer."

I was about to tell her she was wrong. I had been known as many things in my life: officer, private detective, liar, drunk, asshole. But *writer* was new to me, especially since I'd not yet written a word.

"Deputy Johnson told me about you," Barbara said. "He says you're writing a book about Cold Mountain. You know there's already a book about that."

"So I've heard."

"I'm a writer too. I have a blog. It's about southern cooking. I write down all the steps of a recipe and post them along with pictures I take with my phone. My last one was about pinto beans. It's a popular blog—I have over thirty readers. You should look it up; it's called BarbsCountryKitchen.com."

As Barbara spelled out the website address, I heard a sound behind me. When I turned, a skinny man about my age was walking toward me. He wore greasy blue coveralls and a camouflage ball cap with the Ford logo stamped on the front. His limp was much worse than mine. His left leg dragged behind him like a broken tree limb.

The man hobbled up to the counter and looked directly at Barbara, ignoring me altogether. His body odor was ungodly, and I took a step to the side to get out of its range. One step didn't work. I needed to take about fifty more.

"What do you want now, Floppy?" Barbara asked.

"It's the same as last time. Someone's broke into my garage."

"Is anything missing?"

"No, but my things is out of order. My tools and stuff. I keep my things organized, and when I went in this morning, my plug wrench wasn't where I left it yesterday and my jumper cables was on the floor, not on the hook where they's supposed to be. I know, because I keep my things organized."

Barbara rolled her eyes and let out a deep breath.

The man glanced at the key ring sitting on the counter and cocked his head like a dog reacting to a high-pitched whistle. He then looked over at me as if I'd just magically appeared. His eyes gave me a once-over from head to toe. I looked back at him and smiled. I assumed this was the notorious Floppy Johnson, the grandson of the man who'd claimed to find, then lose, or maybe not lose, a chest full of gold. Dale had said Floppy was crazy, which was always a vague diagnosis at best. But from what little I'd witnessed of Floppy so far, I thought Dale might be right on the money.

"Who are you?" Floppy asked me. "I don't know you, I ain't never seen you before—are you from around here? 'Cause I know just about everybody here and if I'd seen you before, I'd remember you, but you don't look familiar to me. So what's your name and where are you from."

"Floppy, leave this man alone," Barbara said. She then pushed a button on an antiquated intercom system that sat next to her computer. As she spoke, she leaned down so close to the microphone I thought she might take a bite of it.

"Deputy Norris, could you come out front, please?"

A moment later a door behind the counter with PRIVATE written across the front opened and my archnemesis stepped through. Skeeter was wearing his mirrored aviators and rolling a toothpick between his clenched teeth. If my eyes had been lasers, I would have burned a hole through his face.

Skeeter stared at me for a moment, then looked at the key ring sitting on the counter.

"Hey, Skeeter," Floppy said. "You still drive that black 'Stang? I tell ya, I think Sally could take her. Maybe not off the line, but you give me a good stretch a road and Sally'd blow by you like you's standing still. Now my buddy Cecil has a 'Stang, but it's an old five-point-oh and sounds like one of them big motel ice machines when it cranks up. Now, I don't never get that ice when I'm at a motel, 'cause you don't never know what's been in them little plastic buckets. Them nice motels give you them little bags to put in the bucket, but still . . ."

"Floppy!" Barbara yelled. "Go with Officer Norris."

Skeeter gave me a scowl, then turned around and walked back through the doorway. As Floppy followed him, I thought about Skeeter's "black 'Stang" and how much I would enjoy etching the word *prick* into its hood.

"Sorry about that," Barbara said. "Floppy's in here at least twice a month with some sort of emergency."

She glanced toward the door, then leaned forward and lowered her voice.

"He thinks the government is out to get him," she whispered. "The boys used to investigate every time he'd come in with a complaint. But now they just take a statement and forget about it. It seems to calm him down for a little while."

"Why waste the time taking a statement? Why not tell him to get lost?"

Barbara lowered her brows. "Because he's Deputy Johnson's cousin. Now here, let me tell you more about my blog."

14

After what seemed like an eternity of listening to Barbara's plans to monetize her website of cornbread and banana pudding recipes, I excused myself and headed back to the cabin. I spent a couple of hours and a couple of beers lying on the couch regretting that I'd agreed to go to Long Branch with Dale. I didn't really feel like going out. But Dale was not one to be denied. If I didn't show up at his house by seven, he would track me down and drag me out by the ankles.

At 6:58 I pulled up to Junebug's to find Dale standing in the driveway. I could have seen him from a mile away. Actually, I probably could have seen him from outer space. He was wearing an enormous orange University of Tennessee sweat shirt. I realized it was the first time I'd seen Dale out of uniform. I guessed this was his "going out" wear.

When Dale wiggled himself into my Mercedes, I asked him if the couple had come by the sheriff's department to collect the keys.

"They never showed," he said. "And that's the last I have to say on that subject. Now let's go get hammered."

While driving into Waynesville, I fought the urge to comment on Dale's sweat shirt. I wanted to ask him if the sun knew he'd stolen its look. But Dale didn't seem in any mood to joke. He kept rubbing his hands together and taking deep breaths. It was like I was driving him to a job interview.

When we pulled into the Long Branch parking lot, Dale turned to me. I'd never seen him look so serious.

"Now, Davis, listen to me. Tonight I'm gonna make a move on the brewery owner, Beth. And I need you to be my wingman."

"Wingman? What does that involve, exactly?" I said.

"You laugh at my jokes and make me look interesting—not that that will take a lot. And then when me and Beth start hitting it off, you make yourself scarce. Go to the bathroom or wait in the car until I close the deal."

"Make you look interesting, then disappear. Got it. Hey, nice sweat shirt, by the way."

"It's my alma mater." Dale pronounced the last word the same way he pronounced *tomato*.

"You said you were expelled."

"Yeah, but I went there for a while."

"Well, I drove through the campus of Duke once, but I don't wear their sweat shirt."

Dale snarled. "You're a shit wingman, you know that?"

*　*　*

Long Branch had taken a page out of the microbrewery design handbook—reclaimed wood tables, chalkboards, vintage lightbulbs surrounded by small wire cages, shelves of books and board games. It was like every microbrewery in the country used the same interior decorator.

Dale and I found a high-top table near the bar and sat down.

"I'm not fucking with you, Davis. Tonight's about two things: one, not talking about BMWs, key rings, or books you ain't writing, and two, me taking Beth home."

"I'm your ride, dumbass. You really think the owner of this brewery is going to jump at the chance to ride back to your dad's house with me and a guy who looks like the mascot for Florida orange juice?"

"Brother, how long have I known you, a month? You ain't seen me work my magic. Tonight's going to be a lesson for you."

As we argued that point, I noticed Dale glance over my shoulder toward the bar. Suddenly his eyes grew wide and his jaw lowered a few inches.

"What's the matter?" I said.

Dale didn't answer. He didn't have to. A second later a cute young woman holding two menus stood next to our table. Her short blonde hair curled outward just before it hit her shoulders, and she wore a very—and I mean very—low-cut black tank top with the brewery's name printed on the front. At least I think it was the brewery's name—the woman's breasts were so large that the printing was stretched to the point of being almost illegible.

" 'Evening, fellas," she said. "Can I get you a beer?"

I took a menu while Dale continued to stare at the woman's chest. I glanced up at him every few seconds, worried he might fall into a hypnotic trance and start walking zombie-like around the restaurant.

"I'll have a pint of the Dark Secret IPA," I said.

The waitress nodded and turned to Dale. "And what about you, sunshine?"

I laughed, and Dale snapped back to consciousness.

"Yeah, me too," he said.

The woman smiled and walked away. Dale's eye followed the path of her Daisy Dukes all the way back to the bar.

"Holy shit," he said. "That girl's shorts are so tight you can see her ovaries."

"She seems to be your target demographic."

Dale frowned. "What the fuck are you talking about? That woman's exactly my type."

"Should I start my wingman duties when she comes back?"

Dale gritted his teeth and shook his head. "No. That girl's hot, but tonight's about me and Beth. I'm gonna stay focused."

I studied the menu, trying to decide what my stomach could handle. "Do you want to split a burger?"

Dale looked at me with disdain. "That's the gayest fucking thing I ever heard. I ain't splitting shit with you."

The woman returned with our beers and took our food order. Dale got the burger with everything, and I settled on a cheese quesadilla.

"What's your name?" Dale said to the woman as she collected our menus.

"Daiquiri."

"Like the drink?"

"Yep. I'm a little bit sweet, a little bit sour, and too much of me will make your head spin."

I jerked my head toward Dale. I wanted to see how focused he could remain after hearing a line like that. I was impressed. He rolled his shoulders and bit his lip but didn't lose sight of his goal.

"Well, Daiquiri, would you tell Beth I'd like to speak to her?"

"Who's Beth?"

"The owner of this place."

Daiquiri laughed. "The owner's name is Diana."

I snorted, and some beer dripped down my chin. Daiquiri shook her head and wandered away. I placed my hand on Dale's shoulder and gave him a consoling smile.

"Lesson one. Get the fucking name right."

*   *   *

The IPA was very good, crisp and hoppy without a lot of malt aftertaste. I guessed they used Pacific Northwest hops, which have a stronger citrus flavor than German hops. I loved it. It was the kind of beer I could drink all day, every day. Not that that was an especially high bar.

I finished my beer before Dale finished his, which was a first. He seemed distracted.

"Thinking about your strategy?" I said while looking around for Daiquiri.

"I could've sworn her name was Beth."

I caught Daiquiri's eye and held up my empty glass. She gave me a nod and walked toward the bar.

"Come on, man, liven up," I said. "I'm ready for a lesson in the art of the pickup."

Dale straightened his posture and downed the last half of his beer. "And you're gonna get it, buddy. You just watch."

A few minutes later I noticed a woman walking from the bar toward our table. She was carrying a single beer in her hand. As she approached,

I realized she was the same woman I'd seen at El Bacaratos, the one who'd driven off in the vintage Mercedes. She stopped at our table and raised the beer.

"Who is this for?"

I pointed at Dale, who sat like he was posing for a passport photo.

"Hi, I'm Diana. Or is it Beth? I'm not really sure."

She was beautiful. I'd caught a glimpse of it when she walked past me at El Bacaratos, but here, with her standing close to me, I could see she was on another level. Perfect skin. Green, shimmering eyes. Soft, wavy hair. But it was her dimples that really yanked my crank. Dale had described her as "hot as shit," and my assessment was that she was absolutely gorgeous.

Dale cleared his throat and began to speak in a voice I'd never heard from him before. It was authoritative and confident and somehow free of obscenities. I figured it was his official voice, the one he used when he testified in court.

"I'm Deputy Dale Johnson, and this here's Davis Reed."

We both shook Diana's hand. It was warm and soft, and I wanted to put it in my pocket.

Diana pointed at Dale's beer. "Do you like the IPA?" she asked.

This was when Dale's lesson in how not to pick up women officially began. He talked about the beer as if it were a science project, breaking down every nuance the way a restaurant critic deconstructs a Michelin-starred meal.

"So therefore," Dale went on, "I believe the IPA is the best gauge of a brewer's competence."

Diana nodded politely. "So do you like it or not?"

"It's great," I said, jumping in to save Dale. "I'd like to get a couple of growlers before we leave."

"Sure, just tell Daiquiri. Hey, nice to meet you both. Thanks for coming in."

As Diana walked away, Dale stared at me like I'd just picked his pocket.

"What the fuck are you doing?" he said. "Don't interrupt me when I'm working my magic."

I shrugged, then began wondering how a woman like Diana had gotten into this business. She didn't look like any brewery owner I'd ever met. They were usually guys with bushy beards and potbellies. I liked Diana's style much better. Much, much better.

I scanned the bar and watched a few guys nurse their beers between stealing glances at Daiquiri. One guy, who had his back to me, wore a black T-shirt with the Ford Mustang logo printed on the back. On the sides of his buzz-cut head I could see the tips of plastic earpieces hanging over the backs of his ears. My temperature rose a few degrees.

I wondered if Skeeter was there looking for bad guys like me. Guys that needed punishing. I thought about telling Dale how Skeeter had pulled me over and then keyed my Mercedes. In the end I decided to keep that to myself. Skeeter was my business, and I didn't need Dale trying to talk me out of my revenge.

*　*　*

Daiquiri brought our food, and Dale devoured his burger in less than five minutes while I picked at my quesadilla. When Daiquiri returned to clear our plates, I asked her if she happened to know anyone who drove a red BMW 2002. As soon as I asked the question, Dale kicked me under the table and I yelled "Shit!" much louder than was polite.

"Are you okay?" Daiquiri asked.

"Sorry. Yeah, I'm good. So does that car sound familiar?"

"Can't say it does. Why you asking?"

"I found a set of keys that belong to the owner. I'm trying to track him down to return them. The back of the BMW is covered in Long Branch bumper stickers. I thought he might be a regular or even work here."

"Sorry, can't help you."

I asked Daiquiri for two growlers of Dark Secret IPA. When she walked away, I avoided Dale's glare by focusing on one of the TVs mounted above the bar.

"Don't ignore me, motherfucker," Dale said. "First you get all up in my shit when I'm trying to hit on Beth, or Diana, or whatever the fuck her name is, and then you go and start talking about them damn keys again."

A few minutes later Diana placed two growlers on our table. "These are on me," she said.

Dale inhaled sharply and pushed out his chest.

"Thank you very much," he said. "This is a fine—"

"So, are you a deputy too?" Diana said to me.

"No, I'm a writer." It was still a weird thing to say.

"Really? What do you write about?"

"I'm working on a book about the plane crash on Cold Mountain."

"I didn't know a plane crashed up there."

"Yes, that occurred in 1949," Dale said, wiggling his way back into the conversation. "It was a B-52 bomber with eight war heroes aboard. A sad, sad story."

"It was actually 1946," I said. "And it was a B-25. Five men were on the plane—they all died in the crash."

Dale huffed at my correction and made a comment about Daiquiri not being very attentive. "I'm going to the bar to get another beer," he said. "I think our waitress retired."

When Dale was gone, Diana laughed and said, "He's something, isn't he?"

"Yes, he is. But he's actually a pretty good guy. I think he's just nervous. He was planning on asking you out."

Diana laughed again. "I see. Well, he's off to a pretty bad start."

"I'm supposed to be his wingman, but I don't think I'm fulfilling my duties."

Diana flashed her dimples. "I think you're doing a fine job."

I was certain I was blushing, but I powered through it. "Hey, didn't I see you at El Bacaratos a couple nights ago?"

Diana cocked her head. "Were you standing by the counter when I was leaving?"

"Yeah, that was me."

Diana sat down on Dale's stool. "So tell me more about this book."

* * *

As far as my book was concerned, there wasn't much to tell, so I guided the conversation around to my home-brewing hobby. As I talked about hops and fermentation and IBUs, Diana sat spellbound. I was spellbound too. Her eyes were so soothing I wanted to crawl in her lap and let her feed me cookies. I fell into such a trance I didn't notice Dale standing behind Diana until a wadded-up cocktail napkin hit my face. I figured that was my cue to drop back into wingman mode.

"Dale brews beer too," I said. "He's got quite a knack for it."

Dale put a full pint glass on the table and squeezed between us. He then started a dissertation on brewing techniques using words I'd never heard him say before, like *consequently* and *statistically*. Diana listened patiently for a few moments, then put her hand on Dale's arm.

"Would you be a sweetie and get Davis another beer?" she said. "I want him to try the coffee porter."

Dale suddenly looked like a kid whose ice cream scoop had fallen off the cone.

As he stomped off, I told Diana there was a very slim chance he would return.

"That's the point," she said.

"So how long have you owned this place?" I asked.

"I started the brewery a couple years ago. Then I added the restaurant last spring. It's not exactly a gold mine, but it pays the bills. Hey, would you like to get some guacamole one night? I'd love to hear more about your book and maybe try some of your beer."

"Yeah, I'd like that," I said. "But my phone doesn't really work very well around here, so I'm not sure . . ."

"Do you have an email address?"

Diana pulled out her phone and added my name and email to her contact list. As she tapped the screen, I grabbed one of the growlers and inspected the label, which showed a finger pressed against a pair of closed red lips. Above the logo were the words DARK SECRET IPA.

"So what's the dark secret?" I asked.

Diana put her phone away and winked. "Wouldn't you like to know?"

15

By the time Dale and I climbed back in the Mercedes, his mood had dramatically improved. He was in love.

"Can you believe that Daiquiri girl? God! Damn! I talked to her a little bit up at the bar. I think she was impressed I'm a deputy. You gotta work that shit, know what I mean? Women love a man with a badge."

"I thought you were interested in Diana. That was the whole point of going there tonight."

Dale had a mild seizure.

"Aw, she's too skinny. Got a body like an ironing board. And she's snooty as all get-out. No, I'm telling you, Daiquiri is the woman for me. Little bit sweet, little bit sour, make my head spin. God! Damn!"

Dale connected his phone to the car's stereo system and played "Is This Love" by Whitesnake. While he sang along, I somehow resisted the urge to vomit.

* * *

When we pulled up in front of Junebug's, Dale was still riding his Daiquiri buzz.

"Brother, we need to go back there tomorrow night. I'll pay. You can have that grilled-cheese bullshit you like."

He reached over to the back floorboard and grabbed one of the growlers Diana had given me.

"What are you doing?" I said.

"One of these is mine, dickhead."

83

Dale got out of the car and walked toward the front of the house. As I pulled away, I rolled down the window and yelled, "That sweat shirt makes you look like a three-hundred-pound Cheeto!"

Dale didn't turn around. He just reached behind his back, extended his middle finger, and walked into the house.

*   *   *

Back at the cabin I poured a glass from the growler of Dark Secret, took a pill, and fired up the laptop. I had one new email. It was from Laura, and I hesitated for a few minutes before opening it. I got up and circled the table a couple of times, anticipating what the email might say. I finished the beer and poured another. When I was halfway through that one, I sat back down and double-clicked on the message.

Davis,

You have hurt me for the last time. Do not come back here. Do not contact me. Stay away.

Laura

And that was that. It was the communication I'd been waiting for. I wasn't surprised by what she'd written. I knew she had to still be furious with me. But at her core my sister was a softy. She'd forgiven me for many things, both large and small. She'd even forgiven me for missing our parents' funeral. I knew she'd forgive me eventually. It was who she was. I would just have to wait until she was ready. All those hours sitting in my car waiting to photograph a cheating spouse or insurance fraud had taught me one thing: patience. I could wait on Laura. That was actually the one thing I was good at. Waiting.

16

It was another cold morning. My head hurt, my stomach hurt, and my leg felt like it was being pricked by a thousand invisible needles. I made some instant coffee, swallowed a pill, and opened the laptop. I reread the email from Laura several times, not sure what I hoped to discover with each fresh view. It was a waiting game now. Waiting for Laura to forgive me. Waiting for Greg to live or die. Waiting to learn who'd shot me and wondering if they would come to Cruso to finish the job. Waiting for inspiration to strike and a book to begin to take shape. Waiting to become a better man.

I pulled up Facebook and searched for Dale's page. When it loaded, I noticed he'd changed his profile picture. The old one had shown him standing on a wooden boat dock in a sleeveless Bon Jovi T-shirt. The new photo was his official sheriff's department head shot. I figured he had changed it in hopes Daiquiri might look him up.

I opened a new tab and pulled up the website for the *Post and Courier*, Charleston's leading newspaper. I clicked on the NEWS section and entered *storage unit* into the search field. I was hoping to find some new information on the investigation, but the only story that appeared was the same one I'd read close to a month ago.

Police Investigating Robbery at Isle of Palms Self-Storage Facility

A Charleston Police sergeant is in serious condition after being violently beaten during a robbery at a self-storage facility.

Authorities were called to the U-Store-It facility on Isle of Palms at 11:31 p.m. Thursday after the sounds of gunfire were reported. Sergeant Greg Evans was found inside an open storage unit suffering from what a police spokesperson described as a "brutal and savage beating."

Another man, Davis Reed, suffered a gunshot wound to the leg during the robbery.

Both victims were transported to the Medical University of South Carolina.

Further information was not immediately released.

The story was factual but misleading. A better version would have read:

Police Investigating Clusterfuck at Isle of Palms Self-Storage Facility

A dirty cop is in a coma after his brother-in-law discovered he was trafficking drugs and then proceeded to beat the living shit out of him. An unknown assailant, driving a gray Audi sedan, then shot the brother-in-law in the leg and absconded with several cases containing drugs and cash.

An Internal Affairs investigation is now under way.

I closed the newspaper's website, pulled up Google, and typed *Cold Mountain* into the search field. With no news of the storage unit investigation and no ring of keys to distract me, I figured I might as well do some actual book research.

The first page of results focused on the book and the movie. Like the newspaper report of the storage unit debacle, it showed how fiction is more popular than fact.

On the next page I browsed through a couple of results that dealt with the actual mountain, then for the hell of it typed *Cold Mountain gold*. The first few results were for local jewelry stores and "We Buy Gold" businesses. One of the links toward the bottom of the results was for an amateur treasure hunters' website called Ray Hicks Treasure Guide. When I clicked on the link, the first thing I saw was a photo of a frighteningly tanned man with a white beard holding a handful of dirty coins. According to the photo's caption, this was Ray, who was described as the world's greatest treasure hunter.

Below Ray's photo was a map covered with dots denoting his treasure-hunting sites. I clicked on a dot located at the western end of North Carolina, and a new page appeared.

Posted by Ray. December 20th 2011

Is There Gold Buried on Cold Mountain?

Hello fellow hunters! You've read the book! You've seen the movie! But did you know Cold Mountain may hold a lost treasure! That's right! According to some locals millions of dollars in gold bullion may be buried somewhere among the lush hills of the mountain best known as the setting for a confederate love story!

A B-25 Bomber crash landed on the mountain in 1946 and some believe the plane was carrying a stash of stolen gold bullion! Could this gold be strewn among the hardwood forests of the most famous mountain in the Blue Ridge range?!?

If you would like more information on the Cold Mountain Treasure click the link below to order my e-book, "Digging Up Your Fortune!" This book will furnish you with first-hand knowledge, tips, tricks, and the do's and don'ts of finding hidden treasure! It's a how-to book on how to become financially independent! Order Today!

The world's greatest treasure hunter hawking an e-book seemed a bit suspect, but not nearly as troublesome as his affinity for exclamation points. I spent a few more minutes looking around Ray's website but didn't find any more information on Cold Mountain or the rumor of buried gold. "They ain't no fucking gold," is what Dale had said, and I was inclined to believe him.

I made another cup of coffee, then clicked on Google and searched for Long Branch Brewery. The first link took me back to Facebook and the brewery's social media page. The profile listed the brewery's hours along with a link to its beer offerings and the food menu. I clicked on the PHOTOS tab and started scrolling through the pictures. Some were interior shots of the restaurant and behind-the-scenes looks at the brewing process. The rest of the images were taken by customers who had tagged the brewery in their pictures. More than a few showed red-faced twentysomethings playing cornhole, the devil's gift to breweries, or raising pints of beer in a toast toward the camera.

I scanned the photos for Diana. It took a few minutes, but I finally found a picture of a group celebrating what I guessed to be a birthday. They sat huddled around a table while a young woman blew on a candle poking out of the top of an oversized cupcake. In the background I could see Diana leaning back against the bar and smiling toward the celebration. She was gorgeous, even in a snapshot like this. Next to her, sitting on a barstool, was a man facing away from the camera and wearing a yellow T-shirt with the Long Branch Brewery logo emblazoned across the back. Diana was close to him, their arms almost touching. I zoomed in on the picture to get a better look, but the more I zoomed, the more the picture blurred.

The details of the image were fuzzy, but if I squinted just right, I could see a shiny object near the man's waist. It was a tiny mess of square silver pixels surrounded by flecks of brown and orange. The devils suggested I was staring at a large ring of keys. The angel shrugged. I shrugged back and swallowed another pill.

17

I threw on some clothes and hopped in the Mercedes. A few minutes later I pulled into the parking lot of El Bacaratos. I called Dale to ask him if the couple had picked up the keys.

"They came by this morning to collect 'em," he said. "But guess what? The keys wasn't here."

"What do you mean? I handed them over to Barbara yesterday."

"Yeah, Barbara says you did, and she says she put them in her desk drawer. But when that couple came by this morning, the keys was gone. Barbara was pretty embarrassed and said the couple was rightly pissed. Especially the dude."

"What did he say?"

"Barbara said he went on bitching about this and that. Said we was unprofessional and that kind of shit."

"Did they give their names or leave a number?"

"Nope. The dude said they'd check back later today and that them keys had better've turned up."

The keys disappearing made no sense to me. I also didn't understand why the couple kept refusing to give anyone their names or leave a number where they could be contacted. If their goal was to act suspicious, they were doing a good job of it.

"Could Barbara have just misplaced the keys?" I said. "I mean, could she have looked in the wrong drawer or something?"

"That ain't very likely. Barbara keeps her shit tight. If she says them keys are gone, then they're gone. You know, Davis, I shouldn't have let you fuck around with those keys. I should've made you give 'em to me yesterday morning."

"I wish I had given them to you. Then I wouldn't have gotten stuck listening to Barbara ramble on and on about her damn blog. I should've snuck out when your cousin came in."

There was a long pause, followed by, "What do you mean, my cousin?"

"Floppy. He came in when I was talking to Barbara. He said someone had broken into his garage."

Dale grunted like he was trying to open a stuck jar lid. "Did he see them keys?"

"Yeah, they were on the counter when he came in."

"Motherfucker! I betcha my left nut he took 'em when Barbara wasn't looking."

"Seriously? Why would he take them?"

"Floppy's a klepto-fucking-maniac. He'll take anything that ain't bolted down. Calls hisself a collector, but he ain't nothin' more than a hoarder."

I tried to imagine what Floppy's house looked like—and smelled like. I didn't care for the thought.

"Why didn't you tell me he was your cousin when I asked you about him? When we were watching the game, you never mentioned that you were related."

Dale grunted again. " 'Cause that ain't nothin' I like to admit. The man's as crazy as a shit house rat."

"So how are you two connected?"

"Floppy's granddaddy, Ol' Gerald, was Daddy's uncle."

"Okay. So that makes you and Floppy, what, like third cousins?"

Dale hissed. "Fuck if I know. Or care."

"Or maybe it's second cousin once removed."

"I wish it was all the way removed," Dale screamed.

"What about Floppy's parents?" I said. "Are they still around?"

"Nah. Floppy's daddy died in 'Nam a few months 'fore Floppy was born. Then Floppy's momma got that depression shit some women get after they have a young'n and ended up slittin' her wrists in the bathtub.

Momma and Daddy said they thought about taking Floppy in, but I was just a curtain climber back then, so they had their hands full with me. I'm a handful, in case you ain't noticed."

Dale was more than a handful, but I wasn't going to give him the satisfaction of acknowledging it.

"So where'd he go? I mean, where did Floppy live after his mother died?"

"Ol' Gerald took him in. Raised his grandson to be just as crazy as he was."

I laughed. "So your great-uncle was Gerald Johnson. The man who claimed to have found a chest of gold up on Cold Mountain."

Dale exhaled so loudly I could almost smell his breath through the phone.

"I'm gonna tell you two things right now, Davis. One, there never was no fucking gold. And two, you get your ass up to Floppy's garage and get them keys back."

It was my turn to exhale. "Why should I go up there? He's your cousin and you're the one with the badge."

"Well, unlike you, dickhead, I have a job. I gotta be at court at eleven, some dumb fuck challenging his DUI charge."

Dale bitched for a couple of minutes about having to appear in court, then gave me directions to Floppy's garage.

"And listen," Dale added. "Floppy ain't to be trusted about nothing; he's as much a liar as his granddaddy was. He ain't gonna admit he's got those keys, so there ain't no reason asking. You're going to have to poke around and see if you see 'em laying around somewhere."

"So he's supposed to let me just wander around his garage as if I've misplaced something? He'll kick me out in five minutes."

Dale started giggling.

"Five minutes, my ass. Davis, you'll be lucky to get yourself out of that place before nightfall. Now go on. Get!"

18

I followed Dale's directions to an area called Sunburst. The winding two-lane road led through a valley dotted with modest homes, trailers, and the occasional cow field. After a few minutes I came upon a small lake with a several cabins situated along its edge. A sign near the road read LAKE LOGAN EPISCOPAL CENTER. It was a picturesque spot, and I figured if there was a god, this looked like as good a place as any for him to hang out.

After another couple of miles I spotted a blue cinder-block building surrounded by junk cars and rusty appliances. I was afraid it was the place I was looking for.

I pulled into a dirt lot in front of the building and parked next to a primer-gray Ford Explorer sitting on four columns of bricks. I hesitated a moment before getting out of my car, wondering if there was a guard dog somewhere on the premises. The last thing I needed was a junkyard dog gnawing on my one good leg.

The building held two garage bays, and both were so full of junk I couldn't imagine fitting a vehicle inside either of them. As I stared at the building, Floppy materialized out of the cluster of junk. He slowly dragged himself to the edge of one of the bays, then stopped and stared in my direction. I finally stepped out of my car, figuring if there was a dog prowling about, it was probably as lethargic as Floppy.

"I work on them foreign cars, if that's what you's gonna ask," Floppy said as I approached.

He was dressed in the same greasy outfit as the day before, and as I closed the gap between us, his body odor hit me like a cloud of noxious gas.

"Hey, wait a minute," he said. "Didn't I see you yesterday at the sheriff's office? You's talking to Barbara."

"Yeah, that was me. My name's Davis Reed. I'm a friend of your cousin Dale. I'm renting his cabin for a few months."

Floppy waved his arms like he'd just walked into a spider web.

"He ain't no family of mine! He thinks just because he wears a uniform and carries a gun that he's better than me. Well, he ain't. I got more knowledge between my ears than that fat ass has in his whole body. Do you know he can't even find Kansas on a map? I showed him a map one time and challenged him to find it, and he pointed to South Dakota. Can you believe that? And he walks around acting all cocky. Just because you're a deputy don't mean you're smart; just means you didn't fail out of tech school.

"I'm Gerald Johnson, by the way, named after my granddaddy. People call me Floppy 'cause of my leg. When I walk, it sorta flops behind me. I was struck by lightning back when I was in high school. I was out at the football field after a game one evening with my metal detector looking for coins and rings and stuff. Did you know people lose things like that all the time at sportin' events? You can find some good stuff if you got a good detector. Anyways, I's hunkered down with the detector and had my headphones on, 'cause you can't always hear the detector when it beeps—it's subtle and such—and sometimes you can't always hear it unless you got a good set of headphones. So I didn't notice they was a storm coming up, and dang if I didn't get struck right in the leg. Threw me halfway up the bleachers. Set my pants' leg on fire. They didn't find me till the next morning."

While listening to Floppy, I made a mental note to kick Dale's ass the next time I saw him.

"So what can I help you with?" Floppy asked. "That kraut wagon giving you some trouble?"

I thought about how to get inside the garage to take a look around. It obviously wasn't going to be hard to keep the man talking, but there was no way I was going to let him near my car.

"I'd like to talk to you about Cold Mountain. I'm writing a book about it and talking to some of the locals to find out more about the folklore and history."

"There's already a book about Cold Mountain. But I guess they's enough about that mountain to write another one."

"I'd appreciate any help. Can we go inside and talk about it?"

"I know everything there is to know about that mountain. My grand-daddy used to bear hunt up there all the time. Did you know a black bear can eat a man in less than nine minutes? It's true. People don't worry about black bears as much as they worry about grizzlies, 'cause grizzlies are real nasty and can probably eat a man in less than five minutes—I don't have the statistics on that—but black bears are mean too if you catch them at the right time. I was chased by a black bear once. People say you're supposed to play dead if a bear's chasing you, but it's awful hard to play dead when you're worried about dying.

"Speaking of bears, I used to go with this woman had a bear paw tattooed on her right titty. I called it her tit-too cause it was on her titty. Get it? I don't understand women that get tattoos on their titties. Do they think they need something to draw attention to their titties? I mean, we's gonna look at their titties no matter what's there. It's like them nipple piercings. Now why would a woman go do something like that? Put a piece of metal through a perfectly good nipple? That's like a man stick-ing a nail through his pecker. Ain't no reason for that. I tell ya, some thing's I just don't understand."

I looked over Floppy's shoulder into the junk-filled garage and decided I was on a fool's errand. I took a step backward while glancing at my watch.

"You know, actually I should probably get going. It's later than I thought, and I'm sure you're busy."

"I ain't got no tattoos. A lot of people 'round here do, but I didn't never see no point in it. Dale's got a tattoo of a skull wearing a cowboy hat with the words Lynyrd Skynyrd under it. He got it about twenty years ago, and I said what the heck did you get that for, your momma's gonna kick your butt when she sees that. But his momma died 'fore she ever saw it. I ain't never smoked, but she smoked a lot and that lung cancer ain't no good way to die. I guess there really ain't no good way, if you think about it. I was lucky I didn't die that first time I got struck by lightning. That was the bad one that fried my leg. The second time just stung. I don't know, maybe the second time you're struck don't hurt as bad. I'd like to talk to people who've been struck by lightning more than once. I've heard they's a group of people on the internet who's been struck by lightning multiple times, but I don't trust the internet because you don't know who you're talking to. You could be talking to somebody who says they been struck by lightning a couple times but really they's just some pervert trying to find out where you live."

I had to yell Floppy's name twice to interrupt his stream of consciousness. Once he stopped talking, I told him it was nice chatting with him but I was going to head on out.

"But hey, didn't you want to ask me about something?"

For a moment the old Clash song "Should I Stay or Should I Go" rattled in my head. I wanted to find out if Floppy had the keys, but talking to the man was like playing Whac-A-Mole. I looked again over Floppy's shoulder into one of the garage bays and noticed a refrigerator wedged between two workbenches. I pointed toward it and said, "You got any beer in that fridge?"

Floppy gave me the same look Dale had given Daiquiri's ass.

"Heck yeah," he said. "Come on in."

19

When we walked into the garage, Floppy hobbled over to the refrigerator door and pulled out two cans of light beer.

"Dale likes that fancy beer," he said. "But beer's beer, if you ask me."

He handed me a can and pointed to an oil-stained bench next to a hydraulic lift.

"Now what did you want to know about?"

"What can you tell me about Cold Mountain? My book deals with the plane that crashed up there in the 1940s."

Floppy didn't hesitate an instant. With rapid-fire delivery, he told me everything from the mountain's elevation to the names of the trails that webbed across its acreage to the variety of trees that grew out of its soil. As he spoke, I sipped the light beer, which tasted like dirty water, and glanced around the garage hoping to catch sight of the missing keys. It was like searching through a landfill. Every surface was covered with tools and junk and garbage. It would have been hard to find a haystack in the place, much less the needle inside it.

"Now, people say wormy chestnut ain't an indigenous tree to these parts, but it's an indigenous tree if you consider that it was brought here by the Spanish who planted it in order to make cabinets and furniture out of it once it matured. Now, I don't like wormy chestnut myself—I prefer oak because it's a much hardier wood, although some say it's not as attractive. But then again, you can't always account for taste."

When I'd had as much botany as I could take, I stopped Floppy mid-sentence and asked him if he would show me around the garage.

"Oh yeah, I got a lot going on here. I work on all types of vehicles. Now, I don't know much about them electric cars, but it's no matter, 'cause they ain't none of them around here nohow. I changed the oil in a Jaguar once. Did you know a Jaguar can cost over sixty thousand dollars? I don't know who'd spend that kind of money on a car—"

I interrupted again. "Mind if I get another beer?"

"No, help yourself. I buy 'em by the case over at the Walmart. I keep 'em for customers and such—they like it much better than them garages that just have a Pepsi machine."

Over the next hour and five beers, Floppy showed me every inch of his garage. During that time I learned how the government was spreading chemicals through the vapor trails of airplanes, how climate change was a fraud perpetrated by the green-energy lobby, and how the United Nations had helped fake the moon landings. One thing I didn't discover was a set of keys.

I finished the last sip of the last beer and tossed the can in an overflowing garbage bin sitting next to a welding machine.

"It's been great talking to you, but I really need to get going," I said. "Thanks for the beer."

I walked out of the garage and heard Floppy dragging his foot as he followed me to my car.

"Hey now, wait a minute," he said as I slipped behind the driver's seat. "You was talking about that plane crash on Cold Mountain. Are you trying to find out about that gold?"

20

I drove back to El Bacaratos and called Dale from the parking lot. He answered on the first ring and, as usual, didn't bother with a hello.

"How'd it go with Floppy, dickhead? You two best buddies now?"

For a second I considered telling Dale I'd had a very pleasant chat with Floppy and he'd handed over the keys, no questions asked. But lying took energy, and Floppy had worn me out.

"I ought to kick your ass for sending me up there," I said.

"Brother, you couldn't kick my ass even if both your legs worked right."

"That man is insane. He thinks the moon landing was faked."

Dale laughed. "Yeah, and you wondered why I didn't tell you we was kin."

"He also swears his grandfather found a chest of gold from the bomber crash, and get this, he says your dad and Sheriff Byrd stole it when they were kids."

Dale groaned. "I've listened to that bullshit for years. Floppy's fucked up in the head. I think all them welding fumes has burnt his wiring."

"Well, I looked all around the garage and didn't see the keys. But I don't how anybody could find anything in that shop—there's stuff strewn everywhere."

"You didn't flat out ask him about 'em, did you?"

"How could I? I couldn't get a word in edgewise, between the conspiracy theories and the talk about some woman with a bear paw tattooed on her boob."

"Oh yeah, Tanya. I remember her. I should see if she's on Facebook."

* * *

I drove to the sheriff's department and parked in the same VISITORS spot I'd used the previous day. I wanted to talk to Barbara about the keys and find out if she thought Floppy might have taken them.

"Did you look at my blog?" Barbara asked when I stepped up to the counter. "I wrote a new post last night. It's a recipe for heavy-cream biscuits."

"I haven't had a chance to check it out yet," I said. "But I promise I will."

Barbara smiled in a way that communicated *That's sweet, but you're full of shit.*

"Listen, Dale told me that the keys I turned in yesterday are missing."

"That's right," Barbara said. "A young couple came in early this morning to pick them up, but when I went to pull them out of my desk drawer, they were gone."

"Do you have any idea where they could be?"

"I don't know. They threw a big fit and then stormed out the door."

"Not the couple, the keys."

"Oh. I put the keys in this drawer right here."

Barbara opened the top drawer of her desk and waved her hand over the contents like a magician gesturing over a magic hat. The drawer contained multiple lip balms, notebooks, a compact, and a travel-sized pack of incontinence pads. Barbara caught me staring and slammed the drawer closed.

"I lock the drawer every night before I leave. And I'm the only one who has a key. I have personal items in here, and no one else needs access to it."

"But the drawer is unlocked while you're here, right?"

Barbara nodded.

"So anybody could have opened it and taken out the keys when you weren't at your desk."

"I'm always at the desk."

"Surely you go to the restroom."

Barbara frowned and folded her arms.

"What about that guy that came in yesterday while I was here?" I asked. "You said he was Dale's cousin."

"Floppy?"

"Yeah, Floppy. Could he have taken the keys when you weren't looking?"

Barbara seemed to consider the idea for a moment, then quickly shook it away with a jerk of her head. "Absolutely not."

Just then Dale appeared in the doorway behind the counter, the same one I'd watched Floppy and Skeeter disappear through the previous day.

"What are you doing?" Dale said.

"I was just talking to Barbara about her blog."

"No, he wasn't," Barbara said. "He was asking me about the missing keys."

Dale shot me a look and I shrugged in return.

"Get your ass back here," he said.

* * *

I went around the counter and followed Dale through the doorway. We walked down a long hallway past several rooms with open doors. Through one doorway I saw Sheriff Byrd sitting behind a large desk. He was staring at a computer monitor while speaking to someone on his desk phone. He glanced at me as I walked by, and I waved with a wiggle of my fingers. He didn't return the gesture, but his hound-dog jowls dropped another quarter of an inch, so I was satisfied.

At the end of the hall we turned left and passed through a set of double doors propped open with two red bricks. We entered a large room containing several metal desks. A few deputies milled around the room, each one giving me a sour look as Dale pointed to an empty chair next to one of the desks. Maybe they thought I was under arrest or had been brought in to give a statement. Maybe they were like Sheriff Byrd and thought I was here to "sniff around" the department. I honestly didn't care.

"How was court?" I said to Dale as I sat down.

Dale took off his duty belt and placed it in a drawer, then wedged himself into the office chair behind his desk.

"They didn't call the case," he said. "Gotta go back tomorrow. But I don't mind. There's this bailiff down there got an ass that looks like two coons fighting in a sack."

I tried to imagine what that would look like. "I thought you were interested in Daiquiri."

Dale spread his arms wide.

"Brother, there's enough of me to go around."

* * *

As we talked, I saw Skeeter walk through the doorway. He was still wearing those ridiculous aviators, and I wondered how often he replaced the toothpick he kept clenched between his teeth. When he noticed me, he walked toward Dale's desk. My morning pill had long worn off and my insides were pulsating like I'd swallowed a vibrator.

"You owe me twenty," Skeeter said, holding out his palm to Dale. "I told you the Vols were shit."

It took Dale a good thirty seconds to fish his wallet out of his pants pocket. When he finally wriggled it free, he pulled out two tens and handed them over.

"That game was bullshit," Dale said.

Skeeter smirked and gestured toward me. "What did you pick him up for?"

"General dickheadedness," Dale said. "I'm not sure what the code is for that one."

Skeeter snickered, and I imagined squeezing his nuts so hard his eyeballs would pop out and knock those stupid glasses off his face.

"Being a dickhead is a serious offense around here," Skeeter said. "You best watch yourself."

"You know, I've learned only two kinds of people wear sunglasses indoors: blind people and assholes."

Skeeter took a step toward me, and when I stood up I could see my neck turning red in the reflection of his glasses. The only thing that kept me from knocking Skeeter to the floor was the thought of carving up his beloved Mustang. That and the fact that punching a deputy while surrounded by other deputies is a form of assisted suicide.

"You best watch your mouth," Skeeter said.

"That's a nice goatee. Where I come from, we call it prison pussy."

Skeeter reached to his side and pulled his handcuffs off his duty belt. Dale stood up with a loud grunt and wedged his bulk between us.

"Cool your jets, Skeeter. Davis here's not as big an asshole as he pretends to be."

Skeeter snorted and glared at me over Dale's shoulder.

"Bullshit," Skeeter said. "I pulled him for speeding a couple days ago. He was going seventy-five on 276 up by the golf course."

Dale turned around and shot me a stunned look. "Holy fuck. Did you have a stroke or something?"

I shrugged and continued to give Skeeter my best menacing stare. Dale turned back to Skeeter and said, "Well, if my man here was going that fast, there was surely some good reason for it."

Skeeter and I continued to glare at each other, neither of us willing to back down.

After letting the tension build for a few more moments, Dale put a hand on Skeeter's chest and pushed him away.

"Quit fucking around," Dale said. "And stop pulling over speeders. You got better shit to do than that."

It was good to know Dale had my back, even when I was up against one of his own. I grinned, and Skeeter's face twisted so tight I thought his toothpick might shoot out of his mouth like a dart from a blowgun. He stared at me for another moment, then turned and walked away. When he was passing through the double doors, he glanced back at me and I blew him a kiss.

When Skeeter was out of the room, I turned to Dale.

"What is his problem?" I said.

"Ah, he's just young, dumb, and full of cum. Thinks being a deputy is all about bringing people to justice. Boy thinks he's judge, jury, and executioner. He just ain't learned my social skills yet."

I heard someone say "Yoo-hoo" and turned to see Barbara standing next to the double doors.

"That young couple is out front asking about those keys," she said.

Dale leaned back and stared at the ceiling. "Oh, for fuck's sake."

Barbara's face soured. "Watch your mouth, Deputy."

Dale pushed himself out of his chair and threw his duty belt back around his waist. "C'mon, Davis, let's go talk to these assholes."

"I can't talk to them," I said. "They'll recognize me from the parkway."

"Who cares? Now grow a pair and come on."

21

When Dale and I entered the lobby, I saw the same couple I'd seen a few days earlier at the ranger station. The woman's hair was now up in a tight ponytail, and the man wore a black knit cap with PUB embroidered on the front. They were both captivated by the phones in their hands and didn't look up until Dale cleared his throat.

"I'm afraid we have still not located the keys," Dale said in his official voice. "But I assure you we are diligently looking into it and I'm confident they will turn up. We will contact you as soon as we have them."

The man frowned at Dale, then glanced over at me. I noticed a hint of recognition in his eyes.

"You look familiar," he said.

When I didn't respond, Dale put his hand on my shoulder.

"This is Davis Reed," he said. "He is the gentleman who originally found the keys. He's a private detective."

I bit my lip and fought the urge to punch Dale in the gut.

"So is he going to find them again?" the man said.

I noticed Barbara staring at me from her chair behind the counter, so I threw her my best smile. Like Skeeter, she was not amused at my beam of sunshine.

"Yes, he is," Dale said. "I was just speaking to him about it. We'll have those keys back here in no time."

The man lowered his brows, which sat just below the bottom of his knit cap.

"Where have I seen you before?" he said.

I gave him the same smile both Barbara and Skeeter had rebuffed.

"He's the guy we met on the parkway," the girl said. "We gave him a beer, remember?"

"The writer," the man said.

The girl nodded. "Yeah, he's writing a book about Cold Mountain."

"I told him there's already a book about that," Barbara yelled from behind the counter.

Dale obviously thought this was a good time to make himself scarce. He pushed past me, nodded at the couple, then strolled out the front door without saying a word.

The man looked at me sharply, and I could see distrust in his eyes. I hoped he could see the same in mine.

"Who are you?" he said.

"Like the deputy told you, I'm a private detective."

"Where are those keys?"

I didn't respond. If he was looking for any more answers, he was going to have to give me some first.

"Where's Lester Cordell?" I asked.

The man and woman exchanged glances, but neither answered my question. In the silence I felt my pressure gauge click up a few notches. I wanted to get the couple outside and away from the sheriff's office—that way I could ask my questions with a bit more enthusiasm.

I pointed toward the door and said, "Why don't we take a walk?"

The couple didn't budge. After another exchange of glances, the man took a step toward me and whispered, "Who hired you?"

"Yoo-hoo," Barbara called from her throne behind the counter. "Mr. Reed. Sheriff Byrd would like a word with you."

I turned and gave Barbara another of my best grins. When I turned back, the couple were walking out the front door. I was headed in their direction when a hand grabbed my shoulder. It belonged to one of the deputies who'd scowled at me earlier.

"This way," he said, pulling me back into the lion's den.

* * *

105

Sheriff Byrd was sitting behind his desk, his chin cradled between interlocked fingers. His jowls seemed to be hanging lower than usual, and I wondered if he had to prop up his face to keep it from dripping off his skull.

Byrd pointed to a seat opposite his desk, and I sat down. I figured he'd been talking to his Charleston PD friend Emory and wanted to grill me more about the storage unit affair.

"Son, I've been sheriff of this county for over thirty years," Byrd finally said.

Whew, I thought. *We're going to talk about Byrd's favorite subject—himself.*

"Now, we don't have the same sorts of problems a big city has, but I've still seen my share of wickedness. Evil doesn't constrain itself to the city. No sir. It can manifest in a person's soul no matter where he lives. Do you know the first case that came across my desk after I was elected sheriff?"

"Someone set a dumpster on fire?"

Byrd scoffed. "A body was found in the woods up the river in Cruso. Actually not too far from the cabin you're renting. A couple of boys hunting squirrels found it, half-hidden under a pile of leaves. Bullet hole in the back of the head. Put the fear of God in those boys, I'll tell you that. They ran home and called it in, nervous as all get-out. It was my first week as sheriff and there I was, standing out in those damp woods staring at the first murder this county had seen in five years."

Byrd looked out his office window as if he were pulling memories through the glass.

"The deceased's name was Randy Pless, thirty-two years old. Now, do you think that boy ever thought he'd be lying dead in the woods up in Cruso? Shot through the head like a lame horse? All his years on this earth just leading to those woods and that pile of leaves?"

Byrd looked back at me, his eyes reaching toward me as if I might actually have answers to those questions.

"Did you catch who did it?" I asked, trying to get this story to a conclusion and me out of Byrd's office.

"At the time we didn't have a clue. Randy had never been in any trouble, and there was no clear motive for the murder. We interviewed everyone he associated with—family, friends, coworkers over at the mill. We must have talked to fifty different people, and not one of them could shed any light on why Randy was dead. But then I set up an interview with Randy's boss, a man named Larry Inman. As soon as Larry sat across from me, I knew he was guilty, but he swore up and down he didn't know what happened to Randy. 'Liked the guy,' he said. 'Hard worker and a good Christian man.' But I knew he was lying. You can call it instinct or gut; it doesn't matter. I knew the truth as soon as I looked into his eyes."

Byrd stared straight at me, or rather into me. I wondered what truth he thought he was seeing.

"Were you right?" I asked.

"Yessir, I was right. It took a while, but I finally got a confession out of him. Seems Larry thought there was something going on between his wife and Randy. Fooling around while he was at work and this and that. Larry said he'd confronted Randy about it but Randy swore there was nothing to it. But Larry's wife egged him on; seemed she liked the idea of him being jealous. So she kept stirring the pot, and Larry kept boiling. Then one morning Larry decides to put an end to it, so he asks Randy to go up to Cruso with him to hunt ginseng. They'd been out in the woods for less than fifteen minutes when Larry put a bullet in the back of Randy's skull. Larry piled some dead leaves over the body and went home and ate dinner. Evil. There's not another word for it. And I saw it in his eyes before he ever spoke a word."

I glanced at my watch, the universal symbol for *Is this going to take much longer?*

"My gut is telling me something about you, son. Something I'm not comfortable with."

"I'm not a jealous husband. I'm just a writer."

"Well, you don't seem to be doing much of it. From what I hear, you're spending your time looking for weeds in other people's gardens."

I didn't know what Byrd was referring to. My interest in the keys? Or me asking around about the rumors of the missing gold? Or maybe

Byrd's friend Emory had told him Greg was being investigated for criminal activity and that I was probably involved somehow. And now here I was, "sniffing 'round the sheriff's department," as Dale had put it. Maybe Byrd thought I was looking for an opportunity to find some bad apples in his own crate.

"You know, Sheriff, after we broke guacamole together, I thought we were going to be friends."

Byrd leaned forward and narrowed his eyes. "I am being your friend. I'm telling you, don't waste your time chasing what's not there. You just finish your book. Then head on back to the Lowcountry."

So, like a high school principal, Byrd had called me into his office to give me a long-winded lecture. And like my own high school principal had been, he was wrong about me. Byrd thought I was evil, but I wasn't even evil lite. I'd hurt some people in the past, both physically and emotionally, but I'd done the most damage to myself. I'd spent a long time circling the drain, and those I'd hurt had just gotten caught up in the swirl. I wasn't trouble and I wasn't looking for trouble. I was just trying to maintain a buzz, write a book, and give a guy back his keys.

"Are we done here, Sheriff?"

Byrd picked up a pen from his desk and studied it as if it were a crucial piece of evidence.

"That man who was in that storage unit with you—I hear he's a sergeant with the Charleston PD."

"That's right," I said. "He's actually my brother-in-law."

"According to my friend Jack, someone beat that man like a rented mule."

I looked at my watch again.

"I suppose it was the same person who broke into that storage unit and shot you," Byrd said.

"I don't know, Sheriff. I told you I'm not a detective anymore."

"On the other hand, that man could have been beaten before the shooting occurred. Doesn't make sense to shoot one man, then beat another one; that is, unless you only have one bullet in your gun."

Byrd's gaze moved from the pen to me. I stared right back at him and wondered what he was thinking. If he could spot a liar, he was looking at one, but not a very good one.

"Well, I hear Internal Affairs is on it now," I said. "That should tell you something about what happened down there."

Byrd leaned back and frowned.

"Jack didn't mention that."

I cocked my head. Emory not knowing about the IA investigation surprised me, but I hoped Byrd didn't notice.

"Although he did mention the name Perry Long," Byrd continued.

"He's an old friend of mine," I said. "He's in charge of the robbery investigation. You should talk to him if you want to know what's going on."

"Now, I find that very interesting, son. That a man would be put in charge of an investigation involving his good friend. Is that how they do things down in Charleston? Because up here we call that a conflict of interest."

I shrugged and stayed silent.

Byrd stared at me for a long moment, then nodded as if we had come to an understanding. We both stood.

When I reached the doorway, Byrd said, "Good luck with your book, son. No offense, but I hope not to see you again."

I turned and nodded.

"The feeling's mutual, Sheriff."

22

Since I was in town, I swung by the grocery store before heading back to the cabin. After I commandeered a shopping cart, I pulled out my phone and tapped the icon for my banking app. Checking my bank account was always a distressing exercise. Waiting for the balance to appear was like watching the window of a Magic 8 Ball and not knowing if the answer would be YES DEFINITELY or OUTLOOK NOT SO GOOD.

When our parents died, Laura and I had both inherited $110,000. Our folks didn't have much savings, but the home they'd raised us in was paid off, and it sold ten days after Laura listed it with a Charleston realtor. A month later I received a certified check. It was more money than I'd ever seen. That same day I drove to the Mercedes dealership in my '88 Camry with the cracked windshield and intermittent air conditioning. A couple of hours later I parked my new $65,000 Mercedes SUV on King Street and walked into the Apple store. I dropped a couple of grand on a new laptop and then strolled down to M. Dumas & Sons and Billy Reid for a new wardrobe. It was the first time I'd had disposable income, and I was disposing of it as fast as I could.

I'd thought my inheritance would last forever, like water from the kitchen faucet, available any time I raised the handle. But now, according to my banking app, my balance was down to $2,500. That would have to last until I sold the book I'd not written or got a job. Both seemed unlikely.

I bypassed the produce aisle and filled my cart with the essentials: tortillas, black beans, shredded cheese, and frozen pizzas, comfort food for someone with constant queasiness. For a small-town grocery, the store's beer selection was impressive, and I picked up multiple six-packs from breweries in Waynesville, Asheville, and Brevard. When I checked out, the bill came to a little over $100—eighty in beer and twenty in groceries.

* * *

I was sitting on the deck drinking and shivering when I heard a siren coming up the driveway. A few minutes later the sliding glass door opened and Dale appeared, holding a brown growler. Of course he was still in his uniform.

"What the hell are you doing sitting out here?" he said. "It's cold as fuck."

"What can I say. I love the view."

"It's dark, dickhead. Get your ass inside."

* * *

Dale sat at the kitchen table while I drained the rest of my beer and took a fresh one out of the fridge. When I sat down, I pointed to the Dark Secret IPA logo on the side of Dale's growler.

"I'm surprised you have any of that left," I said. "I thought you'd drink it all the night we got it."

"I did. This is a new one. Got three more at the house."

"You went back to Long Branch? Were you looking for beer or for Daiquiri?"

"Both. I went after I left the courthouse. She wasn't there; they said it was her day off."

I imagined Daiquiri diving under the bar when she saw Dale walk in.

"But I did see Diana," Dale said. "She asked about you. I told her you were a peckerhead."

"You're going to have to make up your mind. Is it dickhead or peckerhead? Because I keep getting confused."

"I might throw in shitheel now and again to keep you guessin'."

"What did she say?"

"She wanted to know if you got her email."

While Dale sat across from me, swigging from his growler, I opened up the computer. An email from Diana@LongBranchBrewery.com was the at the top of the unread list.

Hey!

I'm free tomorrow night and I'd love to hear more about your book. I'll bring guac & chips and some beer. Send me directions to your place. I'll be there at 6:30.

Diana

I closed the laptop and sighed.

"So what did she say?" Dale asked.

"She wants to come over tomorrow night."

"You know, she ain't as sexy as I first thought. Them weird lines in her face are fucked up."

"You mean her dimples?"

"Yeah, they look like little ass cracks in her cheeks."

I sipped my beer and thought about the idea of Diana coming over. She was gorgeous, smart, and owned a brewery. It was like a genie granting me all three wishes at the same time. But what did I have to offer someone like her? Unless she'd rubbed a lamp and wished for an alcoholic, pill-popping, temperamental slacker, she was going to be disappointed. But I figured one date wouldn't hurt, even though it would probably be our last as well as our first.

"So how'd you leave it with that couple at the sheriff's department?" Dale said. "They give you more shit about them keys?"

"Yeah. Thanks for bailing on me, by the way. You made me look like an idiot."

"You don't need my help with that."

Dale smiled and unsnapped the pocket on his uniform shirt. He wedged his beefy fingers into it and pulled out a small piece of paper.

"Jeff and Becky Ingram," he said, reading from the paper.

"Who are they?"

"That couple that wants them keys so bad. I went outside and wrote down their license plate. I ran the tag after you left."

Dale was a lot of things: obese, ornery, opinionated, and occasionally pretty clever.

"That Jeff fucker's been busted a few times. Same petty shit as Cordell."

"What else did you find out?" I asked.

"Vehicle's registered in both names. They live over in Banner Elk."

"Where is that?"

"Couple hours north of here. Up near App State."

"Never heard of it."

"Appalachian State University. Did you know you can major in beer making there? I shit you not. You can get a degree in brewing beer. Wish they offered that shit when I was going to school."

"You still would have failed."

Dale shrugged; he knew I was right.

"What about Pucker Up Brewery?" I said. "Did you find anything about that? I searched online the day I first met them, but nothing came up."

"I dug around the internet a little bit, but I didn't see nothing. Hell, these hippies start making beer in their garage and suddenly think they's running a brewery. They come up with a name and slap it on T-shirts and stickers and shit, but they ain't making no more beer than me and you are."

I closed Diana's email and pulled up Facebook. I typed *Jeff Ingram Banner Elk* into the search field, and soon the young man I'd first met on the parkway was staring back at me. I clicked on his image, and his Facebook profile filled the screen. It showed nothing more than his name and his profile picture. His photos, friends, and posts were all private. I went through the same routine with Becky and got the same result.

"What made you get their tag number?" I asked. "You've given me nothing but shit about those keys since the day I found them. Why the sudden interest?"

"I don't like their attitude. Especially that Jeff motherfucker, with them tight jeans and little hat. Come down here and act like we're a bunch of backwards rednecks. I'd like to take that hat and shove it up his ass."

"I'd pay money to see that."

"Shit, I'd pay money to do it."

"Where is Cordell? That's the part I don't understand. Why isn't he looking for his keys?"

"I already told you, maybe those keys ain't his."

"But why would one of those keys open Cordell's car if that key ring didn't belong to him?"

Dale shrugged and took another swig from his growler.

"I don't know," he said. "People give friends spare keys and shit to hold for safekeeping."

"Maybe to their house, but not to their car."

Dale shrugged again.

"After you walked out, I asked that couple about Cordell," I said. "They seemed very surprised that I knew that name. Then Jeff asked me who had hired me."

Dale squinted. "Who hired you? To do what? Drink beer and piss me off?"

I raised my glass, middle finger extended.

"Do you still have the address Cordell's car is registered to?" I asked.

Dale manipulated his billfold out of his pocket and shuffled through several pieces of paper. He handed me the piece listing Cordell's Florida address, and I entered the information into Google. The first search result was a map with a red arrow pointing to the address's location. Other results linked to real estate sites listing information about the address, such as house size and market value. A few links connected to background check databases that offered information such as occupant's names, their ages, phone numbers, and so on. Five minutes and $9.99 later, I had a phone number.

"Let me see your phone," I said.

"What the fuck are you doing?"

"Let me borrow your phone. You know I don't have service here."

Dale unhooked his phone from the holster on his belt and entered his pass code to unlock it. I dialed the number, and after three long rings a woman's voice said, "Hello. If you are a telemarketer, I'm not interested."

The voice was slow and crackly. I imagined an older lady in a housedress sitting on the edge of her bed with a small Pomeranian on her lap.

"No, ma'am," I said. "My name is Dale Johnson. I'm a deputy with the Haywood County Sheriff's Department in North Carolina. To whom am I speaking?"

Dale shot me a bird and mouthed *Fuck you.*

"Oh my," the woman said. "My name is Louise Cordell."

Bingo.

"Ma'am, everything is fine. I'm calling because we recently found a red BMW 2002 registered to your address. The vehicle was illegally parked, and we've towed it to our holding facility. We need to get in touch with the owner."

"That's Lester's car. Is he in trouble again?"

"Ma'am, is Lester there now? May I speak to him?"

"Oh no, Lester moved to North Carolina some time ago. I'm his aunt."

"Thank you, ma'am. Do you have a phone number or local address for him?"

"He put his phone number in my phone. How do I look at that and talk to you at the same time?"

I went through a lengthy process with Louise, describing how to view the phone number. As she recited it to me, I wrote it down.

"And do you have a local address for him, ma'am?"

"Yes. He asked me to send him any mail that comes for him. Hold on a minute?"

It was more like five minutes, but Louise finally gave me an address in someplace called Maggie Valley. I thanked her and ended the call.

Dale pointed a giant finger at me. "When I finish this beer, I'm going to wring your neck."

I entered the address Louise had given me into Google Maps. The red arrow on the map pointed to a spot at the end of a short road called Ellison Drive. At the other end of the road, where Ellison met the main highway, was a small orange circle with a knife and fork in its center. I clicked the icon, and the name of the restaurant appeared: Pop's BBQ— "Give Your Mouth a Taste of the South."

I then typed Cordell's number into Dale's phone. After one ring a computerized voice recited the number I'd just dialed and requested that the caller leave a message.

"Straight to voice mail," I said. "C'mon, let's go."

Dale snorted. "What the fuck are you talking about?"

"I've got Cordell's local address. Let's go check it out."

I turned the laptop around so Dale could see the map. He glanced at the screen and frowned.

"That's on the other side of the fucking county. I ain't doing that shit."

"Let's just ride up there and see if we find Cordell."

"Brother, you've got a hard-on for that guy like I ain't never seen. What are you gonna say to him? 'Hey, I found some keys that might belong to you but they's lost again, sorry'?"

I looked back at the map and noticed that to get from the cabin to Maggie Valley, we'd have to drive through downtown Waynesville.

"We can stop at Long Branch on the way, pick up a couple more growlers."

Dale grabbed his phone from my hand and looked at the screen.

"It's nine twenty-two. Long Branch closes at ten. If you don't drive like a nearsighted grandpa, we might make it."

23

As we drove toward Waynesville, Dale wrangled the auxiliary audio cable from between the seats and plugged it into his phone. Soon Dokken's "The Hunter" was blaring out of the Mercedes's speakers. Dale sang along while he dug a tin of Copenhagen out of his shirt pocket.

"Where do you plan on spitting that?" I asked.

Dale glanced around the car, obviously hoping to find an empty bottle or coffee cup. "Dammit, Davis! You need to keep a spit cup in here."

We arrived at Long Branch Brewery a few minutes before ten. A couple of cars and several motorcycles sat in the lot. I pulled into an empty space and told Dale to make it quick.

"Bullshit," he said. "I ain't going in there. I'm in my uniform."

"Weren't you in uniform when you came here after court?"

"Yeah, but I was in my patrol car. People would've reckoned I was on official business."

"I doubt they thought that when you walked out with four growlers."

"Dammit, Davis, they's about to close. Get your ass in there and let's go to Maggie Valley and get this shit over with."

I turned off the car and held out an open palm.

"Are you shitting me?" Dale said.

I didn't move.

"Goddammit, Davis."

Dale opened the door and got out. At first I thought he'd changed his mind and was headed into the brewery himself, but then I realized he couldn't reach his wallet while he was sitting down.

After a minute of finagling, he handed me two twenties.

"Here," he said, throwing himself back into the passenger seat. "And bring me my fucking change."

*　*　*

Inside, a couple of servers wiped off tables and hauled trays of empty glasses toward the kitchen. Three men sat at the bar, dragging out last call as long as possible. I half hoped to see Skeeter among them, although I didn't know what I'd do if he was. Maybe knock off his aviators with a pint glass.

I stepped up to the bar and asked the bartender for two growlers of Dark Secret IPA. He gave me an apologetic look.

"Sorry, buddy, we're closed."

A skinny guy with a ZZ Top beard sitting at the bar chuckled, then picked up his beer and took a long drink. I ignored him, pulled out my phone, and showed the bartender the time.

"C'mon, man. It's only nine fifty-eight."

"He told you they're closed," ZZ Top grunted.

The angel on my shoulder chanted, "Stay calm. Be cool. Stay calm. Be cool." I clenched my teeth for a moment, then leaned over toward the bartender.

"Listen, my friend's waiting for me in the car. I promised I'd get him two growlers. Help me out, okay?"

ZZ Top slammed his beer down on the bar. "Do you not understand the word *closed*?"

Stay calm. Be cool. Stay calm. Be cool.

The bartender glanced at ZZ Top, then back at me.

"We're closed," he said firmly. Then he shrugged and disappeared through a door behind the bar.

I had a couple of choices. I could leave quietly and tell Dale we were too late, or I could make ZZ Top swallow his own beard. Neither would give me complete satisfaction, so I walked behind the bar, pulled two clean growlers off a shelf, and began filling them from the tap labeled DARK SECRET. ZZ Top watched the whole affair with a complacent grin.

When both growlers were full, I stepped back and looked under the bar.

"The caps are in that drawer behind you," ZZ Top said.

I nodded a *thank you*, capped off the growlers, and then tossed Dale's forty bucks onto the bar. As I was limping away, I wondered how close to the door I'd get before ZZ Top tried to stop me. I was just past the shelves of board games when I got my answer.

"Don't you want your change?"

When I turned around, ZZ Top and the two other guys from the bar were walking in my direction. I decided this would be a really good time for Dale to lose his patience and come looking for me.

ZZ Top pushed up the sleeves of his denim shirt to reveal a mural of faded tattoos. His buddies were just as rough, their hands and arms covered in prison ink and their fingers laced with heavy rings that I did not want introduced to my face.

"He's a friend."

The voice came from the door the bartender had walked through a few minutes earlier. It was a voice from heaven. Diana's voice.

I was elated, but ZZ Top and his buddies didn't seem to care and continued their slow march in my direction. As they walked, ZZ Top lifted the bottom of his shirt to reveal the grip of a handgun poking out over the top of his jeans. Diana ran up behind the men and put her hand on ZZ Top's bony shoulder. When she whispered in his ear, he stopped walking, and his minions immediately followed suit.

ZZ Top listened to Diana without ever taking his eyes off me. I didn't like his eyes. They were as dark as coal chutes.

When Diana pulled away from ZZ Top's ear, the man nodded, then tapped both of his buddies on the chest. Soon they were back on their barstools, drinking beer and laughing as if they hadn't a care in the world.

"I always figured I'd die in a brewery," I said as Diana came up to me.

She glanced back at the bar, then nudged me toward the front entrance.

"Did you get my email?" she said when we were by the door.

"The guy with the beard has a gun," I said.

Diana looked again toward the bar, where one of ZZ Top's buddies was now filling a pitcher from a tap.

"Overprotective friends, that's all. So, did you get my email?"

I stared at the men and imagined ZZ Top's beard getting caught in a wood chipper.

"Hey," Diana said, putting a hand on my arm to redirect my attention. "Don't worry about them. Some guys think a woman who owns a bar needs extra security. So did you see my email? I want to get together to hear more about your book."

I looked at Diana and immediately lost myself in her eyes.

"Yeah, sorry, I just saw it a little while ago. The email, I mean."

"So tomorrow night's good?"

"Yeah, that works. I'll send directions to the cabin."

I glanced back at the bar. *With friends like these . . .*

"We're closing up," Diana said. "Now get out of here."

When I didn't move, she smacked me on the ass.

"Don't make me tell you twice," she said, backing away with the cutest smirk I'd ever seen.

* * *

Out in the parking lot I could hear Van Halen's "Hot for Teacher" coming from my Mercedes. I opened the back door of the car and put the growlers on the floorboard. Once behind the wheel, I turned down the stereo and told Dale what had transpired.

"She really smacked your ass?" he said.

I hit Dale's chest with the back of my hand. "What about the guy with the gun?"

Dale shrugged.

"I think if I were lying dead in there, you'd come in and drink a beer before helping me," I said.

"Well, if you was already dead, how could I help you?"

I huffed and started the engine.

"Look," Dale said. "We've got concealed carry in this county. That man's got a right to protect hisself."

"I wasn't threatening him."

"Yeah, but you going in there and acting like an asshole don't help matters."

I pulled out of the parking lot and asked Dale how to get to Maggie Valley. Soon we were out of Waynesville and headed west on a four-lane highway flanked by antique stores and mom-and-pop motels.

"Hey, did you see Daiquiri in there?" Dale asked.

"No. I guess it really is her day off."

Dale shook his body like a dog that had just come in out of the rain. "Whooo! I can't stop thinkin' about that woman."

"Well, earlier you were thinking about a bailiff with a wildlife problem for an ass."

"Yeah, I know, but Daiquiri is leading the pack. I sent her a friend request on Facebook. I tell you, it won't be long till I change my relationship status."

Dale tapped his phone screen, and a moment later "Heavy Metal Love" by Helix started up.

"You ever heard of playing hard to get?" I asked.

Dale snorted. "That shit don't work for dudes. A man's got to show that he's interested."

I shook my head. "Have you ever seen a cat play with a piece of string?"

Dale stared at me but didn't answer.

"What happens if you hold that piece of string just out of the cat's reach? It goes crazy, right? It jumps in the air and swats at it. All it can think about is getting its paws on that string."

"Yeah. And?"

"But what happens when you put that piece of string on the ground right in front of the cat? Suddenly the cat's no longer interested. The string isn't enticing. It's no longer a challenge. Don't you think Daiquiri might become more interested if you stayed just slightly out of reach?"

Dale's face twisted as he tried to wrap his head around the concept.

"I'm the cat," he finally said. "Not the fucking string!"

24

It was almost ten thirty when we passed the sign welcoming us to Maggie Valley. During the drive Dale told me the town was a tourist trap. A long swath of souvenir shops and cheap motels that beckoned visitors looking to get away to the Great Smoky Mountains. The town was also a favorite among bikers who flocked to events with names like Rally in the Valley and Thunder in the Smokies.

"Them bikers don't cause much trouble," Dale said. "They'll be a fistfight here and there and some ole gal'll get liquored up and flash her titties, but it ain't never nothin' the local police can't handle."

A few minutes later I noticed the sign for Pop's BBQ. The restaurant was dark and the parking lot was empty. I pulled into a handicap space next to the front door and dug out a flashlight and a pair of binoculars from the car's center console.

"What are you doing?" Dale asked.

"I'm going to walk around back and see if I can find Cordell's house."

"Why don't you just drive back there?"

"Because I don't want to announce our arrival."

Dale reached around and pulled one of the growlers off the back floorboard. He unscrewed the cap and took a long draw.

"Okay. Don't worry, I'll keep an eye on things here."

I stepped out of the car and was about to close the door when Dale threw a hand in my direction.

"Hey! Where's my fucking change!"

* * *

It was a clear night, and a three-quarter moon hung just above a ridge-line in the distance. It was getting colder, and as I walked across the parking lot, I wondered if I was going to have to eventually invest in a thicker jacket. Surely there was a Goodwill somewhere close.

When I reached the corner of the building, a motion sensor light clicked on, and suddenly the entire parking lot glowed as bright as day. I glanced back toward the car and saw Dale give me a thumbs-up through the window.

I turned off the flashlight and quickly walked to the back of the building, where a rectangular asphalt pad was shrouded in darkness. As soon as I passed the rear corner of the building, another motion light clicked on. I assumed this was the employee parking lot. It was empty except for two blue dumpsters sitting about three feet apart on the lot's far side. I crossed the pavement and wedged myself between the two dumpsters with my back to the restaurant. I knelt down, then stayed perfectly still. After a minute the motion light turned off, and when my eyes adjusted to the moonlight, I was looking out across a flat, grassy field. I raised the binoculars and turned the focus ring. The field stretched out in front of me for about three hundred yards, ending at what looked like the edge of a wide ditch.

On the other side of the ditch, the field continued sloping upward on a slight grade. I could see the grass was cut shorter on the slope. It looked like someone's front yard.

Beyond the yard stood a white, two-story house. The building was dark except for a light coming from one of the second-floor windows. I focused my binoculars on the glowing window but didn't notice any movement.

I scanned the bottom floor of the house from one side to the other. It was too dark to see many details, but I did make out a couple of rocking chairs on the front porch next to a red door. Starting at the door, I lowered the binoculars down a set of steps that led from the porch to a small path. I followed the path to the left and could make out the very faint glow of a few solar-powered walkway lights. The path ended at a small, barren parking area.

I hurried back to the car, damning each of the motion lights that clicked on as I passed under them. Dale was blaring the stereo as I approached the Mercedes, and when I opened the door, he nearly jumped out of his seat.

"Mother! Fucker!" he yelled as I got in. "Don't be sneaking up on me like that."

"The house is a few hundred yards back behind the restaurant. There's a light on, but I didn't see any vehicles parked out front."

"All right then, you found the house. Now let's go home."

I hesitated a moment and rubbed my leg. Just walking to the dumpsters and back had filled it with pins and needles.

I nodded at Dale. "I'm going to go up and take a closer look."

Dale slammed the back of his head against the headrest. "Why the fuck would you want to do that?"

I didn't have a good answer. I just knew something was sticking in my craw. Maybe it was what Byrd had said he'd felt when he interviewed the man who had shot his coworker. Instinct. A gut feeling. Whatever it was, I had it, and it was a relatively new feeling for me. During my time on the force and those years as a private detective, I hadn't cared who was guilty and who was innocent. I just put in my hours and cashed the checks. Instinct never got into the mix. I never once had a gut feeling that told me to dig deeper or look closer. It wasn't that I couldn't connect the dots; I just wasn't all that interested in finding them in the first place.

Until now. Maybe I had something to prove. Or maybe I was procrastinating on my book. Or maybe the angel on my shoulder was giving me a distraction to try to lower my beer and pill intake. Whatever the reason, my gut was telling me to go to that house, leg be damned.

"I'm just curious," I said. "Who knows, maybe I'll find a clue."

"Dammit, Davis. You need to get your head on straight."

I grinned at Dale, then stepped out of the car. "I'll be back in fifteen minutes."

Dale sneered. "If you ain't back in ten, I'm driving this thing home."

*　*　*

I walked back to my spot between the dumpsters and waited again for the motion light to turn off. In the darkness I stayed low to the ground as I made my way across the field. When I came to the ditch, I could see a stream of water flowing at its base. It was too wide to jump over—anything bigger than a puddle would be for me—so I looked in both directions for a crossing point. Using the binoculars, I found what looked like a small footbridge thirty or so yards from where I stood. Once across the ditch I could see a gravel driveway leading to the house.

I stood still for a moment and stared at the illuminated second-floor window. I listened for the sound of a TV or a conversation, but all I could hear were crickets and the faint babbling of the stream behind me.

With the flashlight on its lowest setting, I made my way around to the back of the house, worried that a motion light would turn on at any moment. Thankfully, none did. The back of the house was completely dark. Limbs from a scattering of trees drowned out the moonlight, so I pushed a button on the flashlight to bump up the brightness. Shining the light against the edge of the house, I could see a couple of concrete steps leading up to the building's back door. On the top step sat several brown growlers. I moved closer and saw that all the growlers were empty. One carried a Long Branch logo on its side, the others were blank.

Standing on the top step, I peered through a small window carved in the middle of the door. I couldn't see a thing and wondered if I should risk shining my flashlight through the window.

As I was contemplating that option, a light turned on inside the house. I instinctively jumped aside, and the growlers tumbled down the steps with what sounded like a tray of dishes crashing to the floor.

I jumped off the step and hurried toward the woods behind the house. Peeking around a large tree trunk, I watched the back door, waiting for it to open and Cordell to appear. But the door remained closed.

Maybe Cordell hadn't heard the breaking glass. Or maybe he had and assumed it was raccoons or possums or whatever other kinds of animals rummaged around for garbage at night in these parts.

Suddenly I heard a loud pop. It sounded like a firecracker coming from the second floor of the house. Immediately following the pop, a section of the tree trunk exploded and a piece of bark slapped my cheek. I put my hand up to my face, then pulled it away, looking for blood. I realized the flashlight was still in my other hand and still on, its beam illuminating my white canvas sneakers. I dropped to the ground and turned off the flashlight. Another pop rang out, and dirt shot up into my face.

Lying flat on the ground next to a tree, I thought about the dead man Byrd had seen in the woods. The man named Randy with the bullet hole in his head. Byrd wondered if Randy had ever thought he'd end up that way. Shot dead by a jealous husband, his body stashed under a pile of leaves for two kids to find. Over the years I'd tried many times to envision how I would die. But never once had it involved lying in the woods behind a house in Maggie Valley, North Carolina. Killed by a hipster who thought I was trying to break into his house.

Another pop, and another clod of dirt ricocheted off my face. I needed to move. I turned the flashlight on to its highest setting, then threw it as far as I could to my left. *Pop. Pop. Pop.* The beam from the flashlight danced across the tree branches, then vanished.

I crawled on my stomach, hoping to find better cover by the side of the house. But I was crawling in complete darkness. As I inched across the dirt and dead leaves, my hands finally found gravel. The driveway. I decided to crawl a few more feet, then stand up and make a run for it, or at least what passed for a run. My leg was almost completely numb, and I wondered how much longer it would cooperate before throwing in the towel.

The gravel stung my hands and tore at the material of my jacket. I heard another pop, but nothing near me was disturbed. I assumed the shooter was still aiming at where I'd thrown the flashlight. At least I hoped that was the case. I pushed my knees up under me and adopted a sprinter's squat. The next pop was my cue to take off at full speed, which for me was somewhere between a power walk and a skip.

I heard another pop and felt something whiz past my head. I dropped down on my stomach again and tried to catch my breath. Another pop, this one followed by breaking glass to my left. I looked in that direction and saw a small garage at the edge of the driveway. I crawled across the gravel, then worked my way around the garage until it was between me and the house. Through a dirty window I could see a Land Rover topped with a cargo box.

The Land Rover. I inched around to the front of the garage and yanked up a heavy wood door, then stepped inside. The garage was full of tools and paint cans, and in a MacGyver-inspired moment I wondered if I could fashion together something to help me escape. I tried the handle of the Land Rover's driver's side door, but it was locked. When I tried the rear door, something caught my eye: a metal detector sitting on the back seat where Jeff and Becky's cooler had been. Another pop rang out, and I heard a thump as the bullet slammed into the side of the garage.

I was trapped. If I stayed in the garage, the shooter would eventually come find me, and if I stepped back out on the driveway, I'd be an easy target in the moonlight. Suddenly my thigh quivered, and for a second I thought I'd been hit. I grabbed my pant leg and felt for blood, but then another quiver hit me and I realized my phone was vibrating. My phone!

Like most people I'd become completely attached to my phone. But since coming to the mountains, I'd more or less forgotten about it. The service was so spotty it was practically useless unless I was sitting in the parking lot of El Bacaratos. But out of habit I kept it on me almost all the time. It was a good thing I kept paying the bill.

I pushed the accept-call button and put the phone to my ear.

"What the fuck are you doing!" Dale yelled over the sound of Cinderella's "Nobody's Fool." I'd never been so happy to hear his voice.

"Someone's shooting at me. Drive up here and get me. I'm in a garage near the back of the house."

"Stop fucking around."

I told Dale about knocking over the growlers and the shots that followed. I also told him about finding the Land Rover in the garage.

"Stay put. I'll be there directly."

I knelt next to the Land Rover and waited, staring out the garage door toward the driveway, anticipating the headlights of the Mercedes appearing at any moment. After a couple of minutes my phone vibrated, and I put it back to my ear.

"How the fuck do you start this thing?" Dale said.

"Put your foot on the brake, then push the ignition button next to the steering wheel."

"Where's the key?"

"It's keyless. Just push the ignition button."

"How does it start with no key?"

Another pop rang out, and shards of glass fell onto my shoulders.

"Just do it!" I yelled.

I stayed crouched by the Land Rover for a few more moments, then eased toward the opening of the garage. I wanted to be ready to hobble to the car as soon as Dale arrived. As I waited, I noticed something I hadn't seen when I first entered the building. It looked like a wicker basket poking out over the top of a stack of paint cans. I moved several of the cans to reveal a red bicycle with a basket attached to the handlebars. I shook my head at the thought that entered my mind, but then decided it was just as good as any other. I'd give Dale one more minute. If he hadn't shown by then, I'd take off on the bike.

Ninety seconds later I was pedaling down the driveway on a bike with no gears and a flat front tire. I'd heard another pop as soon as I'd left the garage, but I was too busy pedaling to notice whether the bullet had hit anything. All that mattered was that it hadn't hit me.

The driveway led straight away from the house but then curved around a long bend surrounded by trees. If I could get around the curve, I would be out of sight of the house. Another pop rang out, this one fainter than the others. I was making progress.

Past the curve, the driveway straightened out and sloped down toward a wooden bridge that spanned the ditch I had crossed earlier. I took my feet off the pedals and let gravity pull me down the slope. The handlebars started to shake, and it took everything I had to keep the bike on the road. I glanced behind me again, half expecting to see the Land Rover's headlights trailing after me, but the road was dark. I turned back around just in time to see a car barreling across the bridge just a few feet in front of me. A horn blared, and I swerved off the road just shy of the bridge. The bike dropped down into the ditch and the front tire sank into the mud, sending me headfirst over the handlebars. When I dragged myself out of the ditch and up to the road, Dale was standing next to the Mercedes.

"Where'd you get a bike?" he asked.

"What took you so long?"

"This car is way too complicated. First I had to figure out how to get the seat to go back. Then there ain't no key. Then it took me forever to find the lights. There ain't no reason a vehicle needs to be that difficult."

I didn't know whether to hug Dale or punch him in the face.

"You hurt?" he asked.

My leg had gone from numb to on fire. But it was holding me upright, so I figured I was okay.

"Just my pride. C'mon, let's go."

"You want me to drive? I already got the seat where I like it."

When we were both in the car, I asked Dale what he was going to do. "I'm going to drive your dumb ass home."

"Aren't you going to call for backup?"

Dale ignored me and fiddled with the steering wheel adjustment lever.

"Backup for what?" he said, after raising the wheel so high it looked like he was driving a bus.

"Someone shot at me. Repeatedly. I was almost killed."

"Look, I don't know how they do it down in Charleston, but around here if you find someone prowling around your house in the middle of the night, you fire off a couple of shots to scare 'em away."

"Are you fucking kidding me!"

"A man's got a right to protect his domicile."

I couldn't believe what I was hearing.

"Hey, they's a big difference between being shot and being shot at," Dale said. "You were shot at. Now if you'd been hit, that'd be a different story."

"So you're not going to do anything?"

Dale spun the Mercedes around and sped across the bridge.

"There ain't nothing to do. We found the man's house, and that should've been the end of it. But you had to go all Sherlock Holmes, looking for clues and shit."

"But I did find a clue."

Dale snorted and gunned the engine as we pulled out onto the main highway.

"That couple's Land Rover is in the garage," I said.

"That ain't no fucking clue. It just proves Cordell and that couple is friends. And I told you that in the first place."

"There was a metal detector on the back seat of the Land Rover."

Dale laughed. "Well, shit. We'd better go back. Possession of a metal detector is a serious offense."

We didn't speak for the rest of the ride back to the cabin, expect for when Dale said, "This is your new theme song," just before playing Ozzy Osbourne's "Flying High Again."

When I was driving, it had taken us half an hour to get to Maggie Valley, not counting the stop at Long Branch. With Dale behind the wheel, the return trip took less than twenty minutes.

As Dale walked over to his patrol car, I felt obliged to thank him for coming to my rescue.

"Well, it was worth it just to see you on that bike," he said. "Man, I wish I had a video of you going over them handlebars. I could make some money on the YouTube with that shit."

"So what are we going to do now about the keys?"

Dale pointed a finger at my chest.

"You ain't gonna do a damn thing. I'm gonna run by Floppy's in the morning and tell him to give me them keys or else I'm going to arrest his skinny ass. Then I'll give the keys to Barbara, and whoever comes to get 'em can have 'em."

With that, Dale wiggled into his patrol car and tore off down the gravel road. I limped into the cabin without the energy to grab a beer or open the pill bottle. I dropped on top of the bed fully clothed and was out before the devils could whisper a single word.

25

The next morning I wanted breakfast. A real breakfast. Bacon, eggs, sausage, pancakes, hash browns. A coronary on a plate. It was unusual. Most mornings my head and stomach both hurt so bad just the idea of breakfast was nauseating. But this morning I was hungry. Maybe it was the adrenaline still pumping from the night before, or maybe it was the fact that I'd had less than eight beers the previous day and I hadn't taken a couple of pills before bed. I didn't feel like running a marathon or even limping through a 5K, but I did feel better than most mornings. Maybe being almost killed was the secret to sobriety.

The closest Waffle House was located in Canton next to the interstate exit. I remembered passing it on my way to meet Dale the day he showed me the cabin. The great thing about the Waffle House menu is the pictures. No matter how drunk or stoned you are, you can just point to a picture and soon it will materialize in front of you. I pointed at the menu, and a few minutes later enough food to scatter, smother, and cover my arteries for the next decade appeared before me. It was only eight bucks and it was delicious.

As I was finishing my coffee, I saw a patrol car pull into the parking lot. At first I thought it might be Dale, but since the car didn't skid in on two wheels, I figured it must be another deputy. I watched as Skeeter got out of the car and strutted toward the restaurant's door. He was wearing his mirrored aviators, and between those and his tight uniform and goatee, he looked like he was on his way to a Halloween party.

When he walked in, the waitresses, cook, and a few of the customers welcomed him with shouts of "Hey, Skeeter!" He nodded silently in return, like a celebrity walking the red carpet.

When he finally noticed me, he sneered, and I somehow resisted the urge to throw my fork at him. A moment later he was sitting next to me. I turned to face him, and I could see my reflection in his aviators. My cheek was still red from the ricocheting tree bark, and I noticed a large bump on my forehead, courtesy of the rock that had broken my fall when I went over the bicycle's handlebars.

I'm no psychologist, but I'd summed up Skeeter thirty seconds after meeting him the day he pulled me over. My guess was that he'd been bullied in high school. After graduation he'd probably done a short stint in the military, where he got in shape and learned a little discipline. Then he'd come back to his hometown, earned a two-year degree in criminal justice, and joined the sheriff's department. Now he was the bully and thought every problem could be solved with force. A big fish in a teeny, tiny pond. He was finally big man on campus. Problem was, I didn't attend this school.

The waitress came over and brought Skeeter a cup of coffee. He poured three sugars and two creamers in the cup and stirred the beige mess with a spoon.

"I never fancied you a cyclist," he said. "I hear you have a unique form, ass over end."

When I didn't respond, Skeeter chuckled.

"Oh, yeah, Dale had us in stitches this morning with that story. Said you went over those handlebars like you was slung out of a slingshot. Oh, boy, what I'd of given to see that."

It was one of the rare mornings I felt halfway decent. My mind wasn't foggy and my stomach wasn't churning. I hadn't even taken a pill, yet for some reason the devils were silent. I wasn't worried about losing my temper with Skeeter, because I knew at some point I would enjoy five minutes alone with his vehicle. But until then, I was happy to play the game.

"What's your real name?" I asked. "Is it Reginald or Harold or something like that?"

Skeeter grinned and took a sip of his coffee.

"It's Deputy Norris to you, asshole."

"Well, Deputy Norris, don't worry, I'll be out of this town soon enough. Unlike you, who'll be here for the rest of your life."

"I don't know about that. But I'll tell you one thing—while I am here, I'm going to clean the place up."

I smiled, then blew a bacon burp toward Skeeter.

He shook his head and poured another sugar in his coffee.

"I got eyes," he said, stirring his coffee a second time. "I see things. I take notice."

I pointed at Skeeter's aviators. "Are you telling me those are magic glasses?" I said. "Are you like that guy on *Star Trek*?"

Skeeter snickered and placed his spoon on the counter.

"You think I didn't see you at Long Branch the other night?" he said. "Drinking with Dale, eating a quesadilla? Dale was gunning for that waitress, wasn't he? He sure does have a type. What were you gunning for?"

When I didn't answer, Skeeter raised his eyebrows and took a long sip of his coffee. I didn't much care for Skeeter knowing my business. I thought back to that night and how I'd spotted him at the bar. At some point he'd caught sight of me and I hadn't noticed. It made me wonder how many of the adulterers and insurance frauds I'd staked out over the years had seen me before I'd seen them.

"Mark my words, I'll be sheriff here one day," Skeeter said. "And I hope you're still around to see it."

So Skeeter was an asshole with ambition. I'd always found that to be a dangerous mix.

"You're a dreamer, huh?" I said. "Got big plans?"

Skeeter stared into his coffee as if it were a crystal ball. "You don't know nothing about me."

"So what else do you dream about? Maybe finishing a crossword? Or reading a book?"

Skeeter continued to grin, but I noticed his neck was turning a dazzling shade of red. Either he had eczema or I'd struck a nerve.

"My book will be all words, so you probably wouldn't enjoy it. But there are a lot of books with pictures in them. I'm sure there's a children's section in the library here."

"Shut up."

"But what I'm really curious about is why you're called Skeeter. Is it 'cause you're hung like a mosquito?"

* * *

That was the morning I got arrested. Fortunately, Dale was at the sheriff's office when Skeeter dragged me in with my hands cuffed behind my back.

"What the fuck did he do now?" Dale asked.

"Disturbing the peace," Skeeter said. "And resisting arrest."

I looked at Dale and shrugged. "Resisting arrest was a given."

Dale walked over and shoved Skeeter aside, then unlocked my cuffs and threw them on the nearest desk.

"What the fuck happened?" Dale asked.

"I made a joke, and Deputy Dickhead here got offended," I said.

"What kind of joke?"

I looked at Skeeter and grinned. "Do you want to tell him or shall I?"

Skeeter bit down on his toothpick. "He said my pecker was the size of a mosquito."

When Dale leaned back and laughed, his uniform shirt stretched so tight across his stomach I thought it might pop open at the seams like a tube of refrigerator biscuits.

"Dammit, Skeeter," Dale said, still laughing. "Is that all he did? Boy, you got to get yourself some thicker skin."

Skeeter pointed a finger just inches from my nose and gave me his best alpha-male routine.

"I told you I got eyes," he said. "And they are all over you."

With that, Skeeter picked up his cuffs from the desk and strutted out of the room.

"That boy's got more testosterone than a high school football team," Dale said when Skeeter was gone.

I looked around the squad room for my other archnemesis. "Can you give me a ride to my car? I don't want Byrd to see me here."

Dale plopped down into his desk chair. "Why are you worried about Byrd?"

"I'm persona non grata," I said.

Dale rolled his eyes. "Speak American, dickhead."

"After I talked to that couple yesterday, Byrd called me into his office to tell me a story about some murder he solved years ago. Then he told me he didn't trust me. He thinks I'm up here looking for something."

"Looking for what?"

Dale knew only half of the storage unit story. The half that didn't include me finding cases of drugs or beating Greg. How much Byrd knew, I wasn't sure. I needed to ask Perry about Byrd's friend Emory, but until then I felt it best to stay out of Byrd's sight. A part of me felt bad for keeping Dale in the dark about what had actually transpired down in Charleston, especially since we'd shared quite a few personal stories while sitting on the deck and drinking beer. But just like my plan to key Skeeter's Mustang, some things weren't Dale's business.

"I really don't know," I said. "Can you give me a lift or not?"

*　*　*

During the ride back to the Waffle House, I told Dale a little more about my conversation with Byrd, including Byrd's self-professed ability to spot a liar.

"Well, I tell you one thing," Dale said. "I don't play poker with the sheriff. Not no more, anyway. He can call a bluff better than anyone I've ever seen. I told him he should give up this bullshit and go to Vegas."

I wondered if Byrd would call my bluff and figure out I was the man responsible for my brother-in-law's current condition. I hoped not. I didn't need the local sheriff considering me a violent fugitive.

*　*　*

When we pulled into the Waffle House parking lot, I caught a whiff of the paper mill. I told Dale it smelled like rotten eggs covered in wet sawdust.

"People 'round here says it smells like money," he said.

Dale parked his patrol car next to my Mercedes, then pressed the unlock button for the doors. I hesitated a moment.

"So what happened with Floppy?"

Dale's nostrils flared. "I went by his trailer this morning, but he swears up and down he ain't got them keys."

"And you believe him?"

"Hell no. I don't believe a word that skinny sumbitch says. I poked around the garage, but it'd be hard to find a brush fire in all that mess."

"But you're convinced he has them?"

"Fuck if I know. But if had to bet, I'd say if them keys ain't in his garage, then they's stuck in a drawer in his trailer somewhere. Man's a pack rat, got shit everywhere, and half of it ain't his."

I thought about Floppy's body odor and how it could make the paper mill jealous.

"Where's his trailer?" I asked.

"Out back of his garage."

"I didn't notice it when I was there."

"That don't surprise me. There's so much shit stacked in front of it you can't see the damn thing till you're right up on it."

"You didn't you go in and look for the keys?"

Dale laughed. "Floppy don't allow no one in his trailer, 'specially not me."

*   *   *

I got out of the patrol car and walked over to my Mercedes. As I opened the door, I looked toward the Waffle House and saw several faces pressed against the window, staring back at me. When I gave them a thumbs-up, they all quickly disappeared. Persona non grata, I thought, was something I should probably get used to.

26

By noon I was back at the cabin sitting on the deck with a beer. The first pill of the day was flowing through my veins, and I could feel a pleasant numbness starting to blanket my brain. I stared at the blank legal pad and decided it was finally time to write something. I wrote the numeral *1* on the first line of the pad. Next to that I wrote *Found Some Keys*. From there I continued down the page, listing the events of previous few days. One beer later I wrote *25. Get Inside Floppy's Trailer*. I stared at the list and tried see if there were any dots I could connect. After twenty minutes I gave up. I'd never been a good detective.

I went inside and sat down in front of the laptop. I reopened the email Diana had sent the previous day. I had to admit I liked her forward approach. It reminded me of what a womanizing friend of mine called the *assumed close*. "You don't ask a woman if she'd like to go out," he told me. "You ask if she'd rather you pick her up at seven thirty or eight. You phrase it so it's not a question of yes or no, it's a question of when." This was the same guy who'd told me about the cat and the string. I needed to give Dale his number.

But Diana didn't even give me the opportunity to pick the when. Her email made it very clear that she was in charge. Maybe that was just what I needed—a woman who would take control. Sure, I could engage in conversation and even make a woman laugh every now and then, sometimes intentionally, but I was temperamental, stubborn, moody, private, and generally tipsy. I wasn't consistent enough at being consistent to drive any kind of relationship forward. But this was just a date. All I had to do was focus and not embarrass myself.

I emailed Diana directions to the cabin, closed the laptop, and then considered riding up to Floppy's garage to see if I could somehow get inside his trailer. But my breakfast had put me into a sort of grease-induced coma, and it was about all I could do to walk to the refrigerator for a third beer.

Back at the table I thought about Diana slapping my ass and how it had made me feel. I needed Diana to take charge. I needed her to lead the way to wherever we were going. It's what Dale had done to become my friend. I hadn't invited him over; he'd just kept showing up whether I wanted him to or not. And I did want him to, even though I'd have to be waterboarded before admitting that fact in front of him.

I opened the computer again and pulled up Facebook. I found Dale's profile, clicked on the FRIENDS tab, and saw that he was connected with over three hundred people. I was connected to no one. I'd signed up for Facebook when I started dating Sarah, and for a while she was my only friend. Then Laura and I reconnected, and suddenly I had two Facebook friends. But they had both unfriended me, and I hadn't bothered reaching out to anyone else since. I was a Facebook voyeur. I used the site to see what other people were doing rather than to share the experiences of my own life. It says a lot about your personality when you open Facebook only to be greeted with the announcement *you have zero friends.*

Maybe it was time for me to stop being so closed off. I had no intention of going out and making new friends in the real world, but what could it hurt to reconnect with a few old friends in the virtual one? I clicked the ADD FRIEND button on Dale's profile and then searched for Sarah's and did the same. What the hell, I thought, she might like to hear I'd been shot. Then I thought of Perry. He was one of those friends you might not see or talk to very often but one you knew you could always count on. Since leaving the Charleston PD, I'd seen Perry only a handful of times. Before giving him my statement at the hospital, I couldn't remember the last time I'd seen him in person.

I entered his name in the search field, and several profiles appeared. I narrowed the search by clicking on Charleston, South Carolina, and soon I was looking at his smiling face. Perry was now in his early sixties, but his salt-and-pepper hair was as thick and wavy as it had been the day I'd first met him soon after I graduated from the academy. At that time Perry was a field training officer. For fifteen weeks we worked side by side, him attempting to show me the ropes and me trying not to be an insubordinate asshole.

At the end of my training, Perry reluctantly gave me his stamp of approval, and I was assigned to Team 7, Traffic Division, where I spent a month arguing with jaywalkers and cyclists. After it was reported that I shoved a guy who'd given me some guff about the expired meter ticket I'd placed on his truck, Perry invited me out for a beer. I'd come to respect Perry more than anyone else in the department. He was about the only person on the planet I'd actually listen to.

Over that beer, Perry described the department as a living maze.

"It's almost impossible to maneuver," he told me. "Just when you think you're on the right path, a new wall suddenly appears in front of you. To survive, you have to be willing to climb over those walls, or dig under them. You're not cut out for this, Davis. Go out on your own. Get your PI license and a camera with a long lens. You'll probably make more money, and you won't have a bureaucracy breathing down your neck."

I resigned the following day.

Over the next few years, Perry and I occasionally met for a beer. I'd tell him about the most recent cheating spouse or insurance fraud I'd photographed, and he'd tell me about his golf handicap and the twenty-foot fishing boat he referred to as his mistress because he said that was about how expensive it was to maintain.

During one of our meet-ups, he told me he'd been moved to the detective division. "No more dealing with blue flamers like you," he said. Later I heard he'd become a senior detective. It hadn't surprised me that Perry had learned to navigate the living maze of the department.

I focused on Perry's Facebook profile picture. He was on a golf course, smiling like a kid at an amusement park. I clicked ADD FRIEND and scrolled through Perry's profile. The only public photos showed Perry hamming it up with some of his police buddies, and I was suddenly a bit jealous for the friendships I'd never been able to obtain, much less maintain. "You're not cut out for this, Davis," Perry had told me. I now wondered if he was talking about the bureaucracy of the department or the camaraderie required to be a member of the force.

Then I considered that maybe Perry had been referring to something different altogether. What had he really meant when he talked about having to outmaneuver the walls of the department?

I thought back to my conversation with Byrd at the sheriff's department and how he'd brought up Perry. Byrd had said that a detective being put in charge of an investigation involving a good friend seemed like a conflict of interest. I'd never looked at it that way before. Perry was my friend, and he was protecting me. That's what friends did. But Byrd was right. It was a conflict of interest. Actually, it was worse than that. Perry knew I was guilty of putting Greg in a coma, and he was breaking some major rules by looking the other way. Perry wasn't just climbing over walls; he was smashing right through them.

It made me wonder how far Perry was willing to go. I'd been surprised when Byrd said that his Charleston PD friend Emory hadn't mentioned the IA investigation. But then again, those types of investigations weren't exactly broadcast through the department. Byrd's friend could be out of the loop—although Emory seemed to know who I was and enough about the storage unit incident to tell Byrd something wasn't quite right about it and to keep an eye on me. If he knew that much, it seemed more than likely he'd know IA was on the case.

But if Greg was being investigated by IA, why hadn't they contacted me? I was the only witness in the storage unit fiasco. Perry would give them my statement, but that wouldn't satisfy them. They would want me to recount my discussion with Greg word for word, and they'd want to hear it directly from me, and in person. But no one had contacted me.

Had Perry broken more rules to keep me out of that mess? How would he be able to do that? It didn't seem possible. It was as if there were no IA investigation at all. But if there wasn't, why would Perry tell me there was?

I pondered that question for a moment, despite the uncomfortable feeling it was giving me. I didn't know if it was the angel or the devils whispering in my ears, but something was causing a tremor to run through my veins.

I thought about that night in the storage unit and the figure silhouetted in front of headlights. The figure that slowly raised a hand and sent a bullet into my leg. Had a part of me recognized that figure? Had I somehow known all along who it was?

I stood up and marched around the table in an attempt to outrun the flood of thoughts pouring into my brain. I was being ridiculous. Perry was my friend, my mentor, the one person other than Laura I completely trusted. It was stupid to think he would be involved with Greg's drug hustle.

But the more I tried to talk myself out of it, the more suspicious I became. The idea was firmly planted, and it was going to fester.

I searched my memory, trying to pull up the times I'd talked to Perry over the years. Had he ever mentioned working with Greg? Or any bad apples in the department? And what kind of car did Perry drive? I remembered meeting him at a bar on James Island and seeing him get out of some type of SUV, maybe a Jeep Cherokee or something similar. But that had been a couple of years ago.

*　*　*

I drove down to El Bacaratos and used the browser app on my phone to find the number for the Audi dealership in Charleston. When a chipper woman answered, I asked to be transferred to the service department. After suffering through a minute of "Hooked on a Feeling," a service adviser finally picked up.

"Service, this is Paul."

"I need to make an appointment," I said.

"Sure. Have you been here before?"

"Yes. My name is Perry Long."

I heard a few keyboard clicks.

"Okay, let's see. Yes. Here we go—2017 Audi A6?"

"Yeah," I said frantically. "The gray one. It's gray, right?"

"Yes, sir. It's gray."

27

By the time I got back to the cabin, the devils were screaming and my temper had me looking around for something to break. Instead I put a pill under my tongue and began typing out an email.

Hey Perry,

I'm thinking about trading in my Mercedes for something smaller. Do you like your gray Audi? I need an answer ASAP.

Davis

I wanted Perry to know I'd found him out. He had told me I wasn't cut out for the department, but I needed to show him that I could at least put two and two together. That I wasn't so comfortably numb that I couldn't figure out he was the one who'd been with Greg that night. When Greg had come back to the storage unit and found me poking around, I'd noticed him on the phone with someone. He must have been calling Perry to tell him to come back and help solve the problem at hand. That problem being me.

Greg and Perry both knew me well. They knew I'd spill my guts to someone about what I'd seen in that storage unit. If not to the cops, then at least to Laura, and she'd definitely go to the authorities. Perry had no choice but to shoot me. It was a miracle he hadn't killed me. Maybe shooting me in the leg was his way of being a friend.

When I hit SEND, the devils applauded my rash decision, but the angel grimaced. I knew the angel was thinking, *What if you're wrong?*

I sat at the table for half an hour pondering that thought. Maybe I was being rash. There were a lot of gray Audis in the world, and Perry owning one didn't necessarily make him guilty of anything. It could be just a fluke, even if it was a fluke I didn't like. I'd been wrong about a lot of things in my life, so why should I all of a sudden think I'd finally connected the right dots in the right order?

I considered sending Perry another email. This one to say I'd been joking. But just like my attempt at writing a book, I couldn't come up with the words. In the end I decided to let it be. I would just wait and see how he responded.

I grabbed a fresh beer and headed to the deck. I stared at Cold Mountain, half hoping to see a flicker of light somewhere on its slope. A flicker of gold that I could drive up to and collect without having to limp more than ten feet. But what would I do with a chest of gold? Head to Vegas and try to double it? Fly to South America and disappear? Wherever you go, there you are—isn't that what they say? Where could a new me go that the old me would never find? I'd give up a chest of gold to know that answer.

I looked at my phone for the time. It was almost three, and my Waffle House coma was finally starting to subside. If Diana was coming at six thirty, I had a little over three hours to clean the cabin, shower, shave, and come up with something interesting to talk about rather than a book I didn't know how to write.

Listening to a Dale-approved playlist of eighties heavy metal, I spent the next several hours trying to make the cabin presentable. I cleaned off the kitchen table, wiped down the counters, and vacuumed the living room carpet with a metal canister vac that had probably been manufactured during the Carter presidency. In the bathroom I scrubbed the sink, toilet, and tub. I made the bed, cleaned off the nightstand, and threw all my dirty laundry into a hamper in the closet. On a high shelf in the kitchen I found a couple of scented candles, most likely left over from

Carla. I placed one in the kitchen and one in the living room and let them battle it out with the lingering scent of Dale.

By five o'clock the cabin was cleaner than the day Dale first showed it to me. I went down into the basement and organized my brewing equipment. My setup wasn't much to look at, but it worked well. I had two growlers of my IPA left, and I dug them out from behind a piece of plywood leaning up against the basement's cinder-block wall. I'd hidden them there from Dale, not putting it past him to wander off with them during one of his unannounced visits. I put the growlers in the fridge, then hopped in the shower.

At 6:25 I was looking through the sliding glass door, eagerly waiting for headlights to appear. I was still there fifteen minutes later. Evening was coming quicker these days, and soon happy hour would start in total darkness rather than in the fading light of dusk. Although my happy hour always started soon after waking, so it didn't really matter.

I felt like a teenage boy standing at the window. I wasn't nervous, or even really excited—the pills did a good job at numbing those particular feelings—but I was hopeful. It would be nice to enjoy an evening of real conversation rather than arguing with Dale. But maybe I was just hopeful for the same thing most teenage boys hope for when a girl is on her way over.

As I was looking out into the night, I thought of a discussion I'd had with Dale. We'd been sitting on the deck, drinking beer, and listening to music from his phone. When the song "Heaven" by the band Warrant came on, Dale became sentimental, which was surprising. He sang along for a bit, then shook his head.

"That was me and Carla's song," he said. "She used to love it."

The song was a power ballad. A slow tearjerker heavy-metal bands were obligated to write if they wanted steady radio airplay. I hadn't heard it in years.

"Davis, I'll tell you something. They ain't nothin' worse than missing a woman."

I didn't have a response to that, so we drank in silence for a few moments until the song ended. The next track that played was Dokken's "In My Dreams," a song about a man pining for his ex-love.

"You miss that woman down in Charleston?" Dale asked. "That one that kicked you out?"

"Which one? I've been kicked out more than once."

"That last one—Samantha or something?"

I listened to the song for a few moments while pondering Dale's question.

"No, I don't miss Sarah," I said. "I don't miss anyone."

Dale grabbed his phone and searched for another track to play.

"You're full of shit," he said. "A woman loves you, you'll miss her when she's gone."

"A woman loving you is no good reason to love her back."

* * *

I wasn't lying. Once a woman told me she loved me, I knew she wasn't someone I needed to be with. It was the old Groucho Marx line: I don't want to belong to any club that would accept me as a member. Sarah had told me she loved me a few days after we moved in together. That's when I started to become distant. She put up with it for a while, and then when things didn't change, she kicked me out. I thought about her once in a while, but thinking about someone is not the same as missing them.

When six forty-five rolled around, I started to wonder if Diana had received my email with directions to the cabin. I hadn't checked for a response.

I went to the kitchen and opened the cabinet where I'd placed my laptop when cleaning up. I was about to pull it out when I heard a knock at the back door. Through the panes of glass I could see Diana holding a large cardboard box. I opened the door and took the box from her; it was filled with grease-stained paper bags and two growlers. Diana was wearing jeans, a thick gray sweater, and the same fleece jacket she'd been wearing when I first saw her at El Bacaratos. She stepped into the kitchen, removed her jacket with a graceful spin, and hung it over the back of a chair.

"Sorry I'm late," she said. "I missed the turn, then had a hard time finding a place to turn around."

"Yeah, this cabin is pretty secluded. That's one of the things I like about it."

"Are you hiding from someone?" She gave me the same playful smirk she'd flashed after smacking me on the ass at Long Branch.

"No, of course not," I said, not knowing whether I was trying to convince her or myself.

I nodded at the bags in the cardboard box. "Looks like you brought more than just chips and guacamole."

"Tacos, burritos, quesadillas. I didn't know what you liked, so I brought a selection."

I grabbed a few plates and started sorting out the food.

"Where are your glasses?" Diana asked.

I pointed to a cabinet next to the stove.

"Interesting place to store your laptop," she said a moment later.

I looked up and saw Diana pulling two glasses from the cabinet's bottom shelf. My laptop sat just above them.

"Did you do a quick cleanup before I arrived?" she asked. She smiled, and her dimples tripped me up for a second.

"There's, uh . . . well, there's not really a lot of storage here."

"Do you keep your book research under the sink?"

She winked, and I felt the spark of connection again. It was a spark no amount of alcohol or pharmaceuticals could replicate or impede.

Diana filled both glasses with beer and put the growlers in the fridge.

When the food was on the plates, I suggested we take everything to the living room. It took two trips, but we soon had a Mexican buffet set out on the coffee table. Diana plopped down in the middle of the couch, giving me the choice to sit right beside her or in the recliner beside the coffee table. I chose the recliner. Cat zero, string one.

"So, tell me more about your book," she said. "What made you decide to write about that plane crash?"

I had anticipated the question. It was the same one Byrd had asked me at El Bacaratos. But just like with Byrd, the answer was not one I was comfortable sharing. The documentary I'd seen about the plane crash affected me. Like Byrd said, those airmen had walked away from plenty of dangerous battles only to fly into the side of a mountain. The concept of something coming out of nowhere to take you down was certainly one I could relate to. But it just didn't seem fair. It made me think that experience and determination might not matter all that much. If a crew of highly trained airmen could accidentally fly into the side of a mountain, then why bother training at all? We were all bound to the same fate, so why go through the hassle of trying to prolong the inevitable? It was like the stories you heard about a fifty-year-old runner who fell dead from a heart attack in the middle of a marathon. Or the guy who'd never smoked a day in his life but was diagnosed with stage-four throat cancer. I figured life was like Perry's description of the Charleston Police Department—a living maze. Why bust your ass trying to navigate it when you could just sit still, especially if each path led to the same destination anyway?

I heard Diana clear her throat. "Are you okay? I lost you for a minute."

I wiped my mouth on a paper towel.

"Just trying to come up a with a solid answer to your question," I said.

Diana giggled and grabbed a few chips from a plate.

"When was the crash again?" she asked.

"September 1946. Friday the thirteenth, interestingly enough. No one saw it or heard it. Those men lay dead on that mountain for two days before their bodies were recovered."

"What caused it?"

"The weather was bad, and they were flying way too low. They probably never saw the mountain. Barreled into it at two hundred miles an hour."

Diana pursed her lips and let out a little puff of air.

"So show me what you've got," she said. "I want to read it."

I had been anticipating, or rather dreading, that question as well.

"As soon as I write something, you'll be the first to know," I said.

Diana lowered her eyebrows. "You haven't started writing yet? How long have you been working on it?"

"Only since I've been here, so about a month, I guess. Plus, I've been distracted. This cabin belongs to Dale, and he seems to think being a landlord involves coming up here to push my buttons almost every evening."

Diana laughed and picked at a burrito. "So what did you do before you became a writer?"

"I was with the Charleston police force for a while; then I was a private detective."

"Ooooo. A private detective. So what kinds of things did you investigate?"

I downed the last of my beer and gave Diana my most smoldering stare.

"Things that were private," I said.

I tried to wink, but I was out of practice. When my eye closed, the corner of my mouth shot up in a sneer. Diana looked down at her plate, and I could tell she was trying not to laugh.

"Is that how you got your limp? Investigating something that was private?"

"You're a pretty good detective yourself."

Diana stood up and grabbed our empty glasses. "I'll get us more beer, and then you tell me how you got that limp."

While I tried to come up with an alternate but believable story that would explain my leg injury, I heard Diana rustling around in the kitchen, the sound of drawers opening and closing and cabinet doors smacking against their frames.

"Can I help you find something?" I yelled.

"I'm looking for a bottle opener. I want to try this double IPA that's in your fridge."

The woman was definitely forward, I had to give her that.

"It's bolted to the wall next to the door."

A minute later Diana was back on the couch and two half glasses of beer were on the coffee table.

"So what happened to your leg?"

"It's really a boring story," I said. "I'd rather not talk about it."

Diana slid across the couch toward my recliner. She put her hand on my knee and looked straight into my eyes. "Tell me what happened."

Diana eyes were like perfectly cut opals flecked with spots of pink and blue. They were mesmerizing in a way. Like looking at a hypnotist's pocket watch. I started to feel a little dreamy, relaxed, calm. It was the same feeling I got when the first pill of the day hit my system.

Maybe it was her eyes, or the warmth of her touch, or maybe it was the revelation of Perry's possible betrayal—whatever the reason, I let it all out. I told Diana about Laura and Greg and the drugs and the gun and my temper and the gray Audi and the bullet that went clear through my leg. I told her Greg was in a coma and that Laura had told me to stay away. It was a complete report, minus the copious amounts of beer and pills.

When I finished, Diana's hand was still on my knee. Her other hand was over her mouth.

"Oh my god," she said through her fingers. "You're lucky to be alive."

A couple of people had said those words to me since I'd been shot. I still wasn't quite convinced.

"I don't know. When I woke up, I was in the hospital. My friend Perry was at the side of my bed. He told me someone had called 911 to report gunshots at the storage facility. By the time the Mount Pleasant police and the EMTs showed up, I had lost a lot of blood and Greg was still out cold. We were both taken to MUSC. Since Greg was Charleston PD, the Mount Pleasant police begged off to let Charleston handle it. Perry's a senior detective and was put in charge of the case. He interviewed me at the hospital, and I told him the truth."

"So what did Perry do?"

"He promised to hide the fact that I'd beaten Greg. And he told me he would get to the bottom of whatever Greg was into."

Diana stared at me like I was a lost puppy.

"He also promised to find the person who shot me," I said.

I thought of the storage unit door slowing opening and the figure silhouetted in the light. The figure raised a hand and whispered, *You're not cut out for this, Davis.*

"What are you thinking?" Diana asked.

My eyes began to well up, and I closed them quickly. I didn't want to cry in front of Diana, but I was overwhelmed. I'd always thought Perry was the one person I could count on. But had I been as wrong about him as I'd been about almost everything in my life?

I felt Diana's hand on my cheek; her finger wiped away a stray tear. In that moment I made a decision.

"I think Perry may have shot me," I said.

Diana jerked backward as if I'd punched her chest.

"What? You mean your friend?"

I nodded. "I just found out a few hours ago that he drives a gray Audi. And I think he's lying to me about the investigation."

"Oh, baby," she said. "My poor baby."

Diana put her arms around my neck and pulled me toward the couch. When I was seated next to her, she rubbed the back of my neck and stared at me with her mystical and now watery eyes. I hadn't kissed a woman in a long time, but I was certain I remembered how. I tilted my head and leaned forward. Just before our lips met, I heard the cry of sirens in the distance. It was as if an alarm had sounded. *Davis Reed is about to make out with someone way out of his league; alert the authorities.* As we kissed, the sirens echoed through the hills until they disappeared somewhere up the river. Whatever trouble they were after didn't interest me at all.

28

Five minutes later my head was spinning, my dick was hard, and Diana was nibbling my earlobe. Normally that would have been a dream situation, but my stomach was sending me an urgent message. The beer and Mexican food were locked in a furious battle. I needed a moment alone, and as much as I hated to do it, I gently pushed Diana aside and told her I'd be back in a minute.

"Take your time," she said. "I'll start cleaning up."

In the bathroom I splashed some cold water on my face and popped a pill, hoping it would negotiate a truce between the beer and the food. But as I stared at myself in the mirror, I realized my queasiness probably had nothing to do with what I'd eaten. It was anxiety. I'd told Diana too much. I'd opened up like a patient on a psychiatrist's couch. I hadn't confided in anyone in a long time. It had been ages since I'd shared my feelings rather than pushed them back with medication and alcohol.

I stared at myself in the mirror and thought about what I'd become. I was not the man I wanted to be. I didn't want to be a recluse. I didn't want to be crippled with anger. I didn't want to be constantly numb. I wanted to be a man who could wake up and feel good about himself instead of a man who didn't really care if he woke up at all. Maybe Diana could pull me out of that hole. Even if it was a hole I'd dug myself. Maybe she could lift me out of it and convince me to put down my shovel.

While I continued to stare in the mirror, I heard noise coming from the bedroom. I wondered if Diana had crawled into my bed. The woman was forward, after all. I hoped she hadn't—my stomach couldn't handle it. What kind of man hopes a gorgeous woman doesn't throw herself into his bed on the first date? An idiot who stares at himself in the mirror amazed at how big of an idiot he is.

When I opened the bathroom door, the bedroom was empty. I went through to the kitchen to find Diana standing by the counter staring at my legal pad.

"What's all this?" she asked.

I grabbed the pad and tossed it onto the table.

"Nothing," I said. "Just a distraction."

I opened the fridge and pulled out a fresh beer. My stomach didn't need it, but my head did. "I found some keys a few days ago," I said. "I've been trying to locate the owner to give them back."

Diana nodded and started packing up the leftover food. I hoped it wasn't the first phase of her exit plan. I didn't feel up to a night of unbridled passion, but I was eager for another ear-nibbling session on the couch.

"Where did you find them?" Diana asked.

"Up on the parkway, on the trail at Black Balsam. That's about as close to Cold Mountain as I can get with my leg the way it is. I saw the keys lying on the ground."

I didn't want to tell Diana that I'd actually stepped a few yards off the trail to take a leak and found the keys sitting under a bush.

"One of the keys fits a red BMW 2002," I said. "Dale and I found the car parked at Graveyard Fields. There were a couple of Long Branch stickers on the bumper. Do you know who drives that car?"

Diana shook her head.

"Well, it doesn't really matter," I said. "The keys are lost again anyway. I gave them to the sheriff's department, but they've misplaced them."

Diana continued to pack up the food, and I thought about telling her of my adventures with the keys. I wondered how much she'd seen on the legal pad. Probably not much, I thought. If she'd seen the part about me being shot at, she would surely have asked. I wanted to get Diana back to the couch but didn't think another story about me stumbling into a shooting was the way to do it.

As I was trying to come up with a new conversation starter, Diana reached for her jacket. I limped over and grabbed her hand.

"Don't go yet," I said. "I can make some coffee. It's instant, but it's really not that bad."

Diana grinned but didn't answer. She suddenly looked tired. I didn't blame her. The woman had thought she was going to share an evening with a writer and beer aficionado, and instead she'd wandered into a therapy session.

She hesitated for a moment, then slid past me and grabbed a fresh beer out of the refrigerator.

"That's the spirit," I said.

*   *   *

When Diana resumed her place on the couch, I sat down next to her. Who was I kidding? Like Dale, I was the cat, not the string.

"Let's not talk about Perry," I said. "At least not any more tonight. I'm still trying to process the whole thing."

Diana nodded but seemed distracted. It was as if a cold front had blown through the cabin. She didn't want to be on that couch, it was obvious. I wasn't boyfriend material; I was a project. A fixer-upper that was probably not worth the time or effort. She was just being kind and trying to come up with a way to let me down easy.

As I waited for the hammer to fall, I noticed a blue glow illuminating the trees just past the deck. I walked over to the sliding glass door to get a better look.

I was about to step outside when I heard someone yell my name from back in the kitchen. When I turned around, Dale stormed into the living room. His fingers were clenched tight around the grip of his service weapon, and his face looked as if someone had just told him that Carla and I were dating.

Dale glanced at Diana for a second, then focused his glare back on me.

"What's going on?" I said. "Why are you holding your—"

"Shut the fuck up," he yelled.

155

He grabbed my elbow and pulled me across the living room and into the kitchen. It then occurred to me what he might be doing.

"Is this some kind of plan to impress Daiquiri?" I said. "Act tough in front of Diana so she'll go back and tell Daiquiri what a badass you are?"

Dale shoved me up against the refrigerator and leaned in close. His mouth was full of tobacco, and I wondered how long he could go before having to spit.

"Tell me everything," Dale said. "Tell me everything, or I swear to god I'll haul your lyin' ass in right now."

I tried to push Dale off me, but it would have been easier to move the refrigerator.

"What are you talking about?"

"Cordell," Dale screamed, spraying a mist of tobacco juice over my face.

I glanced back toward the living room and wondered what Diana was thinking. When I looked back at Dale, his face was red as a bottle of hot sauce. I wondered what he was thinking as well.

"What's gotten into you?" I said, as calmly as possible.

Dale snorted. "Where'd you find those keys?"

"What? I told you. I found them on a trail. At Black Balsam."

Dale shook his head while I tried to wiggle out from between his belly and the refrigerator.

"Tell me the truth. Tell me everything you know about Cordell and them keys."

"I don't know any more than you know."

"Davis, you're about to be in a world of shit." Dale's words gurgled, like he was trying to talk to a dental hygienist while having his teeth cleaned.

"Go spit in the sink before you drown," I said.

Dale leaned in closer. His breath was baiting my nausea.

"I'm on my way to the parkway right now," Dale said. "A couple of campers found Cordell's body up at Graveyard Fields. Looks like he died a few days ago. About the same time you came across them keys."

I stared at Dale's tobacco-stained lips, trying to wrap my head around the words that had just passed through them.

"He's dead?" I said. "But why?"

"You tell me."

I don't know if it was Dale's breath, the Mexican food, or the news about Cordell, but whatever caused it, the reaction came quick and I vomited a brown mess all over Dale's chest.

"Goddamit, Davis!" Dale screamed, throwing his hands in the air and backing away as if I'd just pulled a knife on him. As he walked toward the sink, I bent over and puked again on the linoleum floor.

"For the love of fuck!" Dale yelled.

I leaned back against the refrigerator and took a few deep breaths. Across the kitchen Dale unbuttoned his uniform shirt and threw it in the sink. The white tank top he was wearing underneath was so thread-bare it was nearly transparent. The material stretched against the mass of his stomach like plastic wrap over a plate of leftover mashed potatoes. On his bicep I could see the Lynyrd Skynyrd tattoo Floppy had mentioned.

As Dale washed my puke off his shirt, he turned and glared at me. Then he glanced to my right. I followed his gaze and saw Diana standing in the doorway leading to the living room. She was surveying the kitchen like it was a crime scene.

"Is everything okay?" she said.

Dale and I glanced at each other, then back at Diana.

"Yeah, sorry." I said. "Everything's fine. I just got a little sick."

Diana stood still for a moment, then navigated around my vomit to the kitchen table.

"I should really get going," she said.

Diana pulled her jacket over her shoulders and tiptoed toward the door. She was almost there when her feet flew out from under her. The next second she was flat on her back, the soles of her boots covered in what I guessed was once a chicken quesadilla.

"Holy fuck," Dale yelled.

I reached down and helped Diana to her feet. I apologized constantly as I led her through the bedroom and into the bathroom to get cleaned up. In the bedroom I changed my shirt and wiped off my face with a dirty towel from the laundry basket, all the while knowing there would be no more ear nibbling tonight, or probably ever. When I returned to the kitchen, Dale was still standing at the sink washing out his shirt. He was seething.

"Tell me what's going on," I said.

Dale shook his head like he still wasn't sure he could trust me.

"Tell me, goddammit."

Dale wrung out his shirt and threw it back into the sink. Then he turned toward me and put his hands on his hips.

"Two campers found a body at Graveyard Fields," Dale said. "One of the campers had gone off to take a shit and stumbled over something. Said he thought it was a log at first, but when he shined his flashlight at it, he saw it was a body. When they called 911, the dispatcher sent it through to the ranger station. Terry got the call and then rode down there to take a look—he thought they might be drunk and just fucking around. When he saw the body, he called the sheriff's department to confirm it. Byrd and three other deputies are already up there. I should be up there too, but I needed to stop here and talk to you first."

"How do you know it's Cordell?" I asked.

"Because who else would have Cordell's driver's license on 'em?"

"Holy shit."

"No shit, holy shit. Terry didn't know no better than to not fuck around with the scene before Byrd got up there. When he saw the body, he looked for identification and found a wallet in the man's back pocket— a Florida license issued to Lester Cordell. Terry said it looked like he'd been shot in the back of the head. But I don't know if Terry's ever seen a dead body before, so I ain't taking his word on how the man was killed."

"But why did you need to talk to me? I don't know anything about this."

"Because it's a fuckin' mess, that's why. I'm gonna have to tell Byrd I know where Cordell lives because me and your dumb ass was there last night. I'm gonna have to tell him somebody took a few shots at you and I didn't report it."

"But you told some of the deputies we went up there. Skeeter knew about me crashing the bike into the ditch."

"I didn't tell anybody where we was. That weren't nobody's business. But now it's Byrd's business, and it's a mess I don't like being in."

I felt another wave of nausea coming on.

"It gets worse," I said. "When they find Cordell's phone, your number is going to be in there. Remember? I called his number yesterday from your phone."

Dale kicked the cabinet underneath the sink.

"Holy fucking shit, Davis. I'm neck-deep in this, and it's all on account of you."

"So what's going to happen now?"

Dale held up his dripping uniform shirt and snorted.

"Well, dickhead, I'm going up to Graveyard Fields to tell Byrd the truth. Then, after Byrd chews my ass six ways from Sunday, he's gonna come down here and talk to you. And your story better be the same as mine, 'cause if I find out you ain't been straight with me, yours will be the next body found laying out in the woods."

I sat down at the table and looked at the legal pad. My story would match Dale's because it was the truth.

"I told you there was something fishy about those keys," I said.

Dale spun around from the sink as if I'd smacked him on the back of his head. "Now you listen to me, Davis, and you listen good. Don't you go telling Byrd any of your bullshit theories about them keys, or that dead hippie, or that asshole couple."

I suddenly wanted to punch Dale in his fat, red face. "Oh, I get it. Byrd doesn't need to know that I'm the one who's thought something was off about this whole thing from the start. And that while I've been trying to figure out what's going on, you've been scratching your ass and trying to fuck anything that'll fog a mirror."

Dale leaned against the sink and crossed his arms over the top of his belly. "You know what? I don't give a shit what you tell Byrd. If you lie to him, he'll catch it. But I'm clean. I ain't done nothin' wrong. "

I heard a sound behind me and turned to see Diana standing in the bedroom doorway. I wondered how much of the conversation she'd heard.

"Are you okay?" I asked.

Diana rubbed her hip.

"I'll be fine," she said. "But I really do need to get going."

"Miss, I'm sorry you had to hear me speak so offensively," Dale said in his official voice. "The heat of the moment got to me, and I apologize."

Listening to Dale's bullshit made me feel like I might puke again.

Diana didn't respond. She simply opened the door and vanished into the darkness.

Dale left a few minutes later after trying to dry his uniform shirt with a thirty-year-old hair dryer he pulled out from the cabinet under the bathroom sink. I cleaned up the mess in the kitchen, then took a long hot shower and wondered if I would ever hear from Diana again. The angel whispered something about the importance of human connection and the value of honesty. The devils chanted *Beer. Pills. Beer. Pills.*

After the shower I changed into sweat pants and a T-shirt and wondered how long it would take before Byrd showed up to interrogate me. I also wondered if he would talk to me at the cabin or if he had enough suspicion to take me in to the station. I opened the medicine cabinet to get the last pill of the day, the one that would help me keep calm while being questioned by Byrd. But the pill bottle was gone.

That was going to be a big problem.

29

Without a pill or two to help me sleep, I tossed and turned until the first birds of the morning started chirping. I got out of bed and made some coffee, then sat down in front of the laptop. According to Facebook, I still had zero friends. Either Sarah, Dale, and Perry hadn't logged on since I'd "friended" them, or they were ignoring me. The latter was more likely than the former.

I typed the name *Diana* into the search field and then paused. I couldn't believe it. The woman had listened to me spill my guts, then watched me literally spill them. She was a woman I'd thought I could really connect with, a woman I'd hoped might save me from myself, yet I didn't know her last name.

I clicked on the email icon to see if Perry had responded to my accusation. But the only new email was from an Indian pharmaceutical company trying to sell me discount hard-on pills. Diana had helped prove I didn't need any chemical assistance in getting blood to flow to my dick. Getting it to flow to my brain was another matter entirely.

I was digging through the brewery's Facebook page, trying to find Diana's last name, when I heard a knock on the back door. I looked up and noticed Byrd and a deputy I'd not seen before staring at me through the panes of glass. I'd figured Byrd would bring at least one deputy with him, and I was glad it wasn't Skeeter. I was glad it wasn't Dale either.

During the night I'd thought about what Cordell's death might mean and who was responsible. It was a good distraction from thinking about Perry or the fool I'd made of myself in front of Diana. Of course, the hipster couple were the prime suspects; they'd lied to me about being at Graveyard Fields, and they were actively searching for the keys. But on the other hand, why would you kill someone and then go to the sheriff's department to collect their property? That would take balls the size of watermelons.

But maybe Cordell wasn't yet dead when the couple came to the sheriff's office. Maybe they confronted him later at Graveyard Fields and that's when they killed him. Then they go to his house in Maggie Valley to collect something, or hide evidence, or who knows what. And that's when I show up and announce my arrival by knocking over a few growlers. They think I'm onto them, so they start firing. And now they were probably long gone.

It was a decent theory, but it was full of holes. It didn't explain what the keys opened or why they had been sitting under a bush near the parkway. It also didn't explain the biggest question of all: why was Cordell murdered? I had thought of one possible answer to those questions, but it was too silly to consider with any seriousness.

Dale was right, I didn't need to hassle Byrd with my theories. I just needed to tell the truth and let the sheriff's department do their job.

When I opened the door, Byrd nodded. His eyes were droopier than usual and his uniform was wrinkled. I figured he'd spent the night up on the parkway.

" 'Morning, Mr. Reed. I need to ask you a few questions."

"I'm a little busy right now," I said. "Maybe we could have lunch one day this week."

Byrd's hound-dog face dropped, and he turned slightly to the deputy at his side.

"Tommy, go wait in the car. I'll call you if I need you."

Tommy frowned at me, and I gave him a quick grin. As he walked away, Byrd and I looked deep into each other's eyes. The man's face gave nothing away, and I imagined sitting across a poker table from him, trying to figure out whether he had a straight flush or a pair of twos. I could tell he was trying to read me as well. Was he looking into the eyes of a murderer or staring at a broke wannabe writer with a pill problem and an alcohol problem and an anger problem and a—

"Let me in, son," Byrd finally said.

I gave my asshole routine a rest and stepped aside to let Byrd into the kitchen. He pulled out one of the chairs from the kitchen table and issued a small sigh of relief when he sat down.

"You wouldn't happen to have a cup of coffee, would you?" Byrd asked.

Instead of answering, I walked over to the counter and grabbed the electric kettle. After I filled it with water and turned it on, I sat down at the table across from Byrd.

"It's instant," I said.

Byrd scoffed.

"With your palate for beer, I thought you would have one of those fancy Italian coffee machines," he said. "I thought a man like you would be drinking espresso, and lattes, and those flavored coffees with the whipped cream on top."

"I'm full of surprises, Sheriff."

Byrd smirked and straightened himself in his chair.

"You're welcome," I said.

"For what?" Byrd asked.

"I gave you the perfect segue. I say I'm full of surprises, and then you say, 'Well, that's actually the reason I'm here.' And then we stop talking about coffee and get down to it."

"You look very tired, son," Byrd said.

I bit my lip and tried to stay calm. Without any pills, my rubber band was already stretched tight.

"Listen," I said. "Before we get started, you've got to lay off this 'son' bullshit. You can call me Mr. Reed or Davis, or hell, you can be like Dale and call me dickhead or peckerhead, but I'm not your son, so don't call me that again. Okay?"

Byrd didn't respond, so I stood up and busied myself with the coffee. A minute later I placed two cups on the kitchen table and resumed my place across from the sheriff.

Byrd took a sip, made a face of dissatisfaction, then stared at me for a good fifteen seconds before speaking.

"You look very tired, son," he said again.

The rubber band snapped—I threw my coffee cup across the kitchen, where it shattered against the refrigerator. I stood up and stared down at the old man with the droopy face and wrinkled uniform, and for a second I thought about how just a few hours earlier an entirely different type of lawman had been standing in the same room washing vomit out of his uniform shirt.

"That's probably the best way to drink instant coffee," Byrd said. He then slung his cup toward the refrigerator, where it settled into shards next to the remains of my cup.

Shit, I thought. I was going to have to mop the kitchen for the second time in two days.

I sat back down, and Byrd watched me closely. My anger had diminished. I had to hand it to him; the old man was good. Throwing his cup was a pattern interrupt. He'd seen my anger getting out of control and had done something unexpected to shock me and stop the flow. I wished I knew how to do that to myself. Having that capability would be helpful.

"I know why you're here," I said.

"Good. So let's talk about it."

* * *

I told Byrd how I'd gone up to the parkway to try to get close to Cold Mountain.

"For inspiration," I said. "I parked at Black Balsam and walked on the trail for about a hundred yards. I stepped off to take a leak and saw the keys sitting under a bush. No one was around, so I took them to Dale's house."

Byrd sat with his arms crossed and watched me carefully.

"Dale told me to take them to the ranger station at Mount Pisgah. We went up there together the next morning."

"Why did Deputy Johnson go with you?"

"I don't know for sure, but it was probably so he could talk to this ranger named Joanne. She's . . . well, she's kinda busty."

Byrd nodded as if he understood perfectly.

I continued, telling Byrd how Joanne had recognized one of the keys and how that had led us to Graveyard Fields and to the red BMW and blue Land Rover.

"No one was around, so I opened the door to the BMW with the key Joanne had picked out. I was looking for a registration or anything that might tell me the name of the owner, but I didn't find anything other than some receipts for beer and gardening supplies."

Byrd leaned forward.

"Then what did you do with the keys?"

I told Byrd how I should have taken the keys back to the ranger station immediately, but Dale was in a hurry and I'd decided to drop them off later when I could talk to the rangers about my book.

"But the day got away from me," I said.

Byrd nodded again, and I wondered what he'd gleaned from that comment.

"Dale came over the next day and said he'd run the license plate of the BMW and that the car was registered to someone named Lester Cordell. I did an internet search but didn't find anything. That was the same day I had lunch with you."

Byrd nodded in agreement.

"The next morning I drove up to the parkway to see if the BMW was still parked at Graveyard Fields. It was, but the Land Rover was gone. Then I drove to the ranger station and saw the Land Rover in the parking lot."

I told Byrd about talking to the hipster couple and how they'd acted suspicious.

"The girl was calm and friendly," I said, "but the guy seemed anxious and uncomfortable. He told me they had just gotten up to the parkway, but I knew he was lying, since I'd seen their vehicle two days before at Graveyard Fields. After they left, I went into the ranger station and talked to Terry. He told me the couple asked if anyone had turned in a set of keys."

I went through the rest of the story. How I'd gone back up to Graveyard Fields the next morning and noticed the BMW was still there. How

Dale had asked me to bring the keys to the sheriff's department. How I'd given the keys to Barbara and how Dale's cousin Floppy came in while I was there. And about how Dale told me the keys were missing the next day.

"Dale thought Floppy had probably walked off with the keys," I said. "So I went up to his garage to look for them, which was a massive waste of time. Then I went back to the sheriff's department to talk to Barbara to see if she had any idea of what had happened to the keys. While I was there, the couple came in. They were just as suspicious then as they were when I talked to them up on the parkway. When I asked them about Cordell, they clammed up and headed for the door."

I told Byrd how Dale had gotten the name of the couple and how I didn't have much luck trying to find out about them online.

"So by this time you thought something was really amiss," Byrd said. "And you went out searching for Mr. Cordell."

"That's right. Dale gave me the Florida address Cordell's car was registered to. I dug around online and got a phone number. I called the number from Dale's phone because I don't have service up here. The woman who answered said she was Cordell's aunt and that Cordell had moved to North Carolina. She gave me his phone number and local address. I used Dale's phone to call, but it went right to voice mail."

"So you and Deputy Johnson then drove to the address Mr. Cordell's aunt had given you?"

"Yeah. We parked at a restaurant a few hundred yards from the house, and I walked up to see what I could find. The BMW wasn't out front, so I went around to the back of the house. That's when someone started shooting at me. I ran and hid in a garage. The Land Rover was parked there. It was locked, but I saw a metal detector on the back seat. I finally got away and met Dale near the restaurant. I wanted him to investigate, but he shrugged the whole thing off. He said if you go snooping around someone's house in the middle of the night, you shouldn't be surprised if they take a few shots at you."

Byrd nodded and shrugged his shoulders. "And you assumed this house was owned by Mr. Cordell?"

I paused for a moment, wondering where Byrd was going with that question. "Well, it's where his aunt said he lived. I didn't really think about whether he owned it or not."

"See, a good detective would have run a property search to find the owner's name. We have a very good online mapping system here in this county. Just click on an area of the map and it will tell you who owns the land, when they bought it, how much they paid for it. Technology amazes me sometimes."

Byrd was right. I had done a property search on the Florida address but not one on the house in Maggie Valley.

"So Cordell doesn't own that house?"

Byrd shook his head.

"So who does?"

Byrd's grin made me think about the speech he'd given me in his office. The one about how evil can manifest itself in anyone.

"I do."

Byrd unhooked his holster and placed his gun on the table.

"Now where are those keys, son?"

30

When I saw Byrd's gun, I immediately thought of Diana. I don't know why she popped into my head. Maybe it was because I thought I might die in that kitchen. Or maybe I thought my temper would explode and I'd strangle Byrd before he could get off a shot. Either way, I was probably never going to see her again.

I looked at Byrd's gun, then raised my eyes and stared directly at the old man's face. The quintessential bad southern sheriff, I thought. I should've seen it coming. The way he'd distrusted me from the beginning. The way he'd warned me to not go around asking questions.

Byrd was still unreadable. His face gave nothing away. He looked at me like a mannequin staring out through a store window.

"Do you want some more coffee?" I asked.

"I don't much care for your coffee," Byrd said. "No offense."

"None taken, but honestly, the gun is offensive enough. Mind if I make a cup?"

Byrd shrugged and tilted his head toward the kettle. He watched me closely as I got up and stepped over to the counter. With my back to Byrd, I filled the kettle and put a scoop of instant coffee into a fresh mug. The water boiled quickly, and after I filled the mug, I turned around. Byrd was now holding the gun in his hand, pointed at my chest.

"If you're thinking of throwing that coffee in my face, don't."

The thought had actually occurred to me. Someone pointing a gun at your chest makes your mind go in interesting directions.

I resumed my place at the table while Byrd kept the gun pointed in the general direction of my heart. I wondered where my anger was. The fight-or-flight response should have kicked in by now, but I was calm. It was a strange feeling. It was different from feeling numb, and I kind of liked it.

"I was never a good detective," I said. "But I knew there was a mystery surrounding those keys. I guess I had what you'd call a gut feeling."

Byrd shifted in his chair. I could tell the gun was getting heavy in his hand.

"And what is your gut telling you now?" he asked.

During the night I'd thought about the dots I'd collected: the BMW, the locked trunk, the receipt for garden tools, the metal detector in the back of the Land Rover. Knowing now that Byrd owned the house where Cordell was living was another dot that seemed to connect perfectly. Suddenly my silly theory didn't seem so silly anymore.

"It's telling me somewhere, somehow, those keys unlock a bunch of gold," I said. "The same gold that dropped out of the sky onto Cold Mountain seventy years ago."

Byrd propped his arm on the table—the gun was definitely getting heavy. I thought about what kind of damage that gun could do at this close range. *Plenty* and *enough* were the only two answers I could come up with.

"I think Cordell and that hipster couple found some of that gold," I said. "Maybe on purpose but most likely by accident. Dale said you know everything that goes on in this county, that you have your finger in everyone's pies. And if you own that house in Maggie Valley, you must have rented it to Cordell. You'd certainly know what he was up to. You knew he was taking that gold off the mountain and storing it somewhere. Probably storing it in the house he was renting, the house you own. You were going to wait until he'd found all he could find, and then you'd help yourself to it. But something happened between Cordell and that couple. I'd guess there was a fight and Cordell's keys came off during the struggle. One of those keys, or maybe several of them, lead to the gold. Without the keys, the hipster couple was stuck. And now so are you."

Byrd looked at me like I was speaking gibberish.

"You've been suspicious of me from the beginning because you thought I was here searching for the gold," I said. "I'd been researching Cold Mountain for a book, and you figured I'd come up here from Charleston because I believed there was 'gold in them thar hills.' It was dumb luck that the waitress at El Bacaratos mentioned it when we had lunch together. But you were quick to put me off the idea. You know, there's a man who swears you stole that gold from his grandfather years ago. You didn't steal it then, but you're trying to steal it now."

Byrd put his gun back in his holster.

"You're right about one thing," he said. "You're not a very good detective."

Byrd's two-way radio suddenly crackled to life.

"Sheriff, it's Skeeter. Come back."

I bristled at the sound of my archenemy's voice.

Byrd pulled his radio off his belt and put it in front of his droopy face. "This is Byrd. Go ahead."

"Sheriff, I'm at Mr. Cordell's residence. You need to get up here. We've got two more bodies."

Byrd's face finally cracked. He was shocked, and it showed.

I was surprised too. If those two bodies belonged to Jeff and Becky Ingram, the couple who'd been trying to get the keys, and Byrd didn't know they were dead, then someone else was involved in this mess. Byrd was probably thinking that someone was me.

It didn't take Byrd long to regain his composure.

"I'm on my way," he said into the radio.

"Are you going to tell me not to leave town?" I said. "Am I a person of interest?"

Byrd ignored me and spoke into his radio. "Tommy, I need your assistance. We're going to take Mr. Reed in for questioning."

31

Deputy Tommy was a big guy, roughly the size of Dale but all muscle. He put the handcuffs on a little too tight and pushed me a little too hard into the back of the patrol car. Then he drove a little too fast down the winding gravel driveway. He hadn't bothered to put my seat belt on me, and with my hands cuffed behind my back, I bounced around the back seat of the patrol car like a tennis shoe in a dryer. Tommy was turning out to be a prick, but at least he was a consistent prick.

When we reached the bottom of the driveway, the deputy made a quick turn onto 276, and I fell completely over onto the back seat. Lying down was actually more comfortable than sitting upright with the handcuffs gouging into my spine, but two thoughts forced me to push myself up. One, the many asses that had been on that seat, and two, the old law enforcement adage that a guilty man relaxes once he's been caught. Arrest an innocent man and he'll pace for hours in his cell. Put a guilty man in that cell and he'll lie down and sleep like a baby, relieved the chase is finally over. I sat up and acted nervous. Sitting up was hard; acting nervous wasn't.

* * *

Twenty minutes later we pulled into the back of the Haywood County Sheriff's Department. I hadn't seen this side of the building before. Tommy parked near a set of double doors and next to the same black GMC Yukon that had been parked out in front of El Bacaratos the day I met Byrd for lunch. Tommy pulled me out of the patrol car with the same enthusiasm he'd shown while pushing me into it.

171

"Don't bother with the formalities," Byrd said to Tommy. "Put him in the interview room, and I'll deal with him when I get back."

Byrd walked over to his SUV while Tommy jerked me by the arm through the double doors. We walked down a short hallway to another set of double doors next to a keypad attached to the wall. Tommy pressed a few numbers on the pad, and the doors slowly opened inward.

"How many murders do you have in this county each year?" I asked Tommy as we walked down another hallway and past several closed doors that I assumed were offices and conference rooms.

Tommy didn't answer.

"Seriously," I said. "What is it? Like one or two at most?"

Tommy remained silent. When we reached the end of the hallway, he opened a door and yanked me into the squad room where I'd sat at Dale's desk a couple of days earlier. The room was empty. I figured all the deputies and detectives were at either Graveyard Fields or Cordell's house in Maggie Valley. I didn't need Tommy's verification; I knew three murders in this county was big news.

"If you wanted to rob a bank in Haywood County, today would be the day to do it," I said.

Again Tommy had no response. He was doing a good job of ignoring me. Which was fine. He was jerking me around like a rag doll, but at least he wasn't Skeeter.

We went through to a door on the far side of the squad room that opened into a small interview room. When we were inside, Tommy shoved me into a metal chair that sat next to a small table. I leaned forward so Tommy could unlock my cuffs, but he left the room and closed the door without showing me that consideration.

I sat in the interview room for about an hour, thinking about how long it had been since I'd had a pill and wondering if I'd misplaced the pill bottle, which was unlikely, or if Diana or Dale had taken it. That didn't seem likely either. Then I wondered about Xanax withdrawal. For several years I'd taken at least six pills a day, chasing them with large quantities of alcohol. There had to be some kind of comedown after that type of long-term abuse. I hoped I'd be back on the cabin deck before I found out. I had some beer in the fridge, but I'd still have to find some pills. I needed to call Dr. Landry.

After a while I started thinking about Perry. Sitting in a law enforcement interview room made it hard not to. I wondered how I would interview him if he were sitting across from me. What could I possibly ask him other than *Was it you?*

I thought about the gray Audi and how much a car like that cost. Could Perry afford something like that on his detective's salary? What about his golf club membership? I had no idea what one of those cost. And what about the fishing boat he had complained about?

If Perry was living beyond his means, it meant he either was deep in debt or had other means at his disposal. Maybe the kind of means that came from a small-time drug business. And why had he not responded to my email? Any other time I'd emailed him with a question, his response had come within a few hours.

I was considering these thoughts when the door to the interview room opened. I wasn't surprised to see Tommy enter the room, but I was shocked when Diana followed him and took a seat across the table from me.

"The sheriff will be in soon," Tommy said, as he reached behind me to unlock my cuffs.

"I thought you were mute," I said. "Guess it just takes you a while to warm up."

With the cuffs off, I rubbed my wrists to try to get some feeling back in my hands. Tommy walked out without saying another word and closed the door behind him. I looked over at Diana. I wasn't sure why she was there. If I was under suspicion, I wouldn't, and shouldn't, be allowed to speak to anyone other than law enforcement officials or maybe my attorney, which I didn't have, at least not yet. The attorney line seemed like a good opener.

"Are you my representation?" I said.

"No," Diana said. "But I am your savior."

"That might be a full-time job."

"A detective came by the brewery this morning looking for information on someone named Lester Cordell," Diana said. "I told him I didn't know the man and then used a bit of charm to get him to tell me what he knew. He told me Lester was dead and that a young couple had been found murdered in the house Lester was renting in Maggie Valley. He also told me a suspect was in custody. He wouldn't give me a name but he said it was a funny coincidence because the suspect was renting a cabin in Cruso that was owned by a deputy."

"That could have been anyone," I said.

Diana scoffed. "I called the sheriff directly. I told him that he couldn't hold you without charging you and that I was coming to pick you up."

There was no question about it, the woman was forward. I liked it.

"That explains how you are here but not why you are here."

"I'm here because I know you didn't have anything to do with this. And if what I've heard about the sheriff is true, then he'll keep you here indefinitely, or at least until he finds someone else to try to pin this on."

"That method is not unique to Byrd. Shake down the most likely suspect, then move on if that one doesn't pan out."

"But you're not the most likely suspect. I saw your notes, remember. You were trying to find that man to give him back his keys. Then the keys vanished, and that couple—I guess they're the same couple that was killed—were very interested in getting their hands on those keys. You're a detective, and you were trying to figure out why. You're the least likely person to have murdered them."

It seemed Diana had looked at my legal pad longer than I'd thought.

She put her hands on the table, palms up. When I didn't move, she beckoned me forward with her fingers.

"Give me your hands," she said.

I put my hands into hers, and she moved her thumbs over the tops of my knuckles.

"I trust you, Davis," she said. "What you told me last night, the way you opened yourself up to me, that showed me what kind of man you are. If anyone is going to find out the truth, it's going to be you, and you can't do that sitting in here."

I looked away for a few moments and tried to gather my thoughts. Even though I was exhausted, it was exhilarating talking to Diana. She was confident, she took charge, and I really wanted her to nibble my ear-lobe again. And despite her slipping in my puke, she seemed to like me. For what reason, I had no idea. It certainly wasn't because of my winning personality or my bank account. Maybe she did want a fixer-upper. If so, I hoped she was up for the challenge.

"Where is he?" Diana asked, looking at her watch.

Before I could answer, the door opened and Sheriff Byrd walked in. If he was perturbed by Diana's interference, he didn't show it.

"Mr. Reed, you're free to go," he said. "But I'd like to formally inter-view you at some other time."

"So was the interview this morning informal?" I asked. "Because the gun made it seem pretty formal."

Byrd smirked.

"Ms. Ross, thank you for coming down to pick up Mr. Reed," he said. "As you can imagine, we are pretty busy at present, and I just don't have the manpower right now to drive him back up to Cruso."

Diana nodded and slid her chair back from the table.

"Hold on a second," I said. "Your last name is Ross? You're Diana Ross?"

Diana ignored the question and followed Byrd to the doorway.

"Let's go, Davis," she said.

Byrd opened the door and stood aside. As we passed by him, I stopped and whispered in his ear, "She's my savior."

As usual, Byrd's expression showed nothing.

32

Five minutes later we were in Diana's vintage Mercedes driving through Waynesville. My eyes were closed and Diana's hand was resting gently on my knee. Even though I was completely drained, I was happy. I liked the feeling. And for it to continue, I was going to have to change. But with baby steps.

"I need to make a call," I said. "And I need to make a quick stop while we're still in town."

"Sure," Diana said. "Is everything okay?"

I thought about making up some story about blood pressure medication but decided to keep the promise I'd made to myself the previous night. If I was going to raise my standards and be honest with Diana, then I needed to go all in.

"I have a prescription I need refilled," I said. "I take medication for anxiety, and I take way too much of it. I want to stop, but I don't think it's a good idea to go cold turkey."

Diana gave me a curious glance. She looked like she was about to say something but stopped short. I instantly regretted telling her about the pills. I'd already dumped a bunch of my baggage on her and thought maybe my need for anxiety medication was the final straw. But after a moment she squeezed my knee and said, "Of course, baby. Whatever you need."

I pulled out my phone and scrolled through the contacts until I found the listing for Dr. Landry. Ted Landry, MD, was what is commonly referred to as a pill mill. He wrote prescriptions that other, more morally focused doctors wouldn't. His office was a storefront tucked between a thrift store and a takeout pizza joint in North Charleston. He didn't take insurance and didn't ask any questions. All you needed to score Viagra, Valium, Percocet, Xanax, and a host of other pharmaceuticals was cash and a face. I dialed the number, and he picked up on the first ring. He was probably the only doctor in the country who answered his own phone. But seeing as how he was the only person who worked in his office, I figured he had no choice.

"Lowcountry Health and Wellness Clinic," Landry said by way of answering.

"Hey, Doc, it's Davis Reed."

"Davis, how is your anxiety? Is there something I can help you with?"

This was a little dance, just in case someone was listening in. Landry knew exactly what he could help me with.

"It's manageable. But I need a refill on my prescription. I know I'm a little early for a refill, but I'm renting a place for a few months in the mountains of western North Carolina and I've misplaced my medicine. Can you call it in to a pharmacy up here?"

"Of course, but I'll need you to come in for an office visit as soon as you get back."

Office visit was code for "I need you to come pay me cash." I doubted Landry made a habit of calling in prescriptions, but I was a longtime customer, and I'd supplied him with some photographs of his now-ex-wife jerking off his now–ex–business partner in the parking lot of a seafood restaurant at Patriot's Point. So I was deserving of special consideration.

"Not a problem," I said. "Hold on and I'll get the name of the pharmacy for you."

Diana told me there was a Walgreens nearby, and I gave Dr. Landry the information. A few minutes later we were in the pharmacy's parking lot.

I wandered around the Walgreens for twenty minutes while waiting for the prescription to be filled. I looked at a few magazines and then strolled down the personal-care aisle. I studied the condom selection and wondered if I was giving in to wishful thinking. I hadn't gotten laid since Sarah kicked me out—actually more like three months before she kicked me out. The scary thing was that not getting any hadn't really bothered me. I was content being numb. But Diana had hit a nerve. A few of them, actually. I grabbed a three-pack of Trojans just in case those nerves kept tingling. I then walked over to the food section and picked out a six-pack of Lagunitas IPA.

When my name was called over the PA system, I went to the pharmacy counter and asked if I could pay for everything there. The woman in the white coat who rang up my purchases must have wondered about my intentions. Ninety Xanax, a six-pack of beer, and a three-pack of condoms. To really blow her mind, I should have also thrown down a roll of duct tape, a bag of lollipops, and a bottle of personal lubricant.

When I got back in Diana's car, I apologized for taking so long. She glanced at the beer and smiled. I'd put the condoms in my jacket pocket. I didn't want her to see those.

As we drove through Waynesville, I thought about what to do next. It wasn't easy. I was exhausted from lack of sleep, and anxiety was pulsing through my veins like a low-level electrical charge. My plan was to wait as long as possible before taking a pill in hopes the tension would eventually subside. If I could wait it out, maybe I actually could go cold turkey. With Diana by my side, I figured anything was possible. Like my new commitment to being open and honest, giving up the pills would be another step in my path to recovery. I would trade being numb for being real, being angry for being peaceful. I would write a book, enjoy a healthy romantic relationship, and maybe even drink less than ten beers each day. Although dating a brewery owner was going to make that last one tough.

"So what's your plan, baby?" Diana said, putting her hand back on my knee and snapping me out of my fantasy world.

I straightened up in my seat and tried to clear the spider webs from my brain. Back in the interview room Diana had said that I was the one with the best chance of finding out the truth about the murders. But if she thought I was a master detective, she was in for an unpleasant surprise. I had connected a few dots to put the missing keys together with the lost gold, but as far as plans went, the only thing I could think to do was what I'd done back in my private-detective days.

"I'll guess we'll just have to wait," I said.

Diana didn't seem to care for that answer. She took her hand from my knee and planted it firmly on the steering wheel.

"Look," I said. "If I start poking around, Byrd will throw a hook into me that even you might not be able to pull out."

I didn't want to tell Diana my theory about the murders and what I thought the keys led to. I didn't feel I was being dishonest with her. It was just that the idea of Byrd being involved in a murderous plot to steal a bunch of gold was too embarrassing to say out loud. Plus, I had no idea who had killed Jeff and Becky. Unless it was Byrd, and his being surprised when he heard the news was just an act for my benefit. But that was hard to wrap my head around. I could see Byrd trying to screw some hipsters out of a pile of gold, but I couldn't see him murdering anyone. It was just too crazy a scenario, but then again, so was the idea of being shot in the leg by a guy you'd thought was your good friend.

Diana shook her head.

"We need to find the keys," she said. "That's the most logical next step."

I knew Diana was trying to protect me. She obviously thought Byrd considered me a suspect and that if I didn't solve the murders, I might end up going down for them. She was taking her role as savior seriously.

"If Byrd thought I was responsible for those murders, he would have never let me walk out of that interview room," I said. "Plus, I bet you two growlers of Dark Secret those keys will turn up by the end of the day."

Diana grabbed my inner thigh and gave it a squeeze. All the blood in my brain suddenly headed south.

"Really," she said. "Who has them?"

I imagined Dale and a few other deputies in gas masks tossing Floppy's trailer.

"I'm not one hundred percent sure. But I think Dale will have his hands on them soon, if not already."

"What will Dale do with them?"

"I guess they'll be placed in evidence, since they belong to a guy who was murdered. But in this town, you never know."

We passed the sign welcoming us to Cruso, and I wondered for the hundredth time about the identity of the old crab. Byrd, Junebug, and Dale all seemed eligible for the title.

A few minutes later we turned onto the gravel road that led up to the cabin. Diana put the vintage Mercedes into low gear and inched up the driveway at a snail's pace. When we finally pulled into the clearing below the cabin, I noticed a brown Volkswagen Rabbit parked next to my SUV. I'd never seen the vehicle before. It was muddy and dented, and the back bumper had been replaced with a long metal cylinder capped at both ends. I figured it belonged to Dale. It looked like something he might drive.

When I got out of Diana's car, she stepped out as well. I wanted nothing more than to crawl into bed next to her. Not for sex; that could wait. I just wanted to fall asleep in her arms. After a few hours I would wake up and she would start nibbling my ear; then we could move on to other activities.

I walked around the car and stood next to Diana. She threw her arms around me and gave me a soft kiss on the cheek.

"It's so peaceful up here," she whispered. "It's like another world."

Diana was right. Cruso and the cabin were a different world, and with her in my arms, it was a world I could begin to envision myself living in permanently. I hadn't come to Cruso looking for anything more than solitude, but solitude had never served me well. What I needed was connection. And trust. And intimacy. I was finally open to all those possibilities.

Diana swiveled next to me and pulled out her phone. She tapped the screen a couple of times, then put her arm over my shoulder and pulled me close until our cheeks were touching.

"Smile," she said as she held up the phone in front of our faces. A moment later she squeezed the phone, and I heard a soft click.

"Our first selfie," she said.

I turned to face her and could feel my eyes welling up again. I'd not had a drink or a pill in more hours than I could count, and I was okay. My savior was already a miracle worker.

"Hey, y'all!"

Diana and I both looked up at the same time. Floppy was standing on the deck, the deck that could be accessed only through the living room. He was wearing brown camouflage pants and a green camouflage jacket. He looked like an anorexic tree.

"What are you doing here?" I yelled. "And how did you get in my house?"

Floppy reached into one of his jacket pockets and pulled out a large set of keys. The keys I wished I'd never found.

"I let myself in," he said.

33

"**W**here did you get those keys?"

We were sitting around the table in the cabin's kitchen. Floppy had taken off his camo jacket to reveal a camo T-shirt. Seemed he was dedicated to the theme.

"I am not at liberty to discuss that," he said.

Boom. There it was. The anger I'd not felt since Byrd called me *son* that morning was now back in all its glory.

"I'm not fucking around," I screamed. "Where did you get those keys?"

Floppy looked at Diana as if my language had offended him.

"I'm not fucking around either," Diana said. "Where'd you get them?"

Floppy pushed back from the table and stood up.

"Now, I don't take kindly to being talked to like this," he said. "I just stopped by to see if you wanted to talk about your book. I know everything there is to know about Cold Mountain and that plane crash. But if you don't want my help, then I'll be on my way."

When Floppy moved toward the door, I jumped up and grabbed his T-shirt with both hands. I shoved him back against the kitchen counter. He was light as a feather, and I thought it wouldn't take much to pick him up and toss him off the deck.

"You're not leaving here until you tell me about those keys."

"I'm going to report you for battery," Floppy said. "I'm gonna call 911 and have you arrested for harming my person. I hope you have good insurance, because I think you gave me whiplash."

He rubbed his neck like he was giving testimony in a hit-and-run.

"You broke into my house," I said. "And I have the right to beat the living shit out of you if I feel threatened. And you not answering my question makes me feel threatened."

Diana walked over to us and put her hand behind Floppy's head. When she began to rub his neck, his eyes rolled back.

"Come sit down," she said. "Don't worry about Davis; he's just had a hard day."

"Well, he'd better watch it," Floppy said. " 'Cause I know tae kwon do, jujitsu, judo, and tai chi."

Diana led Floppy back to his chair. When he was seated, he pointed a grease-stained finger at me. "And I wrestled in high school."

"Is that any better?" Diana asked.

"A little bit," Floppy said. "Not so much pressure. You know, I used to go with this massage therapist for a while, and she'd cover me in oil and rub me down like I was a side of beef. I'd say, 'Damn, Tanya, careful with the merchandise, I ain't no tenderloin.' But she'd just rub and rub till I felt like a wet noodle."

Diana sat down and gave Floppy a taste of her dimples.

"What's your name?" she asked.

"Floppy. Floppy Johnson. I live up at Sunburst. Got me a garage. I work on all types of vehicles, domestic and otherwise."

"That's good to know," Diana said. "I've got an '84 Mercedes that seems to always have something wrong with it."

"Yeah, I can work on them German cars. Mercedes, Audis, Volkswagens."

"Ever work on a BMW 2002?" I asked.

Floppy looked at me like I was a fortune teller.

"I sure have," he said. "Did a full service on a red one for a man just a couple months ago. Now, you don't see many of them 2002s these days. We got our fair share of 325s and such around here, but an old 2002 is pretty rare. Now, most people don't think I can work on a 325, but I got one of them machines that you plug into the computer in the car and it'll tell you everything that's going on. But I don't care for them cars with computers, because them computers are tracking you everywhere you go. People can hack into them and find out where you've been. It's all connected back to the government."

I took one of my growlers out of the refrigerator and poured a glass. Baby steps.

"Hey, can I have one of those?" Floppy asked.

"No," I said.

"C'mon, buddy, I'm not going to use my martial arts skills on you. I mean, I would if you tried to hurt me, but she said you was just having a bad day, so I guess I forgive you for getting up on me like you did."

I responded by taking a sip of beer.

"Ah, man, I gave you a bunch of my beers at the garage."

Floppy looked at Diana. "He needs to be more hospitable," he said.

"Baby, give him a beer," Diana said.

I grabbed a Lagunitas from the fridge. I hated to waste it on a guy who drank Coors Light, but I wasn't about to give him any of the beer I'd brewed. I popped the top and handed it to Floppy.

"Tell me about the guy with the BMW," I said.

Floppy looked closely at the bottle's label, then took a long draw.

"This tastes like pinecones," he said. "Ain't ya got no other beer?"

"Tell me about the guy with the BMW," I said again.

Floppy rubbed his chin for a minute as if he were mulling over the meaning of life. It was the longest stretch of silence I'd ever experienced in his presence.

"He came by the garage asking if I could do an oil change, and I said I could but that he'd be better off getting a full service because that would save him some money in the long run. He asked how long it'd take, and I said oh, about an hour and a half, and he said okay. Now, most people have somebody come pick 'em up when they have a service done, seeing how it takes so long, but he said he'd just wait around. That car was beat up real bad, had a big dent in the door. I told him I could try to get that out, but he wasn't interested in that. So I changed the oil and such, checked all the fluids and the brake pads. I'm real thorough when I do a service."

"And that's it?" I asked. It was a stupid question, because with Floppy I'd quickly learned that there was never a *that's it*.

"Well, the weird thing was, when I was all finished, I couldn't find the man. He weren't in the garage, and I didn't see him out in the lot. Finally found him back behind my trailer. Now, I don't like people messing around near my trailer, but he said he was just looking at my collection of stuff. I got a lot of interesting stuff back there, old furniture and appliances and whatnot. So I wasn't too mad finding him back there. He paid me in cash, 'cause I don't take credit cards. Now, I don't have a credit card myself, 'cause did you know, when you use a credit card, all your information goes into a big computer, and—"

"Stop!" I yelled.

Floppy shivered and took another sip of beer.

"Did you ever see that guy again?" I asked.

"Oh yeah. He came by another time. Brought me a jug of beer. It was called Black Magic or something, tasted like this stuff. I didn't much care for it, but I drank it anyways 'cause I don't like to waste nothing. I use the jug to spit sunflower seed hulls in. Did you know sunflower seeds is real good for you? It's true, they can lower your cholesterol. Now, I ain't never had high cholesterol. Could be on account I eat so many sunflower seeds."

"When was this?" I asked.

"Back about a week or so, I guess. He asked if I could replace the lock on his trunk. I didn't have nothing that matched, but I took one of the door locks off an old Explorer that was sitting out front and made it work. See, I'm real handy with stuff like that; I can take just about anything off one vehicle and make it work on another."

I picked up the key ring and found a key with the word FORD embossed on the top. I hadn't tried to open the BMW's trunk with that key the morning Dale and I first found the car, because why would anyone think a Ford key would open a BMW trunk? Of course, that was before I met Floppy.

"That man lived in Maggie Valley," I said. "Your shop is, what, a good half hour from there? Seems like a long way to drive for an oil change."

"Now, I take that as an insult," Floppy said. "I'm real good at what I do, and he probably heard about my reputation and such. Hey, did you know Maggie Valley was named after a real person? It's true. Most people don't know that; they think it's just a made-up name. But Maggie was a real-life woman. Her daddy set up the first post office in that town, and then . . . hey, wait a minute, you said *lived*. You said that man *lived* in Maggie Valley. Did something happen to him?"

I dropped the keys onto the table.

"Yeah," I said. "His name is Lester Cordell. And someone killed him."

Floppy jumped up. "Well, I be danged! I heard on my scanner they'd found a body up on the parkway. Was that him?"

I nodded.

"And I heard they found two more over at Maggie Valley. Was that at his place?"

I nodded again.

"Well, I be danged," he said.

* * *

It took twenty minutes and another neck massage from Diana to get to the truth. Floppy had taken the keys from the sheriff's department, just as Dale suspected. He'd lifted them from Barbara's desk when she was in the restroom and put them in his jacket pocket and then forgotten about them. He'd really come up to the cabin to talk to me about my book, and when he found the door was locked, he'd remembered the keys and started cycling through them to see if one would fit the lock. One did, and he'd come inside and then gone through to the deck to wait for me.

I believed Floppy's story that he had come over just to talk to me. Since I'd been patient with him at his garage, he'd probably figured I would let him ramble on all afternoon. The poor guy was just looking for an ear to bend.

"It's my cousin Dale's house anyway," Floppy said. "I didn't break into your house; I entered my cousin's house. Ain't nothing wrong with that."

I pointed across the kitchen to the door where Floppy's camouflage coat was hanging from the knob.

"Can you think of any reason why one of those keys would fit that door?"

"I don't know," Floppy said. "I was pretty surprised when one of them did. But then I thought maybe them keys belonged to you, since I saw you at the sheriff's department that day."

"How long has Dale owned this house?" I asked.

Floppy wiggled in his chair.

"Well, technically, Dale doesn't own it," he said. "His daddy does. I think Junebug bought it off Sheriff Byrd about the time Dale got married. Why somebody'd marry that fat moron, I don't know. I ain't never been married, but I've come close a time or two. They was this one girl—"

"So Sheriff Byrd used to own this house?" I asked.

"Yep, he sure did. He used to rent it out to tourists and such, but then Junebug bought it off him, and Dale and Carla moved in. Have you ever seen Carla? She's pretty as all get-out. Way too pretty for Dale. Looks like that girl that played in that movie—what was it called? The one about the woman lawyer that wore pink all the time. Now, I don't go to movies much, since the theater in Waynesville closed down a few years ago. People say you can watch all kind of movies on your computer these days, but . . ."

While Floppy rambled, I grabbed Diana's arm and tilted my head toward the living room. When we were standing by the sliding glass door, I asked to borrow her phone.

"Who are you going to call?" she asked.

"I need to talk to Dale. While I call you go back and sit with Floppy. Make sure he doesn't steal anything from the kitchen."

Diana squinted. "What are you going to tell Dale?"

"I'm going to tell him to come get the keys. The last thing I need is for Byrd to find me and those keys in the same location. And I want to know if he has any idea why one of the keys on that ring opens this cabin."

Diana put her arms around my neck and stared into my eyes for a long moment. I was embarrassed for losing my temper in front of her, but Floppy had a way of pushing my buttons. Plus, I hadn't taken a pill in hours. It was a miracle I hadn't totally lost it and cracked Floppy's skull.

Diana must have read my mind. She kissed me on the cheek, then moved her mouth close to my ear.

"It's going to be okay," she whispered.

Diana unlocked her phone and handed it to me. As she strolled back toward the kitchen, she turned and gave me a wink. I winked back, and this time it came naturally.

Diana's phone was identical to mine, a mini computer with more processing power than the control modules that helped land a man on the moon. I tapped the phone icon and entered Dale's number. After six rings I was connected to his voice mail. I redialed and got the same result. I figured either Dale was busy or he didn't answer calls from numbers he didn't recognize. I pulled up the messages app, reentered his number, and typed *It's Davis. Call me at this number ASAP!* I hoped that would get his attention.

While I waited for Dale to call, I stared at the phone display and pondered a thought. The angel whispered something about respecting a person's privacy and establishing trust, but the devils screamed, *Do it! Do it!* I glanced toward the kitchen, then back at the phone. I hesitated for a moment, then began scrolling through Diana's messages. Not the coolest move to make, but I wanted to know more about the woman I'd fallen for. She certainly knew more than enough about me.

The most recent message, dated that afternoon, was from someone named Louis. The message read *Thinking about you.* Diana had not responded. I felt a ping of jealousy and made a mental note to somehow work the name Louis into conversation with Diana to see if it elicited a reaction.

The next message was from Daiquiri, asking Diana to call the brewery about the upcoming payroll. There were a few back-and-forth exchanges between Diana and Daiquiri, but all seemed brewery related.

I scrolled past a few other messages until I noticed that Diana had sent one to someone listed only as L.C. The message said *Where are you?* There was no response.

Someone—it might even have been Perry—had once told me, "Coincidences mean you're headed in the right direction." I hadn't understood

what that meant at the time, and I wasn't sure I understood it now. But Diana texting *Where are you?* to someone with the same initials as the man I'd spent the past few days looking for pointed me in a direction I didn't like.

I thought about the photo I'd seen on the Long Branch Facebook page, the one with Diana standing next to a guy whose back was to the camera and with what might have been a set of keys dangling from his waist. At the time I hadn't thought much of it; I'd noticed several guys with belt-clip key chains when Dale and I visited Long Branch for dinner. But now wasn't then.

I took a few steps toward the door leading to the kitchen and heard Floppy say, "Now, I don't use deodorant myself, 'cause it's full of aluminum, and aluminum can mess with your genes and make you grow tumors under your arms the size of softballs, and that's just . . ."

Deciding it was safe, I walked back to the sliding glass door and tapped the icon for Diana's photos. I scrolled through the images, hoping not to see a picture of Cordell or a red BMW or anything that might plunge a knife through my heart.

The longer I scrolled, the more foolish I felt. The photos were a scrapbook of Diana's life, but not one of them suggested she had anything to do with Cordell or keys or buried treasure.

I tapped the back arrow to get to the main menu of the photo's app. From there I scrolled to the bottom of the screen and selected RECENTLY DELETED. There was only one photo displayed, and it sucked the air out of my lungs.

The photo showed Diana sitting on the hood of a red BMW 2002. Sitting next to her was a man in a trucker hat pulled down over a nest of curly black hair. It could've been the same guy sitting next to her in the Facebook photo, but it was definitely the guy in the mug shot Dale had shown me. Lester Cordell. On the other side of Diana, Jeff leaned against the hood and flashed a sideways peace sign. I figured Becky had probably taken the photo. It was obviously taken at the house Cordell was renting from Byrd. In the background I could make out the restaurant where Dale and I had parked the night someone used me for target practice.

I stared at the photo and realized that the woman I had bared my soul to, the woman I'd thought was going to be my savior, was completely full of shit. I should have known. I'd let the honeymoon phase blind my judgment, or at least what there was of it. I'd whitewashed the red flags. The biggest one being that a gorgeous, smart, successful woman had fallen for me.

I was still staring at the photo when the phone suddenly vibrated in my palm.

"Whose fucking phone is this?" Dale said when I answered.

"It's Diana's."

"Damn, Davis. You already hittin' that piece of plywood?"

"I'm an idiot."

"Yeah, tell me something I don't know."

"Listen, I need you to come to the cabin right now."

Dale laughed. "Brother, do you know how busy I am? Byrd's flippin' his shit. Every deputy in this county is working overtime."

"I mean it, Dale. Get up here right now. I have something for you."

Dale huffed. "Unless you've got them keys and the person who killed them three hippies, I ain't got no time for your shit."

I looked through the sliding glass door at Cold Mountain. Its peak was shrouded in a dark cloud.

"I've definitely got one, and I might have the other."

There was a long pause.

"Twenty minutes," Dale finally said. "And if I get up there and you're bullshitting me, you best be ready for a beating."

34

When I walked back into the kitchen, Floppy was rambling about alien autopsies at Area 51 and Diana was tapping her fingers on the table like she was waiting on test results.

"Floppy, shut up," I said, handing Diana's phone back to her.

Diana stood up and put the phone in her pocket.

"Baby, I should really get back to the brewery."

I stared down at the linoleum floor and shook my head.

"Just hold tight, okay? Twenty minutes."

There was a long moment of silence, which, with Floppy present, was a near miracle.

Finally Diana spoke. "Okay, sure," she said. "But I need to use the restroom."

I sat down across from Floppy and jerked my head toward the bedroom door. I couldn't look at Diana. I didn't want to see her face. I didn't even want to feel her presence.

I could sense the anger beginning to vibrate inside me. The rubber band was getting taut. I was going to confront Diana; there was no question about that. But I was going to wait until Dale was present. I needed a witness and someone who would keep me calm.

Diana came around behind me. She put both of her hands on my shoulders and leaned down and kissed my cheek.

"I'll be right back, baby," she whispered.

When Diana disappeared through the bedroom door, I stood up and grabbed the Walgreens bag off the counter. I popped three pills with my last swig of beer and put several more in the coin pocket of my jeans.

"What did you just take?" Floppy asked.

I grabbed a fresh beer out of the fridge and sat down.

"What else can you tell me about Cordell?" I said.

"I hope it wasn't OxyContin, because that stuff's poison," Floppy said. "You know, I had a buddy got hooked on OxyContin, and he ended up shooting himself in his living room with his own shotgun. Pulled the trigger with his big toe is what they said. Splattered his face all over one of them big flat-screen TVs. They confiscated that TV, said it was evidence, but I don't see how something like that could be evidence. I think one of them boys down at the sheriff's department just wanted themselves a new TV."

I thought for a second about the giant TV perched atop the whiskey barrel in Junebug's living room.

"I don't have a TV myself; ain't nothing worth watching these days nohow. Now, when I was a kid, I liked that *Hogan's Heroes* program. Did you ever watch that? Did you know that man who played Hogan was murdered and it's still unsolved? Somebody ought to investigate that. You know, them Hollywood types are all into orgies and whatnot, so it probably had something to do with that. I was invited to an orgy one time, but I didn't go 'cause I didn't want to be in a room with a bunch of naked dudes."

I was hoping the pills would kick in soon—otherwise my vision of tossing Floppy off the deck might turn into reality. "Stop talking," I yelled. "Just shut up for a second and listen to me. This is important. I need you to focus. What else can you tell me about Cordell?"

Floppy thought for a moment.

"Well, he was real interested in Cold Mountain and the history of the area and such. He knew about that old plane crash, and I told him about my granddaddy finding that gold and how it was stolen from him. He asked me about how much my granddaddy found and where exactly he found it. Said he was an amateur treasure hunter and thought it would be fun to go look for any gold my granddaddy didn't find. I told him he's wasting his time. Granddaddy found all that gold, then Junebug and Byrd went and took it from him. They was just boys when they did it, but they never have fessed up to it. Granddaddy told me all about it 'fore he passed."

As Floppy talked, I felt the pills beginning to work their magic. It was like sinking into a warm bath. I shouldn't have taken three; one would have been enough. The numbness was enveloping me, and I was having a hard time focusing on Floppy. The timing was bad, because for once I actually wanted to hear what he had to say.

"Hold on," I mumbled. "How do you know your grandfather found all the gold? If there was gold on that plane when it crashed, it would have been scattered all across the mountain."

Floppy shook his head. "No sir. Granddaddy told me those Army men pushed the gold out of that plane before it crashed. It was in a reinforced steel trunk, bolted up tight with big padlocks."

"But they didn't know they were about to crash," I said. "The weather was bad and they didn't see the mountain. They had no warning."

"I know that. Granddaddy figured they'd already planned to get rid of that gold. Why do you think they ain't no record of any gold being on that plane? Them men stole it when they was overseas fighting the war. Most people don't know it, but American soldiers looted a lot of stuff during World War II. I mean, the Germans and the Russians and Japanese did more, but Americans took a fair amount of stuff too. So Granddaddy figured them men on the plane stole that gold from the Nazis and then hid it till they could find a way to get it far away from any Army base. So when they was assigned to fly that plane from Michigan to Florida, they decided to push that trunk out over the middle of nowhere. Somewhere nobody'd come across it. Then they'd come back sometime later and collect it. But they crashed and died, so that plan didn't work out too well.

"Anyways, Granddaddy found that gold between Graveyard Fields and Black Balsam. He's up there with his coon dogs hunting and sees that steel trunk laying there just as pretty as you please. He didn't have nary an idea what was in it, but he didn't care. He figured he could use the trunk for something. But it was heavy as all get-out. He went back home and rounded up Junebug and Byrd to help him pull it down out of the woods. Said it took them most of one day to get that trunk down off the mountain and loaded up onto his flatbed Ford. When they got back to Granddaddy's house, he fired up his acetylene torch and cut through the locks. Opened that box up and nearly had a heart attack right then and there. Did you know acetylene burns higher than almost all other fuels? That's why it cuts so well. Now, I have a real good acetylene setup. I can cut through just about anything. There was this one time . . ."

I would have told Floppy to shut up, but I was too busy fighting sleep. The pills and beer combined with Floppy's bizarre story and my anger at Diana were making my head spin. I placed one arm across the table and lay my head down in its crook. Floppy could ramble as long as he wanted; I just needed a short rest. I was imagining two young boys filling up a backpack with gold bricks when Floppy said something that snapped me back to sobriety.

"What did you just say?" I asked.

"I said that woman's been in the bathroom a long time."

I jumped up from the table and hurried through the bedroom. I knocked on the bathroom door, but there was no answer.

"Diana?" I said, knocking a second time.

I put my ear against the door and could hear water running but no other sounds. I tried the doorknob, but it was locked. I stepped back and raised my foot to kick in the door but found it hard to balance. My head was spinning and my brain felt as if it had shrunk to the point where it might come loose and roll out one of my ears.

I yelled for Floppy, and in a few seconds he was standing beside me.

"Help me kick open that door," I said.

"Is she okay?" he asked.

"Just help me!"

Floppy put his hand on my shoulder. "Ain't no reason for that," he said. "Kickin' in the door will most likely split the doorjamb; then you'll have to replace it, and that can be a real pain if you don't have the right kind of wood—"

"Open this door!"

Floppy reached into his pants pocket and pulled out the largest multitool I'd ever seen. He turned it over in his hand a couple of times, then flicked open a long steel hole punch.

"This is how you open these kinds of doors when they's locked," he said.

He put the skinny steel rod into the hole cut into the center of the doorknob. I heard a soft click, and when I twisted the knob, it turned effortlessly.

"See, these kinds of push-button locks have this small hole on the one side so you can—"

"I know that," I yelled. I pushed past Floppy and opened the bathroom door a few inches.

"Diana?" I said.

When I didn't get a response, I opened the door fully and stepped inside. The bathroom was empty but the sink faucet was running. Floppy stepped in next to me, and we both looked around.

"She ain't in here," he said, as if I needed confirmation of the obvious.

I pulled the shower curtain back just in case Diana was hiding in the tub, which was all I could think to do at the moment. She wasn't there.

"Guess she went out that window," Floppy said.

I looked at the small open window on the opposite side of the bathroom, where a pale-yellow curtain flapped lazily against the cool fall air. I tried to think about what was going on, but my head wasn't ready to cooperate. The thoughts were coming slow, a series of blurry pictures I couldn't bring into focus. Why would Diana disappear through my bathroom window? Had she seen me from the kitchen scrolling through her photos and text messages? Was she so embarrassed that she'd lied to me that she'd climbed out the bathroom window rather than face me and admit the truth?

Then a small glint of clarity began clicking through my synapses. I hurried back into the kitchen and examined the table.

"Motherfucker," I yelled.

Floppy wobbled up next to me.

"You oughtn't to say *fuck*," he said. "Now, it ain't as bad as saying *goddamn*, but it still ain't a good word to say. Dale says *fuck* all the time on account his vocabulary ain't as extensive as mine. I say *sumbitch* sometimes, but that's about as far—"

I grabbed Floppy's shoulders and shook him like a vending machine that had cheated me out of a dollar.

"Where are the keys?"

Floppy looked down at the table and rubbed his head.

"Well, if you're talking about them keys that I had earlier, they was right here," he said. "That woman was messing around with them while you was in the other room. Who were you talking to in there anyways? Did you know the government can listen in to any call you make from a cell phone? I don't have a cell phone myself because—"

I stomped on the linoleum.

"Shut up. Please shut up. I need to think."

Through the exhaustion and numbness, I could come up with only one idea. I didn't like it, but it was going to have to do.

"Let's go," I said. "She couldn't have gotten far."

Floppy's face lit up like a slot machine hitting a jackpot.

"I'll drive," he said.

I walked over to the sink and splashed some cold water on my face.

"You're going to have to."

* * *

The two of us limped down to the clearing where Floppy's car was parked.

"This old Rabbit don't look like much," he said, "but she's got some special modifications. She'll blow the doors off just about anything on the road."

Floppy slung himself in the driver's seat. When I opened the passenger side door, I didn't like what I saw. The seat had been removed to make room for a large Igloo cooler held in place with two bungee cords. I glanced at the back seat, but there was no back seat either. It had been replaced by what looked like two miniature hot-water tanks.

"You can sit on this," Floppy said, hitting the top of the cooler with his fist. "It's sturdy; you won't hurt it."

I climbed in and straddled the cooler. As I shifted my ass to try to find a comfortable position, Floppy reached under his seat and pulled out a red bungee cord with metal hooks attached to each end. He secured one hook to a metal ring next to his seat and then handed me the other end of the cord.

"Put this over your legs," he said. "They's a bracket over by the door. Hook this to it. You're gonna wanna be strapped in."

I didn't like the sound of that, but I followed the instructions. Floppy turned the ignition, and the Rabbit sputtered and jerked. After a few tries the car came to life, and I saw a plume of black smoke rise in the reflection of the side mirror. Floppy revved the engine a couple of times, and the car shook like a dragster on the starting line. The engine was deafeningly loud, and I wondered what type of "modifications" Floppy had made to it. My biggest fear was that the car would explode and Floppy and I would end up in pieces scattered through the woods.

With the bungee cord secured across my legs, I wrapped my fingers tightly around the cooler's side handles. I turned to look at Floppy. He was now wearing a pair of dark wraparound sunglasses and grinning wildly. He grabbed the gearshift, a small rod that rose between the seats with a black eight ball on its top, and wiggled it back and forth.

"This car's a stick?" I asked. "How do you drive a stick with your bad leg?"

Floppy cackled like a frightened hen.

"Don't worry about that," he said. "You just hold on."

35

The Rabbit took off like most rabbits do—abruptly. We tore down the gravel drive at a pace that would have made even Dale clench his ass cheeks together. As we bounced down the drive, I flashed back to a bar I used to frequent back in Charleston. The place featured an old, dusty mechanical bull that served more as decoration than as challenge. But every so often someone would get tipsy enough to climb on top of it and yell for the bartender to throw the switch. Three seconds later the unlucky drunk would be lying flat on the bar's hardwood floor. Maybe they could have lasted longer if they'd had a red bungee cord wrapped over their legs.

* * *

When we hit 276, Floppy turned left toward Waynesville and pushed the Rabbit to the point I thought the doors might shake off. Floppy's right leg, the good one, was furiously working all three pedals: accelerator, clutch, and occasionally, but not often, the brake. I looked out the window as we passed the campground where I'd first laid eyes on Dale. As I watched the RVs fly by in a blur, a terrible thought went through my foggy brain—I was most likely going to throw up.

"Can we catch up to Diana without killing ourselves?" I said.

"You're safe with me," Floppy said. "I used to drive short track; I know what I'm doing."

As we entered the passing zone by the golf course, Floppy buried the accelerator into the floorboard and pointed to his right.

"I used to scuba dive in them ponds out there," he said. "I'd sneak out late at night when nobody's lookin' and dive down and find all kinds of golf balls. Them balls is like white gold. People pay a dollar apiece for them things. Can you believe that? I don't scuba dive no more on account I heard somewhere the air in them scuba tanks can make your lungs swell up like you've been breathin' paint thinner, but that's where I used to do it. Right over there. Look."

Floppy pointed again, but I was too frightened to look anywhere other than straight ahead.

We rounded a sharp curve without slowing down, then raced past Cruso's lone gas station. While Floppy rambled on about a two-dollar scratch ticket that had produced an eight-dollar profit, the car began to sputter and jerk. A part of me hoped we were about to break down. It would end our chance of catching up to Diana, but it would also end the chance of me being found dead strapped to an Igloo cooler.

As the engine hiccupped, Floppy pumped the accelerator like he was trying to stomp out a small fire.

"C'mon, girl," he said.

Soon the car was roaring again and Floppy patted the dashboard as if it were a loyal dog that had just obeyed a command.

"Sally runs on old cooking grease," Floppy said. "I go around to them fast-food restaurants like Hardee's and such and get the old grease they fry food in. It ain't no use to them. They just give it to me. I let it settle in some tanks I got back at my garage to get the little bits of food and such out of it. It's clean fuel and it don't cost me a cent. Of course, I had to modify Sally's engine, but that ain't no big deal for someone like me. Yeah, I've done all kinds of stuff to ole Sally here. Even welded together a pressurized pipe for her back bumper. Got an air nozzle on the side, so if I was to get a flat tire, I could fill it up from that bumper. I tell you, Sally's something special."

Floppy turned to me as if we were out for a leisurely Sunday drive.

"Sally's the name of my car. In case you was wondering."

We took a small curve, then entered a long straightaway where a patrol car with its lights ablaze barreled toward us. Floppy tapped the brake, and my ass slid forward on the cooler until the bungee cord pulled tight across my waist. The patrol car streaked past us, then spun around in the middle of the road and gave chase.

"Dagnabbit!" Floppy said. "Them boys ain't got nothin' better to do than pull me for speeding?"

Floppy slowed down, then pulled into a dirt driveway and turned Sally off.

"Now you let me handle this," he said. "I know how to talk to the authorities."

A few seconds later Dale was standing next to my window. He jerked my door open, but when I tried to get out of the car, the bungee cord was pulled so tight I couldn't unhook it from the bracket.

"Get the fuck out," Dale said.

My brain was still foggy, and the bungee cord was like duct tape trapping me against the cooler. Dale watched me struggle for a few seconds, then pulled out a pocket knife and held it uncomfortably close to my bad leg. When he slit the cord, it separated with a loud thwack. The tension snapped it upward, where it smacked Floppy in the face.

"Dang it, Dale," Floppy yelled. "You got no business stoppin' me. I was driving at a speed safe for conditions. And you ruined my best bungee cord. I'm going to the station and fill out a report."

Dale ignored Floppy as I got out of the car. I bent over and put my hands on my knees, fighting the waves of nausea.

Dale took a step back. "Are you going to puke again? 'Cause I still ain't kicked your ass for the last time."

I stood upright and tried to pull myself together. I needed to tell Dale what was happening, but I wanted to get the facts straight. I wanted him to know I was telling the truth and telling it accurately.

"Listen closely," I said. "Diana knows Cordell. I think they may have even been dating. Floppy took the keys from the sheriff's office. One of the keys on that ring opens the door to your cabin. Diana stole the keys and took off. And Byrd is involved in all this somehow."

When I was finished rambling, Dale spit a few ounces of brown fluid onto the dirt driveway and rubbed his head.

"Are you drunk?" he said.

I took a few deep breaths and tried a technique I'd learned at the South Carolina Criminal Justice Academy. The instructor had told us that if we were in a situation where we felt anxious or panicked, we should breathe deeply and try to find our "center," a theoretical location that existed somewhere in our sternum. Once we'd located this place, we should imagine it filled with a ball of energy radiating a calming white light, then expand that ball of energy until it encapsulated our entire body in peace and tranquility.

I closed my eyes and found my center. There was indeed a ball of energy there. It was huge and glowing bright red. I tried to turn it white, but it wouldn't change. My ball of energy was beyond my conscious command. Like a lot of things in my life, it controlled me rather than the other way around.

"What the fuck are you doing?" Dale yelled. "Open your eyes and tell me what the hell is going on."

I gave up on the energy ball and repeated everything I'd just said, as slowly and calmly as I could.

"Are you fucking serious?" Dale said.

"I'm dead serious. Floppy brought the keys to the cabin and used one to unlock the door. Then Diana took them and disappeared out the bathroom window."

Dale bent down and sneered at Floppy through the open car door. "I knew you had them fucking keys." He then looked back at me. "But why would Diana take 'em?"

I hesitated a moment. "You're not going to want to hear this," I said.

Dale smacked the top of my head. "I don't want to hear any of this."

"Diana took those keys because they unlock a shitload of gold."

Dale laughed so hard I worried he might swallow his tobacco.

"Oh, for the love of fuck, Davis, there ain't no gold."

Floppy threw open the driver's side door and came around next to me. He rubbed a red mark on his cheek and stared at Dale with disgust.

"That gold is real," Floppy said. "You know it is. Your daddy helped steal it."

Dale took a step toward Floppy. "I'm gonna jerk a knot in your ass if you don't shut the fuck up."

"Your badge don't scare me. We're kin, and that means we's equal."

My nausea was starting to pass, but my head felt like it was being squeezed in a vise. I also felt like I had been transported to another dimension. I'd just raced down a curvy two-lane road on an Igloo cooler and was now standing between a skinny man dressed in head-to-toe camouflage and a fat man dressed in a tobacco-stained deputy's uniform listening to them to argue about whether or not a treasure trove of gold had fallen from an airplane in the 1940s. Maybe the town should change its tagline from *Cruso: 9 Miles of Friendly People Plus One Old Crab* to *Cruso: Get Ready for Some Weird Shit.*

"If my daddy had stolen that gold," Dale said, "I'd be living on a beach knee-deep in pussy, not chasing your dumb ass all through Cruso."

"Hang on," I said, trying to wriggle my mind from the vise. "Let's think about this. Whether or not the gold exists doesn't really matter. But those keys obviously open something worth killing for. And Diana wanted them bad enough to disappear with them."

"Why did you say Byrd's involved in this?" Dale asked.

" 'Cause he helped your daddy steal that gold," Floppy said.

Dale put his hand on the grip of his side arm.

"Floppy, I will shoot you dead right here," he said. "Kin or not, I will lay you out in this driveway if you say another word about that fucking gold."

Floppy huffed and looked down at the dirt, where Dale's tobacco spit had now formed a large brown puddle.

"Byrd came to question me this morning," I said. "I told him the truth. And when I told him about going to Cordell's house and someone shooting at me, he said that Cordell didn't own the house, that he did."

Dale shook his head. "I told you Byrd owned rental houses around the county. Him renting that house to Cordell don't mean shit."

"Floppy told me that Byrd used to own your cabin," I said.

"Yeah, he sold it to Daddy a few years back. That don't mean shit neither."

"Well, one of the keys on the key ring unlocks the cabin door. And when Byrd was questioning me, he pulled his gun and asked me where the keys were. He seemed much more interested in finding the keys than finding out who killed Cordell."

Dale spat out another load of liquid and wiped his chin with the back of his hand. He looked at me, then at Floppy, then back at me again.

"None of that means shit," he said, but I could tell he was unconvinced.

"It means something," I said.

Dale rearranged his face back to its normal smug look. "If you weren't answering Byrd's questions, then I ain't surprised he pulled his gun on you. I'd a done the same thing."

"Is that normal procedure around here? Ask questions at gunpoint?"

"If the occasion calls for it. What did Byrd do after he questioned you?"

"He got the call about the couple being found dead in Maggie Valley. It seemed to genuinely surprise him. It surprised the hell out of me too. Then he took me to the station, and I sat handcuffed in an interview room alone for a couple of hours. Then Diana came and Byrd let me go. She drove me back to the cabin."

Dale arched his eyebrows.

"Why did she come to fetch you?" he asked.

"I thought maybe she liked me, but now I'm pretty sure she thought I could lead her to the keys."

Dale let that statement hang in the air for a moment. I could tell he was trying to process all the information I'd given him. There were a bunch of dots, and he and I were both trying hard to connect them all. Problem was, we were forming different pictures.

"What about Cordell's car?" I said.

"They towed it down from the parkway this morning to process it. And I'll save you the trouble of asking—there weren't no fucking gold hidden in the trunk."

"Was there anything in it?"

"A few gallon-sized Ziploc bags and a couple of receipts from some motel near Savannah. They was also one of them prepaid debit cards you can get at Walmart. We checked it, weren't no money on it."

I imagined Cordell putting some of the gold bars in the Ziploc bags and driving down to Savannah to sell them. He wouldn't want to be carrying around cash, so a prepaid debit card would make sense.

"What about Cordell's phone?"

"Ain't never found it. Wasn't on his body and we didn't find it in the car. Whoever shot the man probably slung it in the bushes or kept it, which would be pretty fucking stupid."

"It wouldn't be stupid if they needed his phone to get to the people he was selling the gold to."

Dale shook his head. "You really are a fucking idiot, you know that?"

"Did you look in the Land Rover?" I asked. "And that cargo box on the roof?"

Dale nodded. "The Land Rover was clean," he said. "And that cargo box was empty. Okay? Are you satisfied now?"

I wasn't, so I peppered Dale with questions for another ten minutes. I wanted to know what had been found at the house Cordell was renting and if there was any chance the two campers who'd found his body at Graveyard Fields could be involved. But according to Dale, the house was clean and the two campers were local guys who were beyond suspicion.

"Looks like the same gun was used in all three killings," Dale said. "We found a nine-millimeter casing near Cordell's body, and that hippie couple both had nine-millimeter shells lodged in their skulls."

"Have you determined when Jeff and Becky were killed?" I asked. "I mean, were they already dead the night you and I went to Cordell's house?"

Dale nodded.

"The ME says they's killed that same night. Now, whether it was before or after you were up there snooping around ain't no one sure. That's one of the reasons Byrd brought you in to the station."

"One reason? What was the other?"

Dale hesitated a moment, then grinned. "To search the cabin," he said.

That made perfect sense. While I was sitting handcuffed at the station, some deputy had been digging through my stuff. Then, between Dale vouching for me and the cabin being clean, Byrd had let me go.

"So what now?" I asked.

"You and numbnuts here are going back to the cabin," Dale said. "And Davis, you stay out of this. You have no authority to go sniffin' around, 'cause whenever you do, I'm the one who ends up with his ass in a sling."

I didn't like the idea, but I was in no position to argue. "So what are you going to do?"

Dale kicked the dirt, then seemed to make a decision.

"I guess I'll make a quick look for Diana."

"Her last name is Ross," I said. "Her name is Diana Ross."

Dale squinted. "Like the singer?"

Floppy opened the Igloo cooler and pulled out a Coors Light.

"That's funny," Floppy said. "They don't favor a bit."

36

As Dale tore off in his patrol car, I climbed back into Sally and took my place on the cooler. Floppy dragged himself into the driver's seat and fumed.

"I ain't never liked him," Floppy said. "Even when we was kids, he was a butthole. He's just a bigger butthole now."

I pictured Dale as a kid, chubby and obstinate, sitting in the back of a classroom, tired from "all this learnin' bullshit."

I looked over at Floppy.

"Listen to me carefully. You need to tell me the truth. Did your grandfather really find some gold?"

"He sure as heck did!" Floppy said.

"And you're convinced Junebug and Byrd stole it?"

Floppy nodded like a bobblehead doll. "Yessir! My granddaddy never told a lie. Even 'bout that UFO."

"If Junebug and Byrd stole the gold, why are they still here?" I said. "Why wouldn't they have taken off to the Caribbean and lived like kings?"

"Well now, they's a couple of reasons for that. First, they was just boys when they stole that gold, so they couldn't do much with it. I guess they hid it and made a pact to not touch it or tell no one about it until they got older."

"Yeah, well, they got older, and it still doesn't seem like they ever spent any of the money."

Floppy cackled. "You ain't from around here. You don't understand these people. Do you think Junebug wants a yacht or a big mansion? You think Byrd wants anything other than being sheriff? Maybe they had big dreams when they was kids, but when they grew up, them dreams changed. Plus, even if they did want to spend it, it ain't that easy. You can't just roll a wheelbarrow of gold into a bank and tell 'em you want to trade it for cash. They squirreled away that gold way back when, and it's stayed squirreled away. I guarantee you that. By the way, did you know squirrels . . ."

* * *

The ride back to the cabin took fifteen minutes. Without a bungee cord to hold me down, I'd told Floppy to keep Sally under forty if possible. During the ride I ignored Floppy's ramblings and thought about Byrd and Junebug. Two old friends who'd grown up together and then gone in separate directions, Byrd toward law enforcement and Junebug toward a few decades at the paper mill.

But the idea of either of them having access to a cache of gold was ridiculous. If the gold did exist, it had most likely been hauled off by the military just after the plane crash. And if the military hadn't recovered all of it, then what remained was still scattered across the face of Cold Mountain. Or it had been until an amateur treasure hunter named Lester Cordell got lucky and stumbled onto it.

* * *

When we arrived at the cabin, I thanked Floppy for the ride and apologized for getting rough with him.

"I wasn't kidding about knowing martial arts," he said. "I can take care of myself."

I nodded, then stepped out of Sally. Before I closed the door, I reached in and slapped the top of the cooler.

"I may get you to install one of these in my Mercedes."

Floppy beamed. "You just tell me when, buddy. I can do it."

* * *

Inside the cabin I grabbed a beer from the fridge and took a seat at the kitchen table where I'd sat with Floppy and Diana not much more than an hour earlier. I thought about Diana and shook my head. The more I thought, the more it shook. The angel on my shoulder was heartbroken, but the devils were relieved. They knew things weren't going to change after all.

*   *   *

I opened the laptop and found two new emails, one from the Indian pharmaceutical company and another from the Nigerian prince, once again asking for my assistance in getting millions of dollars out of his country. I thought about emailing him back and telling him I could use his help getting millions of dollars in gold off a mountain, or out of a locked chest, or more likely out of thin air.

I pulled up Facebook and wasn't surprised to learn I was still friendless. Since I now knew Diana's last name, I searched for her page. I found it, but it was private. I went to the brewery's Facebook page and took another look at the photos posted by customers. I found the image I'd already seen of Diana leaning against the bar; I now figured the guy next to her with his back to the camera was most likely Cordell. I studied the other photos closely. Before I'd just been hoping for a glimpse of Diana, but now I was looking for anything that might shed some light on where she'd gone.

I pressed the arrow button on my laptop to cycle through the photos. I'd gone through ten or more when I heard the angel whisper, *Go back.* It was like when a word pops into your head and you're not sure why. Then you look down and see the word on the cover of a magazine sitting on your coffee table. You read the word without even realizing it, but your unconscious picked it up. I pressed the back arrow to find what my unconscious had spotted.

It took a minute, but I found what I was looking for in a photo taken from somewhere near the brewery's entrance. I didn't see Diana in the photo, but in the top left corner, near the bar, I could clearly make out Cordell. I thought this was what my unconscious had picked up, a small image of the man I'd been trying to find for the past week. *Keep looking,* the angel whispered. So I did. I scanned every pixel of the photo until I finally found it. A man sitting at the bar, turned in Cordell's direction, a long beard flowing like a waterfall from his chin.

* * *

While the devils stoked my temper, the angel worked at calming my nerves. The guy with the beard was a friend of Diana's, so it was natural he'd show up in a photo taken at her bar. What bothered me was the fact that Diana was friends with a guy who looked like a psychotic hobo and walked around with a handgun tucked into his jeans.

Fuck Diana, the devils said.

That had been my original plan, but the devils were now talking about something completely different. Diana was just another person I'd trusted without question. It made me think about my friendship with Dale. If I looked through his photos, would I find a picture of him and Floppy standing arm in arm next to a chest full of gold?

* * *

Diana was a thorn in my side, but I also had another concern: Perry. Not hearing back from him was fraying my nerves. I'd been hoping he'd send an email that would convince me my accusation was ludicrous. An email that would persuade me he'd had nothing to do with the shooting and that his owning a gray Audi was purely a coincidence. But his silence was eating away at that hope.

I was beginning to feel certain about what had happened. There had never been any Internal Affairs investigation. Greg had never been under any suspicion. Perry had removed all of those Pelican cases before the police and EMTs arrived. He'd probably told me IA was involved to convince me that the affair was out of his hands. The shooter would never be found, no charges would ever be filed, and Perry would swear to me he'd tried his hardest but the situation was beyond his control. And I'd be left thinking everyone in the Charleston PD was crooked except for my good friend Perry.

But now he would have to make sure the curtain wasn't pulled back. And idiot that I was, I had given him directions to the cabin along with an invitation to show up anytime.

Deep down I still held on to a tiny glimmer of hope that I was wrong. So far, relying on hope hadn't helped me accomplish very much. But I wasn't quite ready to completely give up on it.

There was a sudden rap on the door. I jerked around so fast my beer toppled over and covered the table in beige foam. The door opened and Floppy stepped in with a sheepish look.

"Can I talk to you for a minute?" he said.

I took a few deep breaths and tried to get my heart rate back into double digits. Then I grabbed some paper towels and went to work on the foam.

"I don't think that's possible," I said.

Floppy frowned.

"Why? Are you busy with something?"

"No, I mean I don't think it's possible that you can . . . just . . . never mind."

Floppy took a seat.

"Hey, I've been sitting out there in Sally thinking," he said. "I like to think about things and try to work them out in my head. I do this transcendental meditation stuff. You ever heard of that? A lot of celebrities do it. Some really smart people do it too. Anyways, there's something real important I need to show you."

I sighed. So much for spending a quiet evening alone waiting for an old friend to show up and kill me.

"Fine," I said. "Show me."

Floppy shook his head. "It don't have it with me. It's back at my trailer. I can drive you up there."

I wasn't going to climb back into Sally, not even if the passenger seat was full of good beer.

"That's okay," I said. "I'll follow you."

* * *

A half an hour later I pulled into the dirt lot in front of Floppy's garage. When I stepped out of the Mercedes, Floppy dragged himself over to me and looked around as if we were about to make a drug deal.

"Come with me," he said.

I trailed Floppy through a maze of junk until we arrived at the steps of a teal-green trailer. Floppy hopped up the steps with his good leg, then turned and gave me a steely glare.

"Now, I don't normally let people into my home," he said. "I got things in here I don't want people to see. My business ain't nobody else's business, you know what I mean?"

I looked around at the menagerie of rusted appliances, broken furniture, and car parts.

"I got it. Your business is your business."

Floppy hesitated another moment, then unlocked the trailer's door and walked inside.

When I entered, my jaw hit the floor. The trailer was crammed from floor to ceiling with junk. Books, folders, magazines, old VHS tapes and DVDs. On the floor sat cardboard boxes overflowing with newspapers and five-gallon buckets full of golf balls, aluminum cans, and silverware. It was like a thrift store having a garage sale inside a flea market.

"I'm a collector," Floppy said, moving a cardboard box off a worn orange sofa. "Here, sit down. Sit right here and look forward; don't be looking around at my things. Sit still and I'll be right back."

Floppy vanished into a back room and returned a few minutes later with a black velvet pouch about the size of a paperback novel. I knew immediately what it was, but I didn't want to believe it.

"Now what I'm about to show you, I ain't never showed nobody," Floppy said.

He untied the end of the pouch, reached inside, and slowly removed a bar of gold.

"When Granddaddy first opened that trunk, he took out this one brick and hid it under his mattress. Then that night, Byrd and Junebug tore off with the rest of the gold. Granddaddy kept this brick under that mattress all them years, then gave it to me the day before he died. He never knew what to do with it. Just like Byrd and Junebug don't know what to do with it. That's why I'm telling you that gold ain't never been spent. It's still out there wherever them two hid it."

"Did you ever show this to Lester Cordell?" I asked.

"Heck no! I told you I ain't never showed it to nobody."

Floppy slid the bar of gold back into the velvet bag and then started limping nervously around the obstacle course he called a living room. "Well, except Tanya. I showed it to her one night when she's up here and we's drinking."

I cocked my head.

"Tanya, remember? She's the one with the bear paw tattooed on her titty. The massage therapist. I shouldn't of showed it to her, but we's drinking and I wasn't thinking straight. I thought she'd keep it secret, but then she goes and shows up here the next night with her roommate, asking me to show the gold to 'em. But I was smart. I told 'em it was a joke. That it weren't nothin' but a piece of iron I'd sprayed with gold flake."

"When was this?"

Floppy looked up as if the answer might be written on the water-stained ceiling.

"Uh, last summer sometime."

"Do you remember the roommate's name?"

"Let me think. It was weird. Like tropical or something."

When Floppy couldn't find the answer on the ceiling, he scratched his head.

"Dang it, I can't remember. But let me tell you, she had a set of titties on her that put Tanya's to shame."

"Something tropical. Like Daiquiri?"

Floppy grinned from ear to ear.

37

Twenty minutes later I was in the parking lot of El Bacaratos.

"What the fuck do you want?" Dale yelled through the phone.

"Did you find Diana?"

"Ain't no one seen her. I got her address and rode up to her house. Big ole place up by the country club in Waynesville. Nobody was home."

"Did you get a search warrant?"

Dale laughed. "Based on what? You and Floppy are the only people claiming Diana stole them keys and ran away, and you two ain't exactly the most reliable motherfuckers on the planet."

I was disappointed but not surprised. "Well, here's something else you're probably not going to believe."

Dale was uncharacteristically silent while I told him about my visit to Floppy's. It wasn't until I reached the part about Tanya bringing Daiquiri to the trailer that Dale finally let out one of his signature snorts.

"Where are you?" he said.

I looked around the parking lot. "I'm at my office."

"I'll be there in five minutes."

* * *

Three minutes later Dale pulled his patrol car next to my Mercedes. I heard a few seconds of Ratt's "Round and Round" before he killed the engine. It was almost ten o'clock. El Bacaratos had been closed for hours, and aside from our cars, the parking lot was empty. Dale opened the passenger side door and climbed into the Mercedes. The car tilted to one side under his weight.

He gave me a tired look and said, "Okay, dumbass, what's your hunch?"

I let him have it with both barrels.

"Daiquiri tells Diana about the gold, and Diana tells Cordell. Cordell figures it can't be too difficult to steal a bar of gold from a hundred-pound man with a bum leg, so he goes up to Floppy's garage, acting like he needs his car serviced to do some recon. But of course Floppy can't keep his mouth shut, and he tells Cordell about the chest of gold his grandfather found and that your dad and Byrd stole it. Cordell doesn't believe that part of the story and figures if there is more gold, it's most likely still somewhere near Cold Mountain. So he and his friends Jeff and Becky, and maybe even Diana, start searching for it. But Cordell is the one who finds it, and he locks it away somewhere. That's when the double-crossing starts. Cordell and Diana against Jeff and Becky, or maybe it was each against the other; who knows. Then one of them kills Cordell. But Cordell's keys are nowhere to be found."

Dale put his hand on my shoulder.

"Maybe you should start writin' fiction."

"Listen, it makes perfect sense. Everyone was looking for the keys because they unlock the gold, wherever it is. Remember that night we went to the brewery and how Diana wasn't very interested in us at the beginning? But then after Daiquiri tells her I found a set of keys belonging to someone who drives a red BMW 2002, Diana starts full on hitting on me. The only reason she invited herself up to the cabin was to look for the keys."

Dale unsnapped his shirt pocket and pulled out a tin of Copenhagen. He pinched a giant wad of the tobacco in his fingers and shoved it between his gums and cheek.

"I knew she was way too hot for you."

I nodded.

"So who do you think killed that couple?" Dale asked.

I reminded him about Diana's overprotective friends, the ones who had threatened me the night we stopped at Long Branch on our way to Cordell's house.

"That don't make no sense. Whoever killed that hippie couple was probably the same person shot at you. Since Diana and them dudes were at Long Branch that night, then it couldn't a been them. Unless they hauled ass up there right after we left the brewery."

"You said the ME couldn't pinpoint the time of death. Jeff and Becky may have still been alive when I was snooping around Cordell's and it was one of them who shot at me. Then Diana and her friends go up there later that night and kill them."

Dale rubbed his head.

"It still don't make no sense. If that hippie couple killed Cordell, why would they be at his house? They weren't nothing there."

I shrugged.

"I don't know. Maybe Diana killed Cordell. Or her friend with the beard did it. So far he's the only one that's been seen with a gun. I don't know if it was a nine-millimeter stuffed in his jeans. Fortunately, I didn't get close to enough to find out. But we need to find Diana. She's involved somehow. Either she's guilty or she's in danger."

Dale nodded.

"I still don't think those keys lead to any gold, but yeah, I'd like to ask her some questions."

We sat in silence for a few moments. When Dale reached for the door handle, I stopped him.

"Hang on," I said. "There's something else I need to talk to you about."

"If it's about gold, I don't want to hear any more of that shit."

I shook my head. "It's about Charleston."

*   *   *

On that first night at the cabin, I'd told Dale the clean version of the storage unit incident. I left out the part about me beating Greg and the cases of drugs and cash. Now I told him the truth, including how I was growing more and more convinced that Perry was the person who'd shot me.

"We need to tell Byrd about this situation," Dale said.

"I don't trust Byrd."

Dale raised a finger. "You can trust Byrd. He's a good man."

"I'm beginning to believe I can't trust anyone. You're about it these days."

Dale smiled.

"Let's find Diana," I said. "Then we'll decide what to do about Perry."

Dale looked out the window and exhaled a putrid bouquet of tobacco.

"Well, we ain't doing it tonight. But you ain't going back to the cabin. You're staying with me and Daddy till this Perry shit's fixed."

I was too tired to argue. I followed Dale to Junebug's house and curled up in a recliner under a NASCAR-branded afghan. The sound of Junebug snoring shook the walls. I pulled a pill out from my coin pocket and swallowed it with spit. Before I drifted off, Dale's snoring started to compete with Junebug's. It sounded like an avalanche approaching. The metaphor was not lost on me.

38

When I woke up the next morning, Junebug was in his recliner watching a cooking show. I tried to shake off the cobwebs as some large woman on the screen pulled the gizzard out of a fresh turkey.

"Where's Dale?" I asked.

Junebug grunted and jerked a thumb toward the kitchen. He then raised a Styrofoam cup to his lips. Coffee. I needed coffee. And a pill. And a beer chaser. And a plan on how to stay alive for the rest of the day, and thereafter.

I watched the gizzard puller for a moment, then heard Junebug spit into the cup. I'd been awake all of two minutes, and my nausea was already in panic mode.

It took several tries, but I finally worked up enough strength to kick down the recliner's leg rest. When I walked into the kitchen, Dale was holding a box of cereal. The leprechaun on the side of the box looked like a child predator. In a way he was, I thought.

Dale poured the cereal into a bowl large enough to soak his feet in. I looked around for coffee.

"There's Mountain Dew in the fridge, if you want it," Dale said.

I sat down at the table and watched him inhale a few hundred grams of sugar.

"So what's the plan?" I asked.

"I gotta go down to the sheriff's office for an hour or so. You stay here with Daddy. I'll be back soon."

Dale finished his cereal, then raised the bowl and slurped the milk. When he wiped his mouth with his shirt sleeve, I shook my head.

"Don't start on me, Davis. I ain't got no patience for your shit today."

*　*　*

I followed Dale out to his patrol car and stood by as he wiggled in behind the wheel.

"I'll be back in a bit," he said. "Now don't you go nowhere. I don't need you getting shot, 'cause I ain't moving all your shit out of that cabin."

"Are we going to look for Diana?"

Dale fiddled with some knobs on the dash, and "Screaming in the Night" by Krokus filled the driveway.

"We'll talk about that when I get back. You just sit tight. And stay away from my beer."

As soon as Dale was out of sight, I climbed into the Mercedes and headed toward the cabin.

*　*　*

It was too cold to sit on the deck, so I plopped down at the kitchen table and stared at my reflection in the screen of the laptop. I checked my email but found no response from Perry. My tiny glimmer of hope was becoming a microscopic glimmer of hope.

I wondered when Perry would show up, and whether he'd arrive under the guise of a friend or just kick down the door and put a bullet in my skull. I didn't have a gun. I was too scared to have one. A guy like me didn't need an easy way out.

I made some instant coffee, then opened the bottle of pills. I fished one out and held it between my thumb and index finger. I examined it as if it were a diamond. How could something so tiny be so comforting? And so debilitating?

As I stared at the pill, a strange thought occurred to me. What if I wasn't numb? Even for just a little while? I'd gone without beer and pills for several hours yesterday, and nothing bad had happened. I hadn't had a seizure or heart palpitations. And my anxiety hadn't ratcheted up to the point where I wanted to drive my car off a cliff.

I'd thought I needed someone like Diana to give me the motivation to stay straight. But what if the feeling of being straight was motivation enough?

Two people I'd cared for and trusted had turned out to be liars, and one of them was probably coming to kill me. I couldn't change those facts, but I could use chemicals to forget them. I could hide out in Dale's living room and watch cooking shows and stock car races with Junebug until the authorities caught up with Perry and Diana. I could stay numb and stay safe.

Or I could be proactive. Someone had once told me it was amazing how much a person could accomplish in a day and how little a person could accomplish in a year. On this particular day I could solve three murders, find a fortune's worth of gold, have a senior detective arrested for attempted murder, discover the truth about a beautiful brewery owner, and enact my revenge on the guy who'd keyed my car.

I squeezed my thumbnail against the score in the pill. It split in two, and I swallowed one piece. Baby steps.

*   *   *

At half past ten I heard the squawk from Dale's patrol car. A couple of minutes later he was sitting at my kitchen table drinking what he said was the worst cup of coffee he'd ever tasted.

"It's instant," I said.

"It's instant shit is what it is. Why don't you get one of them fucking pod things?"

"Do you really want to talk about coffee?"

Dale pushed his mug aside. "I knew you'd come back here, you dumb fuck. You're lucky that Perry man wasn't here waiting for you."

"I'd rather be lucky than smart."

"So far you ain't much of either."

Dale stood up, poured his coffee into the sink, then went out the door without saying a word. He returned a minute later carrying a bottle of Mountain Dew.

"Listen to me, Davis," he said, when he'd sat back down. "Floppy is full of shit almost constantly. And him having a bar of gold, if it is real gold, don't convince me that there's a bunch more of it hidden somewhere."

"It convinced some other people."

Dale nodded. "Now that I do believe. I also believe Diana does have something do with Cordell and that hippie couple."

"Hipster. Not hippie."

"Would you shut the fuck up and listen to me?"

I raised my hands in surrender.

"Byrd's working with the authorities down in Florida, trying to get some intel on Cordell. He was busted down there a few times on petty shit, but petty shit can lead to big shit. He's got Avery County on it too. They're askin' around about that hippie couple." Dale jerked his head. "Fuck you, *hipster* couple."

"Did you tell Byrd about Diana taking off with the keys?"

"No. And I'll tell you why. And if you ever repeat it, I'll snap your neck and drink every ounce of your beer. If Byrd knows Floppy had them keys, he'll bring him in, and I don't want that. Floppy's a pain in my ass, but he's kin, and I don't want him in no trouble. And if Byrd knows you had them keys and didn't call him first, he'll pull your ass, and it won't matter much what I say."

I couldn't help but grin. "You're a big softy."

Dale jumped up and pointed a finger at my face. "I wouldn't think twice about puttin' your head through that window. Now listen to me, Davis. Byrd's got a habit of seeing one thing and nothing else. I don't want that one thing to be you or Floppy, 'cause I'm tied to both of you'ns, as much as I hate to admit it. So me and you can go find Diana and get some answers. And if she's involved with this shit, then I'll take it to Byrd and you and Floppy can stay out of it."

I stood up and spread my arms.

Dale backed up against the sink. "There ain't no romance happenin' here."

"Just a little hug?" I said. "It might help us bond."

"Stop fucking around. Let's go to Diana's. See if she's there."

"I've got a better idea. Let's go to Daiquiri's."

Dale relaxed. "Now that's an idea I can get behind. Get it? Behind. In front of. On top of. To the side . . ."

*   *   *

In the patrol car, Dale called Long Branch to see if Diana was there. She wasn't. He then radioed the department for Daiquiri's address, which turned out to be in Clyde, a small town about ten minutes east of Waynesville. It was the same town where Dale had shot and killed a man during a drug raid. When we drove by a dilapidated apartment complex, Dale pointed.

"That's where it happened," he said. "Dumb sumbitch came out on that stoop right there, gun at his side. I tell you something, Davis, I thought I was going to die that day. He raised that gun and started screaming, and I put one in his belly and one in his chest. Dead 'fore he hit the ground. Boy was only nineteen years old."

"How do you feel about it?"

"That's what the shrink asked me. And I'll tell you the same thing I told her—I ain't lost no sleep over it. It was either going to be that boy or me. And I made the right decision."

We drove in silence for a few minutes, looking for Daiquiri's house. When we pulled in the driveway, Dale killed the engine and turned to me.

"I see that boy's face sometimes when my head hits the pillow. I see him standing there with that gun pointed at me and that crazy-ass look on his face. I kill him every time. Same two shots. Then I go to sleep. But I tell you one thing, once you know you can kill a man and not regret it, that's a stone that don't never roll away."

*   *   *

We walked up a path to the front door, and Dale pushed the doorbell button. A few seconds later a dark-haired woman in a white tank top opened the door with a frown. It was hard not to notice the small bear paw tattooed on her right breast.

"What do you want?" she said.

"Hey there, Tanya. I'm Dale Johnson. We met before. You used to date my cousin Floppy."

"Yeah, I used to rub him down real good."

Dale stammered, then looked at me.

"Tanya, my name's Davis. We're looking for Daiquiri."

Tanya turned her head into the house and yelled Daiquiri's name. She somehow stretched it into four syllables.

A minute later Dale's dream woman was standing at the door next to Tanya. She was wearing a black Metallica T-shirt with the collar cut into a low V, revealing milky-white cleavage that looked like a baby's butt.

Daiquiri smirked at Dale. "You stalking me?"

Dale stood frozen. I figured the sight of four enormous breasts was frying his circuits.

"We're looking for Diana," I said. "It's important we talk to her."

Daiquiri stared at me suspiciously. "You seem to always be looking for someone," she said.

"Have you heard from her? She's not at the brewery today. And she doesn't seem to be at her house."

Daiquiri shook her head. "Sorry, can't help you."

Fuck it, I thought. Might as well lay it all out.

"We're here about the gold," I said. "We know Floppy showed you the bar of gold he has at his trailer."

Tanya laughed. "That gold ain't real."

"I think it is real," I said. "And I think Diana might be in trouble because of it."

Daiquiri crossed her arms over her chest, causing the top of her cleavage to brush her chin. "That ain't real gold," she said. "He told us it was just a piece of metal he'd painted."

"Did you ever mention it to Diana?" I asked.

Daiquiri tried to read me for a moment. "Yeah, I told her. Tanya called one night and said Floppy'd just shown her a brick of gold that was worth about twenty thousand dollars. I was at work and told Diana about it; I thought it was pretty cool. But the next night when Tanya and me went up to Floppy's, he said it was fake."

I glanced over at Dale. He still looked like he'd been tascred.

"Listen, Daiquiri, this is serious," I said. "Three people are dead. And we think Diana may be in danger. We really need to find her."

Tanya and Daiquiri glanced at each other.

Tanya spoke first. "He's in uniform and y'all are in a patrol car, so I have to believe this is official. Is that right?"

"That's right," I said.

Tanya pointed at Dale's face. "I want to hear it from him."

Dale nodded.

Tanya took a deep breath and looked at Daiquiri.

"Don't, Tanya," Daiquiri said. "They're full of shit. There's no gold."

Tanya looked down at the welcome mat, the words HOWDY Y'ALL written into the plastic grass. She let out a sigh, then looked back at me.

"I clean Diana's house once a week," she said. "There's a service door around back with a number lock. The code is zero-zero-six-nine. That'll get you in."

Daiquiri stared daggers at Tanya.

"If she's in danger, then they need to find her," Tanya said.

Daiquiri shoved Tanya's shoulder, then slammed the door closed. I snapped my fingers in front of Dale's face.

"You are useless when tits are involved."

* * *

Diana's house was located on Country Club Drive in a golf course community in Waynesville. The house was a typical McMansion, a mix of architectural styles that didn't really match. It was the kind of house you lived in if you wanted people to think you were rich but you really weren't. Or were rich but didn't have any taste.

We stopped in front of the house. The driveway was empty. I asked Dale to park a little farther down the road. If Diana wasn't home, I didn't want her to come back and see a patrol car.

We drove another fifty or so yards until we came to the parking lot for the club's driving range. There were a couple of cars in the lot and three guys hitting balls off a brown rectangle of grass. They seemed too interested in their practice to notice a fat deputy and a limping time bomb trudging back up the road.

As we walked, I asked Dale what he knew about Diana. I was hoping the guy who had failed at getting her name right might know something about her past.

"She ain't from around here," he said. "I think I remember hearing she moved up from Atlanta a few years back. I don't know where she got the money to start the brewery. All I know is, one day Long Branch weren't there and the next day it was."

Diana's driveway ended at a two-car garage with a gabled roof. Both garage doors were closed, and when I walked over, I noticed a keypad next to one of them. For the hell of it I entered 0069, but nothing happened. A breezeway connected the garage to the back of the house. I'd started walking that way when Dale yelled for me.

"Hey! Let's ring the doorbell 'fore we go breaking in."

From the driveway we followed a curving brick path that led up to the house. The front door was a massive slab of wood with a stained-glass image of a rolling golf hole surrounded by mountains. It was hideous.

Dale pushed the doorbell, and we waited. I placed my ear against the glass and listened for any movement. Dale tried the doorbell again. We gave it another minute and then headed around to the back of the house.

We found the service door Tanya had mentioned, and I entered the code. The lock made a strained grinding noise, then clicked. When I pushed the door open, Dale put his hand on my arm.

"Hold on," he said. "What do you think we're going to find in here?"

I shrugged. "A dead woman? Millions of dollars' worth of gold? Some good beer? Honestly, I have no idea."

"I hope it's just two of those things and not all three."

I nodded. "Me and you both, buddy."

* * *

The service door opened into a large laundry room. A pile of clothes covered the top of a dryer, and a pair of sneakers sat on the floor. As we entered, Dale pulled out his side arm. Better safe than sorry, I thought.

We walked slowly through the room. I let Dale lead the way, since he was holding the gun, and because standing behind him was like standing behind a barn door.

When we entered the kitchen, I noticed a few pieces of mail sitting on a granite island. It was funny seeing Diana's name in print. I wondered how much shit she'd caught, growing up with such a name, and what kind of parents would subject their child to that.

I rooted though the mail. It was mostly junk. I picked up an envelope with a CERTIFIED MAIL sticker attached to the front. I tore it open and pulled out a legal-size sheet of paper.

"That's a federal offense," Dale said.

I ignored him and read the document. It was line of credit notification from Blue Ridge State Bank. On the top of the page, the words FINAL NOTICE were stamped in red ink. The outstanding balance was $250,000. The document made it clear that if the entire balance was not paid by December 1, legal proceedings would begin.

I held up the notice. "She owes the bank a lot of money," I said.

"Yeah, who don't?"

"Maybe she took out a loan to start the brewery? Or to open up the restaurant?"

Dale shrugged and asked if we should split up. I thought about three dead bodies, all shot in the head.

"Absolutely not," I said.

We searched every room on the first and second floors but didn't find anything that might point us in Diana's direction or indicate her involvement with Cordell. When we reached a set of stairs leading to the basement, Dale stopped.

"This is nothing but a big-ass waste of time," he said.

I shrugged, then tilted my head toward the lower level.

The stairs descended into a massive rec room: pool table with red felt, giant TV, dart board, wet bar along one wall.

"Motherfucker," Dale said. "I could use some shit like this."

There was a door set into the wall next to the wet bar. I walked over and gave the knob a good shake, but the door didn't budge. I pulled my debit card out of my wallet and slid it in the crack just above the latch. As I was working the bolt, Dale came over and pushed me out of the way. He grabbed the knob, and with a sudden jerk the door popped open.

"You'd a been standing there all day with that secret-agent bullshit."

I reached past the door and found a light switch on the wall. The room was no bigger than a walk-in closet. On the left, a metal shelving unit held several cases of canned beer and a few growlers. On the right, a mop and a couple of brooms leaned against the wall next to a plastic tub of cleaning supplies. In the back of the room stood a green gun safe. It was roughly the size of Dale.

I'd seen this safe before, or a similar model, on the Steel Freedom website. It was the type of safe that matched a long silver key with black etchings. The same key Dale had joked about when I first showed him the key ring. It was no longer a joke.

Centered in the safe's door was a large metal wheel, the kind you'd see on a submarine hatch. Above the wheel was a silver key cylinder. It's edges were dented and chipped as if someone had worked it over with a crowbar. And above the cylinder were the words STEEL FREEDOM stenciled in black.

"Serious safes for serious people," I said.

Dale pushed me out of the way, grabbed the wheel, and grunted.

I laughed. "C'mon. Let's see you jerk that open."

Dale struggled with the wheel for a few more seconds, then grabbed the safe in a bear hug. It didn't budge. Dale backed away and pointed down at the concrete floor.

"I think this fucker's bolted to the foundation. It's like Fort fuckin' Knox."

"In more ways than one," I said.

"Whatcha mean?"

"I mean I think that safe's full of gold. Or was full of gold at one point."

Dale seemed unconvinced.

"It makes sense," I said. "If Diana and Cordell were double-crossing Jeff and Becky, this would be the perfect place to hide the gold." I pointed at the safe. "That right there is why everyone was searching for those keys."

"You really think there's gold in there?" Dale asked.

I shook my head. "With Diana missing, I doubt it. She's got the key and has had plenty of time to empty this thing. The gold's long gone by now."

"You still believe Byrd's involved?"

I thought about that for a moment.

"No," I said. "That was a stupid idea. I think Byrd probably has a few skeletons in his closet, but you know him a lot better than I do. If you say he's okay, then I should take your word for it. But in my defense, I never believed Floppy's story about Byrd and your dad stealing the gold."

"Sometimes you ain't as dumb as you look."

That was still up for debate.

"Let's get out of here," I said. "Diana's gone. You go back and tell Byrd everything. If he needs to speak with me, so be it."

We were halfway up the stairs when the doorbell rang. Dale turned around and put his finger to his lips, and I was instantly reminded of the Dark Secret IPA logo. We crept to the top of the steps, and I peered around the corner toward the front door. Though the stained-glass golf hole, I could see a figure. It looked disturbingly familiar.

"Would the sheriff's department be here for any reason?" I whispered.

"Don't think so. Don't nobody know 'bout Diana taking off with them keys but me."

I pushed past Dale and walked over and opened the door. If I could have had a picture of the look on Skeeter's face when he saw me, I'd have had it framed and hung above the fireplace in the cabin.

"What the hell are you doing here?" Skeeter said.

He was dressed in black jeans and a black waffle-knit pullover. I glanced around the doorframe and saw his black Ford Mustang parked in the driveway.

"Off duty?" I said.

Skeeter elbowed me out of the way and muttered, "You really wanna fuck with me?"

That was an invitation the devils couldn't resist. I wrapped my arm around Skeeter's neck and tried to pull him down to the floor. With my bad leg, I needed to get him down to have any kind of advantage. Skeeter struggled, and I increased the pressure. He was starting to sink when Dale rushed over, grabbed my arm, and twisted it around my back. Skeeter caught his breath, then sucker-punched me with a right jab.

I squirmed, and Dale pulled my arm up higher against my back. I was afraid Dale didn't know his own strength and my arm might snap off at the shoulder.

"I'm good, I'm good," I said, but Dale held firm. "Let me go, Dale. I'm cool, okay?"

Dale released my arm and shoved me toward the front door.

"Skeeter, what the fuck are you doing here?" Dale said.

Skeeter pushed out his chest. "I came to check on Diana," he said.

"For what reason?" Dale asked.

Skeeter looked at me, then raised his chin. "Because we've been dating."

"Bullshit," I said.

Dale raised a fist in my direction.

"It's not bullshit," Skeeter said.

Staring at Skeeter's aviators, a thought occurred to me.

"Did she ever mention a big set of keys?" I asked.

Dale turned to me with a puzzled look. I shrugged and said, "It's worth asking. He saw them the day I turned them in."

Dale looked at Skeeter and crossed his arms.

"Why do you want to know?" Skeeter said.

"Just answer the fucking question," Dale said.

It was painful to watch Skeeter's brain try to work out the details. He knew the couple who had come into the sheriff's department looking for a set of keys had been murdered. It couldn't be a coincidence that Diana was also looking for a missing key ring.

"Did she ask you to take the keys from the sheriff's department?" I said.

Skeeter ignored me and took a step toward Dale.

"I don't know what he's talking about," Skeeter said. "He's just trying to stir up shit."

"Diana was using you to get those keys," I said. "You seriously think she liked you?"

"Fuck you," Skeeter yelled. "Why don't you put all your shit in your bicycle basket and ride on back down to Charleston."

I rushed toward Skeeter, but Dale stopped me with his forearm. It was like running into a tree.

Skeeter and I stared at each other, the same way we'd done in the squad room at the sheriff's department. When he flashed me a sly grin, the urge to rearrange his face was so strong my hands started shaking. Dale stepped in front of me and pointed a finger at my face.

"Don't go losing your shit," he said.

Dale grabbed Skeeter by the arm and led him to the door.

"You need to get out of here," Dale said. "And why aren't you in uniform? You ain't off today. Ain't nobody off until we solve them murders."

Skeeter didn't bother answering. He jogged to his Mustang, hopped in, and then laid a long patch of rubber on Country Club Drive.

Dale looked over at me and shook his head. "I told you. Young, dumb, and full of cum."

* * *

Back in Dale's patrol car, I couldn't help but feel I'd missed something. It was the same feeling I'd had when going through the brewery pictures on Facebook. I thought hard, but the angel and devils were quiet. I wondered if they'd decided to take the rest of the day off.

"What did Skeeter say back there?" I asked. "He said something important, but I can't put my finger on it."

"I don't know," Dale said. "Told us he's dating Diana."

I nodded. "Diana's pretty persuasive, right? I mean, she has a way of leading people into directions they may not normally go."

"She certainly led your dumb ass to nowhere."

"Exactly. So I'm wondering where she led Skeeter."

Dale smirked. "You really got a hard-on for him, don't ya?"

"I don't think Diana would date a guy like Skeeter."

"Well, you said she's involved with that Cordell fucker, so her taste can't be that great."

I hated being in a list that included a murdered petty thief and an asshole in aviators.

"Diana's a user," I said. "She was using Cordell. And me. And Skeeter."

Dale nodded, then fiddled with the stereo. A few seconds later Judas Priest's "Breaking the Law" was blaring from the patrol car's speakers. It was the same song I'd played when Skeeter pulled me over. I glanced at Dale. He just looked forward and grinned. I couldn't help but grin too.

Dale pushed the patrol car to nearly eighty as we snaked up 276 toward Cruso. When the song's chorus hit, he turned up the volume, and we both nodded our heads in unison to the repetitive guitar riff. The song was simple but catchy as hell. I thought back to how it had been one of my favorite songs when I was in middle school. I drove my parents crazy with it. It was the first track on the album *British Steel*, and I spun it repeatedly on the old Panasonic record player that sat on top of the dresser in my room. Above the dresser, a poster of the band was thumbtacked to the wall. The poster showed Rob Halford, the band's lead singer, outfitted from head to toe in studded leather. He was sitting on a shiny black motorcycle with his leather-gloved fist raised in defiance. Next to him, the band's two guitar players held their instruments as if they were machine guns, firing an arsenal of heavy metal out into my bedroom. At that age I thought Judas Priest was the coolest band in the world and that Rob Halford was the toughest singer to have ever lived. Many years later Halford came out of the closet and announced he was gay. Heavy-metal fans were completely shocked when they heard the news. Halford was shocked that everyone else was shocked. I was surprised too, but then I thought back to his tight, studded-leather outfits and over-the-top machismo. Of course he was gay; it was clear as a bell. Sometimes it's easy to miss the obvious.

"Did you know he was gay?" Dale said, as if he'd read my thoughts. "I mean, that man coulda had more pussy than me and you if we lived ten lifetimes. Who'd a guessed it? Riding out onstage on that big ole Harley looking like a total badass, and the man's as gay as a tangerine."

I nodded, and Dale started laughing.

"Now you, I would've guessed," he said. "Riding that bike with the little basket on the front. You looked cute as all get-out."

Basket. The word was a spike drilled straight into my brain. It was the word my unconscious had locked on to, then held just out of reach.

I turned down the stereo, and Dale frowned.

"You told Skeeter about me crashing that bike into the ditch, right?" I asked.

"Yeah, I told everybody in the department that day, 'cause it was funny as shit."

"Okay, but did you say that the bike had a basket?"

Dale squinted his eyes and eased off the accelerator.

"Back at Diana's, he said, 'You should put your shit in your basket and ride back to Charleston.' "

Dale squeezed the steering wheel as if he were trying to pull it off the column.

"If you didn't tell him, then how did he know?" I asked.

It came to me in a flurry, and I laid it all out for Dale as we drove. Diana was in financial straits, with her debt looming and the bank squeezing her for the loan repayment. She couldn't wait for Cordell and Jeff and Becky to divide the gold; she needed it immediately. She latched on to Skeeter, probably nibbled his ear, and sent him after Cordell and the keys. But Skeeter's a hothead, and he fights with Cordell. The keys come off on the trail, and then Skeeter chases Cordell all the way to Graveyard Fields and kills him. With the keys missing, Skeeter heads to Cordell's house and confronts Jeff and Becky. He shoots them but still comes away empty-handed. Then Diana discovers I've found the keys, and she starts working me. She lucks out when Floppy turns up with them, and then she takes off. She empties the safe and disappears.

Dale nodded. "And then Skeeter shows up at her house, ready to disappear with her. That's why he weren't in uniform."

"Yup," I said. "But Diana screwed him over just like everyone else."

We were silent for a few moments, and then Dale smacked his fist on the dash. "Skeeter searched the cabin. He's the one Byrd sent up there when you was locked up at the station."

I couldn't help but laugh. Skeeter and Diana had set me up. And now that Diana had the keys and the gold, Byrd would probably get an anonymous tip about the murders. Then the cabin would be searched again.

"You know at this point there's probably a nine-millimeter hidden somewhere in the cabin, right?"

Dale nodded. "Yup. And if he's smart, he'd a put Cordell's cell phone there along with it. Tie you up real nice." Dale huffed, then shook his head. "But shit. I gotta be real careful about this. It all fits, but goddamn, it's messy. I can't go telling Byrd one of his men killed three people on account he's pussy-whipped."

We drove in silence for a few minutes. Finally Dale spoke.

"Okay, here it is. I'm gonna drop you off at the cabin to get your vehicle, then you go to Daddy's and stay put. I'll go talk to Byrd, but he ain't gonna like what I got to say. Then I'm gonna have to tell him about this Perry shit too. I shoulda never rented you that cabin. You ain't been nothing but a world of trouble."

"When I first called you about the cabin, you said you knew how to handle trouble."

Dale responded to that with a look of pure contempt.

"What do you think Byrd will do?" I asked.

Dale thought for a moment. "First he'll pull in Skeeter and have a come-to-Jesus with him. If Skeeter lies, Byrd'll catch it. As far as the Perry shit goes, I don't know. I guess he'll call his buddy down in Charleston."

We were five minutes away from the cabin when I pointed to the stereo and asked Dale if he had an appropriate song for the situation. He kept one hand on the wheel while scrolling on his phone. When "Welcome to the Jungle" started up, I nodded approvingly.

39

Dale was still seething when we pulled onto the dirt road that led up to the cabin. I was seething too. Skeeter was guilty of much more than just keying my car and being an all-around asshole. And as much as I wanted to wrap my hands around his throat, I'd now have to let Byrd deal with him. I was also going to have to let Byrd deal with Charleston. I hoped his buddy Emory was on the level and not part of whatever Perry and Greg had going. Crossing my fingers was about all I could do.

As we ascended the dirt road, Dale gave me my orders: "Don't go in the cabin. If there's evidence in there, you don't need to touch it and I don't need to find it. Just get in your vehicle and follow me to Daddy's. Got it?"

I nodded reluctantly. I'd been proactive enough for the day, and I wanted my pills. But what the hell. I could sit at Junebug's and get numb off Dale's beer stash.

When we pulled into the clearing, Dale slammed on the brakes, and my chest pressed hard against the seat belt.

We both stared forward for a moment without saying a word. When Dale reached down and put the car in reverse, I grabbed his arm.

"Hold on," I said. "We don't know what's going on here."

Dale bristled. "The fuck we don't! I'm backing down the road and calling Byrd."

I looked at the gray Audi parked next to my Mercedes.

At least Perry was making himself known rather than sneaking in during the middle of the night to slit my throat. Although maybe not seeing it coming would have been better.

"Look," I said. "I could be wrong about everything. I could be wrong about Skeeter and Diana, and I could be wrong about Perry too. I saw a car like his that night at the storage unit, but that doesn't mean it was his car. And even if it was, it doesn't mean he's the one who shot me. And if it wasn't him, I need him on my side. So before you go calling in the cavalry, let me talk to him and see what's what."

"So you're going up there to have a talk with the man who might have shot you while I wait here in the fucking car?"

I nodded.

"You're gonna get yourself killed, that's what's gonna happen. And then I ain't never gonna be able to rent this cabin 'cause of people worried about ghosts and shit."

I smiled. "I love ya, buddy."

Dale snorted. "Get out 'fore I shoot you myself."

When I opened the door, Dale grabbed my arm.

"Hang on," he said. "You think this Perry man's got something to do with Skeeter?"

It was an interesting thought. But the idea of Perry and Skeeter being connected seemed pretty farfetched, even for Cruso.

"No. Now give me fifteen minutes. If I'm not back by then, call for backup."

Dale filled his mouth with tobacco. "You've got ten."

*   *   *

As I walked around to the back of the cabin, I scanned the trees, just in case Perry was hiding behind one. But all I saw were a few squirrels scampering over the fallen leaves like furry little psychos.

I stopped at the door and looked through the panes of glass. Perry was sitting at the kitchen table. Had I forgotten to lock the door earlier, or had Perry picked the lock? It wouldn't be difficult for someone like him.

When Perry noticed me, he nodded and smiled. I pushed the door open and stepped inside. Then everything went dark.

40

When I opened my eyes, I was facedown on the linoleum floor. It was a good thing I'd mopped it after spewing my Mexican buffet across the kitchen. My jaw felt like I'd been worked over by a Confederate Army dentist, and my mouth was coated with the metallic taste of blood.

I was about to roll over when a sharp pain shot through my side. I buckled and curled up like a baby at nap time. The second kick caught me in the stomach. I spit blood on the floor, then put my hands over my face. The third kick almost pushed my palms through my cheeks.

"That's enough," I heard Perry shout.

I lowered my hands and opened my eyes. Greg was standing over me.

* * *

A few moments later I was sitting at the table wiping my mouth on a bloody shirt sleeve. Perry was across from me and Greg was leaning against the refrigerator. They were both wearing gloves.

So much for that last bit of hope that Perry was innocent.

I looked at Greg and smiled.

"You're pretty feisty for a guy in a coma."

Greg didn't answer, so I turned to Perry.

"I'm sorry about all of this," he said. "I really thought I could keep you out of it, but things have changed."

I couldn't believe I was looking at the man I had trusted for so long. Diana's betrayal was nothing compared to Perry's. I'd known her for only a couple of days before stumbling across her web of lies. It made sense that she could fool me during such a short time. But Perry was someone I'd cared about for years, and now he was almost unrecognizable. He looked the same, but he was not the man I'd once known. He was like a loving father suddenly lost in the wilderness of dementia, and I wanted to shake him until he changed back into the man I could depend on.

"Yeah, I'd say things have changed," I said. "I don't even know who you are anymore."

Perry nodded. "I could have killed you in that storage unit," he said. "But I shot you in the leg and made sure you made it to the hospital."

I laughed. "Oh, is that supposed to make me feel better?"

Perry stared at me blankly. He looked tired, almost defeated.

"So, how long have you been running your game?" I asked.

Perry didn't answer, so I kept going.

"Just so I have this straight, Greg was never in a coma, right? Was that just a ruse to keep me scared and keep me quiet? And what did you guys tell Laura? That it was my storage unit?"

I could imagine Greg telling Laura that he'd discovered I was into some shady business. He'd probably told her he'd lured me to my own storage unit to confront me but that once we were there, things took a nasty turn. I'd lost my temper and beat Greg, and then some dealer or junkie I'd been associating with had shown up and shot me. No wonder Laura had told me to stay away.

Perry sighed. "Like I said, things have changed."

At that, Greg walked over to the other side of the kitchen and picked up a small duffel bag from the floor. He unzipped it and pulled out a long length of rope.

"Where do you want to do this?" he said.

Perry sighed again, then stood up and moved behind me. I looked at my watch. I'd been inside the cabin close to ten minutes. If Dale was going to storm in with guns ablaze, he was going to have to hurry.

"C'mon, Davis, stand up," Perry said.

I hesitated for a moment, then felt the barrel of a gun press against the back of my head. I slowly rose to my feet, and Perry led me across the kitchen. When we reached the door to the basement, Greg opened it and descended the stairs. Perry gave me a gentle push with the gun barrel, and soon all three of us were standing in the damp chill of my brewery.

I watched as Greg threw an end of the rope over one of the thick wooden beams that ran along the basement's ceiling. He then looped the other end around itself and tied it off.

"A rope and a rafter," he said. "I told you that was what you needed."

Greg formed a noose while Perry held the gun to my head.

"Am I killing myself out of guilt?" I asked.

"You couldn't stand the pressure," Greg said.

"Davis." The voice came from the kitchen.

Greg glanced upward, then dropped the rope and pulled a gun from his coat pocket.

Perry put his mouth to my ear. "Don't move. Don't speak."

I heard Dale's heavy footsteps cross the kitchen floor. Perry pushed me underneath the stairs, and Greg joined us in a tight huddle. A moment later I heard the basement door open and the top step squeak under Dale's weight.

I didn't know what to do. If I yelled, Perry would put a bullet in my head, but if I didn't, Greg would grab Dale at the bottom step and turn this into a murder/suicide. The angel and devils were silent, and my temper had been frightened into submission. I was paralyzed.

I could tell Dale was trying to tiptoe down the stairs, but each step groaned as he descended. When he stepped onto the dirt floor, his back was to us. Greg jumped out from the behind the stairs and pressed his gun between Dale's shoulder blades.

"Drop it," Greg said.

Dale growled and dropped his service weapon onto the floor. Greg kicked it away, then pushed Dale against the cinder-block wall face first.

Perry exhaled, and his breath smelled like sour milk. "Go stand next to him," he said to me. "Face the wall."

I limped over to Dale and pressed my nose against the cold concrete. "Sorry," I whispered.

When he didn't answer, I turned to him. He looked like he was in the middle of passing a kidney stone.

"So what now?" I yelled.

Perry's fatigue was turning into frustration. "Just shut up, Davis," he said.

I could hear the rope being pulled across the wooden beam. I figured the murder/suicide idea was now Perry and Greg's official plan. I'd be found swinging from the ceiling, and Dale would be lying on the dirt floor with a bullet in his skull. I wondered if Byrd would think I had killed Dale in a fit of anger when he'd tried to stop me from ending it all. Then Byrd would search the cabin and find the evidence Skeeter had probably hidden. I'd be guilty of four murders. Five if I counted myself. Not too bad for a guy who could hardly summon the courage to eat a full meal.

My thoughts were interrupted by a low rumbling noise coming from outside the cabin. At first I thought the cavalry had finally arrived, but the sound was oddly familiar, like a bulldozer running at full throttle. It grew louder and louder until it seemed it would bust through the cinderblock wall. Then all the sudden it stopped.

"Who is that?" Perry said.

I didn't answer, even though I knew exactly who it was.

"Fucking shit," Dale said.

Perry ran over and shoved his gun into Dale's back. "Who's out there?"

"It's my cousin," Dale said through clenched teeth.

"Is he armed?"

I whispered into the wall. "Only with his mouth and a multitool."

"Neither of you move," Perry said.

I twisted my head around and saw Perry and Greg take a position under the steps. Perry noticed me and pointed the gun in my direction.

Upstairs I heard a knock at the door, followed by the sound of footsteps across the linoleum floor.

"Hey! Anybody here?" Floppy yelled.

The footsteps continued through the kitchen and on into the living room. Perry's eyes followed the sound across the basement ceiling. I listened to Floppy make his way through the house, hoping he wouldn't check the basement. I didn't need to be guilty of another murder.

Soon I heard the basement door open and Floppy hopping down the stairs. When he reached the dirt floor, I turned my head to face him. He stared at me as if I had just asked him the square root of his zip code. He looked over at Dale, who was still facing the wall, then back at me.

"Y'all playin' a game?" he said.

Over Floppy's shoulder I saw Perry and Greg moving forward from under the steps. Greg came up behind Floppy and put the barrel of his gun to the base of Floppy's skull.

"Do you have a weapon?" Greg said.

What happened next was a blur. In one fluid motion Floppy spun around on his good leg and raised his elbow as if it were a battering ram. The force knocked the gun out of Greg's hand, and it scurried across the floor into a dark corner of the basement. Floppy then spun back in the opposite direction, striking Greg in the throat with the edge of his open hand. As Greg staggered backward, Floppy chopped his neck again. Perry slipped around Greg and raised his weapon. Floppy jabbed his arms toward Perry, then scissored his hands around Perry's wrist. A second later Floppy was holding Perry's gun. I glanced at Greg, who was facedown on the floor.

Dale rushed over and put his boot on Greg's back. I heard a grunt and saw Perry throw a jab at Floppy's face. Floppy dipped to the side, then grabbed Perry's arm and twisted it behind his back. Perry howled in pain. Floppy threw an arm around Perry's neck and squeezed. Perry stared directly at me. His eyes were wide and frantic. Then they closed, and Perry went limp. Floppy released the pressure, and Perry fell to the floor next to Greg. Floppy handed Perry's gun to Dale, then casually hopped over to me.

"Who are those guys?" he said.

41

Ten minutes later two deputies arrived. Dale had called for backup before coming in to look for me, but I doubted they would have shown up in time to save us. I guessed I owed Floppy my life. Dale did too. I was grateful, but I knew it would burn Dale's ass for years to come.

The deputies were followed by four volunteer EMTs. Greg and Perry were still out cold. After checking vital signs, the EMTs put both men on orange folding stretchers, then hauled them up the steps.

The deputies bagged Perry's and Greg's guns along with the rope. They chatted with Dale for a few minutes, then went upstairs to wait for Sheriff Byrd.

Floppy stood by my brewing setup and examined the equipment. When I saw him slip my hydrometer into his pocket, I walked over and put my hand on his shoulder.

"I'm glad you showed up when you did," I said.

Floppy shrugged and picked up an empty growler.

"You can pay me back with some beer," he said. "But good beer, not that pinecone stuff. You know, my granddaddy used to make 'shine way back when, and he said good 'shine was as hard to make as French wine. Now, I don't drink wine, 'cause it makes my head hurt real bad, but one time a buddy gave me some dandelion wine, and I tell you what, that stuff was real good."

Dale walked over to us and slapped Floppy on the back of the head. "Go upstairs and bother Mike and Earl."

"You ain't the boss of me," Floppy yelled.

I put out my hand. Floppy stared at it for a moment, then shook it firmly.

"Thank you," I said.

Floppy sneered at Dale. "I'm going upstairs on my own volition. I don't want to be near you no more."

Floppy turned to leave, then hesitated for a moment before turning back around. He reached in his pocket and pulled out my hydrometer.

"I don't need this," he said.

* * *

When Floppy was gone, Dale filled his mouth with tobacco, then jabbed a stained finger in my face.

"You almost got both of us killed," he said.

I sat down on the bottom step and looked up at the beam I would have been hanging from had Floppy not arrived just in time to turn the basement into a dojo. I thought about Laura and what her reaction would have been to my "suicide." I guessed it would have depended on the story Greg and Perry fed her. Although, based on my past history, I doubted she would have been shocked.

"Them dudes is lucky Floppy showed up," Dale said. " 'Cause I woulda ended up killing 'em both."

I rolled my eyes.

"Yep. Good thing. Now let's focus on the other problem at hand. Somewhere in this cabin there's probably evidence that implicates me in three murders."

Dale spit on the dirt floor.

"Don't do that," I yelled. "This is my brewery."

Dale kicked some dirt over the small puddle of tobacco juice, then glanced over at the piece of plywood leaning against the wall.

"That wouldn't be a bad hiding place."

I nodded. "It's where I hid beer from you."

Dale gave me the finger, then grabbed the sides of the plywood. He slid it along the wall, revealing a white plastic bag, tied at the top, with the words *Thank You* written in red on the side.

"I doubt that's full of guacamole," I said.

Dale opened a pouch on his duty belt and removed a pair of surgical gloves. He stretched them over his hands, then carefully untied the bag. I walked over and stood next to him.

The bag contained a nine-millimeter handgun, a cell phone, and a small resealable baggie filled to the brim with white, bar-shaped pills. The devils took notice: Xanax, 2 mg.

Dale exhaled sharply. "These ain't Tylenols."

I shook my head in confusion. I'd been expecting the gun and the phone, but the baggie of pills threw a wrench in my theory. "Where would Skeeter get those pills?"

Dale thought for a moment, then began nodding his head as if all the gears in his brain were finally turning in unison. He held up the baggie and smiled. "This is the gold."

The gears in my head creaked and groaned. Drugs? Was that what everyone had been searching for?

"I see it like this," Dale said. "Them hippies were all dealing, and maybe Diana was too. She latches on to Skeeter for, I don't know, maybe protection, or to have an in with the department, and then things turn sour and he takes out Cordell and that couple."

Dale was onto something. He'd said himself that Skeeter acted like judge, jury, and executioner. If he'd known Cordell and Jeff and Becky were dealing, he'd have thought killing them was justified, especially if he'd felt they were somehow a threat to Diana. I'd thought he'd killed them over gold, but drugs was much more likely.

"So Skeeter kills them and then confiscates the drugs," I said. "He wouldn't sell them, because in his mind that would be wrong. So he dumps them in the bag with the other evidence and plants the bag here."

Dale nodded.

"Skeeter must have taken the pills off Cordell when he killed him," I said. "Jeff and Becky and Diana thought the pills were locked in the safe, and that's why they were searching for the keys."

Dale nodded again. "That fits," he said.

It did fit, but it didn't fully explain Diana's involvement. If she thought drugs were in her safe, she was either after them to get them off her property or she was planning on selling them to get the bank off her back. But the drugs weren't in her safe. They were in my basement. What had she done when she discovered the safe empty? Where had she gone? It didn't make sense. Unless . . .

"There are more drugs," I said. "A lot more."

Dale lowered his eyebrows. "Why do you think that?"

I pointed to the baggie. "How many pills would you guess are in there? Three hundred? Four hundred?"

Dale shrugged.

"Let's say it's five hundred," I said. "Even then that baggie's only worth, what, twenty-five hundred dollars? I find it hard to believe that Diana and Jeff and Becky were going crazy for that amount of money."

"I've seen people go crazy for less," Dale said.

"But that's a drop in the bucket compared to what Diana owes the bank."

I thought about the storage unit and the cases of drugs and cash I'd discovered. Dealing pills is like running a dollar store—it takes a lot of individual sales to make a decent profit. Based on what I'd seen, Greg and Perry had probably been making an extra six to eight grand a month with their game. Not enough to retire to the islands with but enough to buy some toys. To make any real money with pills, you needed to be high up the ladder. The pill business is like those cosmetics companies that recruit people to sell lipstick and eyeliner to their friends. Those friends then beginning selling to other friends, who begin selling to an even wider group of friends. It's a cash-based pyramid scheme.

The pill business also depends on the product line. In Charleston I could buy Xanax off the street for as little as four or five bucks a piece. But that was a pain in the ass and put me in contact with people I'd rather not associate with. That's why I used the good Dr. Landry. The prescriptions he wrote and the pharmacies that filled them were legit. Now, whether it was completely ethical, or even legal, was a gray area. Either way, it was a lot easier than making a deal on a dark corner in a neighborhood I'd rather not be in. But other pills were different. Opioids, like OxyContin, Vicodin, and Percocet—those could fetch up to eighty bucks a pill on the street, partly because they were much more powerful and much more in demand. If the baggie in my basement had been filled with any of those pills, the stakes would be much higher. There had to be more pills out there somewhere. Enough to make Diana and Jeff and Becky desperate.

"When I had lunch with Byrd, he told me prescription drugs weren't a problem around here," I said. "Is he right? 'Cause I thought it was a problem just about everywhere, especially in small towns."

Dale put the baggie of pills back into the plastic bag sitting on the dirt floor.

"Well, it's around but I wouldn't go so far as to call it a problem," Dale said. "I mean, hell, I'll bust a kid every now and then and find he's got one or two of his granny's cancer pills on him, Oxy and shit like that. Or sometimes a dude'll get hurt at work and have a hard time weaning hisself off his pain meds and start looking for other ways to get 'em. But ain't no one trafficking that shit around here. If they are, it's small-time. Like smaller-than-your-dick small."

I started to speak, but Dale cut me off. "But every now and again we'll hear rumors about them bikers that come through. You know, for them rallies up in Maggie Valley? They come up from Atlanta or Charlotte or down from Knoxville, and they's always talk about trades taking place. But so far it's just been talk. We ain't never found nothing. Well, not more than a few ounces of pot here and there."

ZZ Top's "Beer Drinkers & Hell Raisers" started playing in my head.

I reminded Dale of Diana's "overprotective friends."

"What if they were there to pressure her?" I said. "What if Cordell had made a deal with them but then Cordell, and his keys, disappeared?"

Dale cranked up his nodding routine. "A deal gone wrong," he said.

"Exactly. So the bikers are out their cash, or their product, and it's all sitting in a safe that, without the key, would have to be dynamited to open."

Dale grabbed an empty growler off the brewing table and used it as a spittoon. "I'd hate to say it, but I'd rather this'd been about gold."

"Me too. But we've got to find Diana. She's had plenty of time to open the safe and hand over whatever was in it, and she's still missing. That's another reason I think there's a lot more to this."

I tried to imagine the possible scenarios. Even if Diana had given the bikers what they were after, it didn't necessarily mean she was safe. And that was assuming the keys led to what they were after. Plus, Skeeter was still roaming around looking for Diana. No matter how I connected the dots, I couldn't draw a picture that showed her out of danger.

I looked at my watch. "Where the hell is Byrd?"

"He's probably talking to his buddy down in Charleston. He'll want to get that shit straight 'fore he comes up here and talks to us."

I kicked the dirt floor, sending up a small cloud of red dust.

"Call him," I said. "Tell him about Skeeter. Tell him to bring him in. I don't want Skeeter finding Diana before we do."

Dale huffed for a few moments, then pulled out his phone and made the call. When Byrd answered, Dale used his official voice to tell him our theory about Skeeter, including the bag of evidence we'd found in the basement. When he finished speaking, he listened intently to Byrd's response, which I couldn't hear. After a minute Dale said, "Yes, sir," then ended the call.

Dale paced around the basement for a minute before he walked over to me.

"He wants me to bring you in."

A moment later Dale's radio crackled. The dispatcher was female, and in a sweet southern twang, she said, "All stations, all units, be advised. Suspicious situation. Be on the lookout for a black 2015 Ford Mustang. Registration Lima, Alpha, Whiskey, Mary, Alpha, Nora, Niner, Two."

The dispatcher then gave Skeeter's description. I was disappointed when she didn't mention the aviators.

"Well. There ya go," Dale said.

"His license plate is Lawman92?"

Dale shrugged, then picked up the plastic bag. "C'mon, let's go talk to Byrd."

We went upstairs and found Floppy sitting at the kitchen table. He had a glass of beer in his hand, and I knew from the color it was my IPA. I was too tired to be angry.

"Was that BOLO for Skeeter?" Floppy said. "When Mike and Earl heard that, they ran outa here like their momma'd called them to dinner. Hey, do you have any other beer? This beer ain't very good. I think it's gone bad."

Dale grabbed the beer out of Floppy's hand and finished it in one long gulp.

Floppy pointed a finger at Dale. "He don't care if beer's bad. He'd drink a quart of turpentine if he thought he could get a buzz off it."

"Follow us to town," Dale said. "Davis and me have to talk to Byrd, and you've got to give a statement about your Bruce Lee bullshit."

* * *

The three of us walked past Perry's Audi on the way to Dale's patrol car. The devils suggested picking up a piece of gravel from the driveway and scratching it down the side of the vehicle, but then the angel perked up and mumbled something about futility, so I kept walking.

Floppy cranked up Sally while Dale put the bag of evidence in the trunk of the patrol car. Soon we were barreling down the driveway with Floppy right on our tail. I hoped Dale and Floppy weren't planning on racing to the sheriff's office. The last thing I needed was a family-feud sprint through the winding roads of Cruso.

We were almost to 276 when Dale's phone chimed. He slammed on the brakes, and Floppy nearly smashed into the back of us. Dale pulled out his phone and gazed at it as if it were a puzzle.

"What the fuck is this?" he said, handing the phone to me.

I looked at the screen and immediately recognized the app as the phone's "I'm Here" service. The app allows you to let your friends know where you are for a set amount of time. You simply select someone in your contact list, tap I'M HERE, and then that person is alerted with a map and a blinking red dot showing your exact location. I'd mentioned the app to Laura when she first started questioning Greg's late-night disappearances. The only problem was, you couldn't see someone's location unless they chose to share it, which Greg was not prone to do. But now someone had volunteered to let Dale know where they were.

The blinking red dot on Dale's phone was surrounded by light green, which designated a park area. There were no other markings or location indicators on the screen; it was as if the dot were in the middle of nowhere. I zoomed out on the map until a squiggly white line with the words BLUE RIDGE PARKWAY appeared. In the middle of the line, and directly below the red dot, was a green icon designating a hiking trail. I recognized the location: Graveyard Fields.

I scrolled back to the red dot and tapped it. A phone number appeared. I showed the screen to Dale.

"Do you recognize this number?"

Dale squinted, then shook his head.

"Someone's letting you know they're at Graveyard Fields," I said. "Whose number is this? It's not someone in your contact list. If it was, their name would show instead of the number."

"Beats the fuck outa me," Dale said.

I opened the phone app and scrolled through Dale's recent calls. It didn't take long to find the number; Dale had received a call from it the previous day. I tapped the info icon next to the number to see the details. The call had been received at 3:35 and had lasted two minutes.

"Where were you yesterday at three thirty?" I asked.

Dale scrunched his face and looked out the window. After a moment he said, "I was at the impound lot, where they'd towed that BMW and Land Rover. Then you called me and told me to come to the cabin 'cause you had the keys."

A chill struck the back of my neck and traveled down my spine.

"It's Diana," I said. "I called you from her phone, remember?"

Dale's response was drowned out by the roar of Sally's engine. It seemed Floppy was getting impatient.

As the sound died, Dale grabbed the phone out of my hand and pushed the patrol car forward. When we came to the highway, he stopped and looked both ways.

"You know what we need to do," I said.

Dale grunted. "You heard the BOLO. Everybody's out looking for Skeeter right now; that's all that needs to be done. We're going to go talk to Byrd."

I looked both ways as well. To the left was Byrd's office and god knows what kind of waste-of-time questioning. To the right were Diana and some answers.

I stared at Dale. I could tell he was torn.

"It's up to you, brother," I said.

Dale smacked the steering wheel, then gunned the accelerator and turned right. I buckled my seat belt.

42

The next fifteen minutes was an experiment in how not to puke. Dale drove so fast I worried the windshield would shake loose and fly back into our faces. In the curves he used both lanes of the road to straighten the path, and I knew that if we met an oncoming vehicle, it would be the end of everyone involved. I dared not look behind us but could hear Sally's engine roaring so loud that it sounded like it was mounted in Dale's trunk.

When we reached the parkway, Dale ignored the stop sign and spun the patrol car to the left. The rear of the vehicle fishtailed, and Dale corrected by spinning the steering wheel clockwise. When we straightened out, Dale stomped on the accelerator, and we zoomed past the Cold Mountain overlook like a Blue Angel passing over the Super Bowl.

"Why'd she send me her location?" Dale yelled over the sound of the engine.

I pushed my feet into the floorboard.

"Don't talk to me," I screamed.

*   *   *

Dale finally slowed down as we approached the Graveyard Fields parking lot. When we pulled in, I saw what I had been dreading: Diana's Mercedes parked next to three motorcycles. There were no other vehicles in the lot.

Dale killed the engine as Floppy whipped Sally in next to us. We all stepped out onto the pavement and stared at one another.

"What're we doing here?" Floppy asked.

"Remember that woman who ran off with the keys?" I said. "Well, she's out here somewhere." I pointed toward the motorcycles. "And she's in danger."

For once, Floppy didn't speak. He simply nodded his head as if he understood the situation perfectly.

Dale popped open the trunk of the patrol car, reached in, and removed a shotgun and a box of shells. He flipped the gun over and placed the butt of the stock against his hip. He shoved five shells into the loading flap, flipped the gun back over, and then tossed it to Floppy, who caught the weapon with one hand.

I looked at Dale. "Can you do that?"

"I just did," he replied.

*　*　*

The three of us walked across the parking lot to the stone steps that led down to the trailhead. I was still in pain. Greg had worked me over pretty good in the kitchen, and even though my adrenaline was pumping, I didn't know how far I could make it on a rough trail. My condition must have been obvious.

"You wait here," Dale said. "Floppy and me can take care of this."

The angel and devils were in a heated debate, arguing between the options of sitting comfortably in the patrol car and powering through the pain and finding Diana. The angel finally cast the deciding vote.

"I'm coming with you," I said.

Floppy started hopping down the steps while Dale shoved my chest.

"Bullshit," he said. "Floppy can take care of hisself, but you won't make it fifty yards."

I had an idea, but I didn't like it. I knew Dale wouldn't like it either.

"Carry me down the steps, and then I'll be okay," I said.

I thought Dale was going to explode. He stomped his feet and spun around. "Go sit in the fucking car," he said.

I moved behind Dale. "C'mon," I said. "Let me hop on your back."

Dale stomped again. "We're wasting time," he yelled.

I looked down the steps and saw Floppy drag himself around a curve of the trail and out of sight.

"Floppy's going to be the hero again," I said.

Dale snorted, then squatted down as if he were ready to play a game of leapfrog. I pushed off with my good leg but didn't rise more than four inches off the ground. My chest slammed into Dale's back, and I slowly slid down onto the pavement.

"Bend down farther," I said.

Dale turned and gave me a death stare. I grinned. He turned back around, then grunted and bent down onto one knee.

"Is that low enough, motherfucker?" he screamed.

I straddled Dale's back, and he wrapped his arms around my legs. As he pushed himself up, I slung my arms around his neck.

"Not so tight, asshole."

A moment later we were descending the stone steps toward the trail-head. I felt like a kid on vacation, riding on my dad's back so I wouldn't tire out and throw a tantrum.

When we reached the bottom of the steps, Dale stopped, and I slid down to my feet. The trail wound through a stand of thick laurel bushes. We moved forward quickly, Dale in the lead. We'd gone about thirty yards when we came to a long set of wooden steps that snaked down through the trees.

"Goddammit," Dale said, taking a knee.

As we descended the steps, Dale turned his head in my direction.

"I ain't carryin' you back up these fuckers, I'll tell you that right now."

The steps ended at wooden bridge that spanned a small creek. I dropped down and followed Dale across the bridge to a dirt trail. We walked a few hundred feet to a point where the trail forked. Floppy was there waiting.

"Which way?" he asked.

Dale pulled out his phone and handed it to me. The red dot was in the same position as earlier. Since the map was designed for driving directions, it didn't show hiking trails or unmarked roads. The dot was just a tiny red beacon surrounded by a sea of green.

"I can't tell anything from this," I said. "She could be anywhere out here."

My adrenaline was being replaced by anxiety. I thought about the pills in my coin pocket. I could take one and try to even things out, but it would slow me down, and I was slow enough already.

"We need to split up," I said. "Floppy, you take that trail. Dale and I will go this way. If you see something, fire off a shot."

Floppy nodded and took off on the trail heading west. Dale and I stared at one another for a moment, then turned and headed east.

The trail was rough and covered in coiled roots that resembled thick, brown snakes. I tried to ignore the pain in my leg. And my chest. And my head.

"What would Diana and them dudes be doin' out here?" Dale asked.

I tried to think of a reasonable explanation, but reasonable didn't seem to hold much sway these days, so I let my mind wander. There was a part of me that still hoped a trunk full of gold was at the heart of the situation. Maybe because I believed gold involved a better clientele. Sure, people killed one another over money, but drugs was a different business. A mean business populated with mean people. Treasure hunting seemed more genteel to me somehow. A gentleman's game. But with three dead bodies, the point was moot.

"I don't know," I said. "Maybe they brought Diana up here to kill her for some reason. Or maybe they're looking for something Cordell left out here."

I thought about the receipt I'd found in the back of Cordell's BMW, the one for the spade and shovel and other landscaping tools. Then I thought about the metal detector I'd seen in the back of the Land Rover. I'd thought Jeff and Becky were using it to hunt for gold, or Cordell's keys, but maybe they were looking for something else altogether.

"Where was Cordell found?" I said.

Dale stopped and looked around, trying to get his bearings.

"Shit, I don't know," he said. "It was dark. Tommy met me by them stone steps and took me to where everybody was. It was a good fifteen-minute walk. It still may be taped off."

Ten minutes passed, and we came to another fork in the trail. Dale took a bandanna out of his back pocket and dabbed a pint of sweat off his forehead.

"This is fucking pointless," he said. "There's miles of these trails. If we do find something, it'll be by accident."

I didn't want to agree, but Dale was right. Looking for Diana at Graveyard Fields was as futile as looking for a set of keys in Floppy's garage.

The shot sounded like a clap of thunder. It came from the west and echoed over us like a sonic boom. Dale shoved the bandanna back in his pocket, then dropped down to one knee. I hopped on his back like a cowboy at a stunt show.

Dale started to run back the way we'd come, but I yelled for him to stop. I'd studied an online map of Graveyard Fields and knew that the trail Floppy had followed looped around in a giant oval.

"Take this fork," I said. "If we're lucky, it'll be quicker than retracing our steps."

Dale grunted, and we took off toward the west.

Every twenty or so yards, Dale grabbed his belt and jerked his pants back up under his belly while I squeezed my legs together to try to shimmy my way higher onto his back.

We'd gone maybe a quarter of a mile when we heard another shot. It was louder than the first, and I knew we were heading in the right direction.

"Motherfucker," Dale yelled.

He stopped and let go of my legs. I slid down onto the ground.

"I can't carry you no more," Dale said. He was out of breath and looked like he might faint. "Stay here. I'll find Floppy."

Before I could argue, Dale unsnapped his holster and drew his service weapon. He nodded at me and then continued on toward the sound of the shots.

I stood still for a moment, then stepped off the trail into a thick stand of trees. I tried to recall the trail map I'd studied. If the main trail looped around in an oval, then maybe I could bisect it and come out near the bridge. If so, I would have a chance at cutting off the bikers if they were heading back toward the parking lot.

I stepped gently through the woods, trying to avoid the roots and small boulders jutting out from piles of fallen leaves. At one point I was forced to backtrack a bit to work around a jumble of thorns that rose from the forest floor and up into the limbs of the surrounding trees.

A few minutes later I stepped out onto the trail. I looked around and calculated I was probably five minutes or less from the bridge. I headed west at full speed, which was probably no more than two miles per hour. My leg felt like a hollow log full of fire ants.

As I approached the fork near the bridge, I saw a glint of light flash through the trees, as if someone were holding a tiny mirror and angling it toward the sun to signal for help. A few seconds later I heard voices, and I jumped off the trail and ducked down into a thicket of brush.

I pushed some of the limbs aside and saw Diana walking quickly down the trail. ZZ Top was next to her, holding her arm. The two other bikers followed closely behind. Both were carrying metal chests the size of sofa cushions.

When I stepped out of the bushes, the entire group stopped in their tracks. ZZ Top grinned and pulled a handgun from the waist of his jeans. He jerked his head toward the bridge and his buddies headed in that direction, struggling with the weight of the chests.

I raised my hands above my head and dragged myself a few steps toward Diana. ZZ Top stared at me coldly and turned his head slowly from side to side.

"Right there's good," he said.

I stopped but kept my hands held high.

"Let her go," I yelled.

ZZ Top raised the gun, and a second later it jerked in his hand. The bullet flew past me with a whoosh, and I collapsed to the ground. A moment later another shot rang out. I glanced up and saw ZZ Top grab at his shoulder. He then spun to the left and aimed toward the trees. Dale stepped out of the woods with his gun raised. He fired. ZZ Top doubled over, then fell face first onto the trail.

Diana began running in my direction, but Dale ordered her to stop. She froze at a spot twenty or so yards ahead of me.

Dale kept his gun raised as he walked over to ZZ Top, whose arms flailed as if he were trying to swim through the dirt. Dale stepped on the man's wrist, then bent down and pried the gun out of his hand. Dale ejected the magazine and cleared the chamber. He then shoved the gun into his belt, grabbed his radio, and spoke into it. I wondered how long it would take for an ambulance to arrive. I hoped that when it did show, there would be enough EMTs to carry me up all the steps.

I picked myself up and looked toward the bridge. ZZ Top's buddies were standing in the middle of the structure, obviously wondering what to do now that their boss was facedown in the dirt. They looked at Dale for a moment, then at each other. An agreement seemed to pass between them, and they hightailed it toward the parking lot.

They were almost out of sight when a cannon fired. I turned and saw Floppy step out of woods near the spot where Dale had appeared. The barrel of the shotgun was still smoking.

Dale looked at Floppy, then raised a finger and twirled it in a circle like he was ordering another round at a bar. Floppy nodded. Then, simultaneously, they tossed their guns in the air toward one another. The shotgun and the handgun almost collided at the peak of the graceful arc. Dale snatched the shotgun with one hand and Floppy caught the handgun the way a receiver catches a punt.

As Floppy held the gun on ZZ Top, Dale ran across the bridge with the shotgun raised, then disappeared around a curve in the trail.

I felt like an innocent bystander, watching the action safely from the sidelines.

When Dale was out of sight, Diana ran up to me and threw her arms around my neck. She pressed her lips against mine and kissed me passionately. I didn't reciprocate.

"I'm so happy to see you," she said. "I'm sorry I lied to you. I just didn't know what to do."

The devils and the angel all smirked.

A moment later I saw the bikers walking back across the bridge in our direction. They were still carrying the metal chests, but their enthusiasm was greatly diminished. I knew Dale was slow, but even he could catch up to two guys lugging such a heavy load up a steep trail with dozens of steps. Dale appeared a few seconds after the bikers, but something was off. He wasn't carrying the shotgun and his hands were clasped behind his neck. Then Skeeter came into view. He was in uniform, walking a few feet behind Dale, his gun aimed at Dale's back.

I looked at Diana.

"Did you send him your location too?"

When she didn't answer, I limped over to Floppy. He had a gun, but even factoring that out, I felt safer in his presence now that I knew his martial arts skills were legit.

I looked down at ZZ Top. He was no longer moving, and a large pool of blood had collected in the dirt near his midsection. I doubted he would last much longer.

The bikers walked over to us, then stood motionless, holding the chests like valets at a fancy hotel. Floppy glanced at me, and I noticed a sparkle in his eye. I shook my head. Floppy had some impressive moves, but I didn't yet understand the whole situation. The bikers could be armed; Diana could be armed; Skeeter was definitely armed and, like me, was known to have a short fuse.

"Floppy, give her the gun," Skeeter yelled.

Diana strolled up to us and held out her hand.

"I ain't gonna do that," Floppy yelled. "You let Dale go; then we'll talk about all this. Hey, what's in them chests, anyway? You know, I can cut those open with my acetylene setup; it'll cut through just about anything."

Skeeter raised the butt of his gun and brought it down hard on the back of Dale's head. Dale dropped to both knees.

"I'm gonna break your fucking neck," Dale yelled.

Skeeter hovered over Dale and pointed the gun down at his skull.

"Now, Floppy," Skeeter yelled.

I looked at Floppy. "Do what he says."

Floppy hesitated for a moment, then flipped the gun over and held it out. Diana grabbed it and pointed it in our general direction.

"Put down those crates," Skeeter yelled.

The bikers bent down and placed the chests on the ground near ZZ Top. I could now see that the chests were identical. Each was secured with two large padlocks that dangled from thick metal hasps.

"Okay," Skeeter said. "Facedown, hands behind your backs."

The bikers followed the order.

Skeeter yelled for Dale to stand up. When Dale was upright, Skeeter told him to cuff the bikers.

Dale rubbed the back of his head and waddled over to them. He removed a set of cuffs from his duty belt, got down on his knees, and attached the cuffs to one of the biker's wrists. Skeeter walked over and tossed his own cuffs to the ground. Dale picked them up and cuffed the other biker.

Skeeter walked behind Dale and kicked him in the back. Dale grunted and fell onto the dirt.

"You are a dead man," Dale yelled.

Skeeter motioned for Diana. When she walked over to him, he pulled a set of plastic riot cuffs off his duty belt. He handed them to Diana, who nodded and bent down beside Dale.

While Diana secured Dale, Skeeter strolled over. His aviators glistened in the bright sunlight.

Skeeter pointed the gun at Floppy, obviously considering him the greater threat. He was right.

"What's going on, Skeeter?" Floppy asked. "This all don't make no sense."

I wanted Floppy to jerk the gun out of Skeeter's hand the same as he'd done to Perry, but Skeeter was smart enough to stand just out of reach.

Diana walked up and stood next to Skeeter. Behind them Dale and the two bikers lay motionless in the dirt.

Skeeter looked at me and grinned. "It makes perfect sense. I've just stopped a drug deal and caught a man guilty of three murders. Byrd's gonna be impressed."

Floppy scratched his head and looked down at ZZ Top.

"Is he the man killed them three people?"

Skeeter laughed. "Floppy, you are as stupid as you are ugly."

Floppy frowned. "I ain't that stupid. I bet you don't know the capital of Kansas. I know it, but I bet you don't. You probably think it's Kansas City, but that's in Missouri and that's a whole 'nother state altogether. Missouri's capital is Jefferson City. I bet you didn't know that either. But what gets me is why Missouri puts *city* after so many town's names. It's like they's tryin' to convince people that their towns are more than just towns. I mean, we don't do that. They ain't a Waynesville City or a Canton City or a Cruso City or a . . ."

While Floppy babbled, I heard sirens in the distance and wondered who would show up first, the EMTs or a group of deputies who just might believe Skeeter's bullshit story. Of course I was the killer; the evidence was stacked against me. And Dale was obviously my accomplice. He'd been with me that night at Cordell's and he'd been trying all along to throw Byrd off my scent. I wondered if Skeeter would try to throw Floppy under the bus as well.

Floppy droned on about state capitals and geography, but his voice was louder than usual. I was afraid he was going to try to make a move on Skeeter, but then I saw Dale push himself up and creep over behind Skeeter and Diana.

Dale moved faster than I thought he could. He threw a beefy arm around Skeeter's neck and jerked him off the ground. Floppy grabbed Skeeter's arm and pulled the gun from his hand. He then grabbed Diana's wrist and aimed her gun at the sky.

"That's not necessary," she said.

Skeeter's legs jerked wildly as Dale held him a good foot off the dirt. I stepped forward and punched Skeeter's face. The aviators shattered and I finally got a look at his eyes. They were full of fear. A moment later

Skeeter went limp. Dale held him for a few more seconds, then dropped him to the ground.

Floppy took the gun from Diana, then danced a little one-legged jig in the dirt.

"Whoooeeeey," he said. "We've had us a busy day."

43

The EMTs arrived first. They worked on ZZ Top for a while, but it was a lost cause. Looked like Dale now had a second justified killing to his name. I doubted he would lose any sleep over this one either.

Deputies Mike and Earl arrived next, followed by Tommy and a couple of other deputies I recognized from my visits to the sheriff's department. I guessed Byrd was going to be fashionably late.

Since ZZ Top was DOA, the EMTs left him in the dirt for the coroner. They checked Skeeter, who was fine but groggy. He sat with his back against a tree, his wrists and ankles shackled together. A deputy stood close by.

Since there were no lives to save, one of the EMTs took the time to tweeze a few pieces of mirrored glass from my knuckles and wrap my hand in a couple of yards of gauze. I appreciated the attention.

Mike and Earl talked to Floppy and Dale while Tommy and another deputy questioned the two bikers. I wanted to know their story, but Dale had ordered me to stay away from them.

Diana sat on a small boulder near the bridge. I hadn't been ordered to stay away from her, but I wasn't ready to speak to her. I still couldn't figure her out and wasn't in any mood for her bullshit.

Dale had said Diana hadn't attached the riot cuffs to his wrists, that she'd just fiddled with them for a minute and then placed them over his hands.

I wasn't sure if she couldn't figure out how to work them or if she was giving Dale a chance. I figured it was pointless to ask her—she had lied to me too many times.

Dale walked over to Diana and spoke to her for fifteen or so minutes. As they talked, she pulled something out of her jacket pocket that looked like a giant orange cell phone. She held it in front of Dale and pressed some buttons on its face. Dale nodded, then waddled over to the bikers.

Floppy walked over to me.

"Did you see that thing that woman gave Dale?" he said. "Man, I wish I had one of them. I could do all kinds of stuff with that."

"What is it?" I asked. "A GPS?"

"Yessir. Looks like a Garmin Explorer Plus. Them things is accurate as all get-out. It's got topo maps, and you can mark all kinds of way points and places you find that you wanna go back to. That'd be real handy for me. I could use it with my metal detector when I'm out looking for things, then mark where I'd found stuff so I could keep track of where I'd been."

Dale came over to us. He held the GPS up to my face.

"According to Diana, this was what was in her safe. Cordell was dealing, I mean big-time dealing. And he hid his supply in metal chests all around here. He used this to mark the locations."

That connected some dots. But it still didn't explain Diana's involvement.

I jerked my head in her direction. "So what's her part in all this?"

Dale huffed. "She says she was going out with that Cordell dude. And when he found out about her safe, he asked if he could store some of his valuables in it. Gave her some story about his aunt dying and leaving him some jewelry or some such. She wasn't using the safe, so she said okay and gave him the key. Then she says she caught him dealing at the brewery, selling pills to some dudes out back of the kitchen. She claims she had no idea he was into that shit and she dumped him. Then she remembered he'd put some shit in her safe. She started to get real worried about what it was, but he wouldn't come get it or give her the key. She thought it might be drugs and didn't want that shit on her property."

"What about Jeff and Becky?"

Dale nodded. "She says they were Cordell's suppliers, bringing pills over from Banner Elk. When she caught Cordell dealing, he told her the whole story, and he also told her she was tied up in it since they'd all been hanging out together. A threat to keep her mouth shut, I reckon."

I thought of the picture I'd seen of Diana sitting between Cordell and Jeff on the hood of the BMW. I wondered how she could not have known what her friends were up to.

Dale continued the story. Diana had befriended Skeeter at the brewery and asked him to try to get her key back. She couldn't tell him about Cordell's dealing because her safe was probably full of pills. She just told Skeeter that an ex-boyfriend was being an asshole and wouldn't give back her safe key.

"She says she told Skeeter that Cordell could probably be found up here," Dale said. "That he'd gotten into treasure hunting and was looking for gold up near Cold Mountain."

Floppy started to speak, but Dale barked a loud "Hush!"

"So Diana did tell Cordell about the gold Daiquiri had seen," I said. "That's why he went to Floppy's, to snoop around, and that's what eventually led him up here. Then he decides if he can't find treasure, he might as well bury some."

Dale bobbed his head.

"Good a place as any," he said. "Lot safer than hiding it at a house owned by the sheriff."

I pictured Skeeter confronting Cordell at Black Balsam. He had the hots for Diana, and seeing her ex-boyfriend had probably raised his temperature. When Cordell saw a deputy approaching, he most likely had tossed the keys into the bushes. He wouldn't want to be caught with keys that opened chests full of pills. Then Cordell takes off down the trail toward Graveyard Fields. Skeeter finally catches up with him, shoots him, and takes his cell phone.

"She says Skeeter agreed to help but then later told her he couldn't find Cordell," Dale said. "So she told him where he lived and that some buddies of his were staying there with him and that maybe they could help find her key. You know what happened next."

Of course I did. With Cordell missing, Jeff and Becky started searching for the keys and the chests of pills. Then Skeeter went to Cordell's house, confronted Jeff and Becky, and realized the whole thing revolved around drugs. He lost his temper and killed them both. Then I show up snooping around, and he takes a few shots at me for good measure. Then he searches the house, finds a small bag of pills, and decides that since I'm there that night, I'd be the perfect fall guy.

"So what about the bikers?" I asked.

Dale shook his head. "Well, there's where it gets a little sticky. Diana said she'd seen them bikers in the brewery a time or two talking to Cordell. But then when he went missing, they came looking for her. The one with the beard told her he'd made a business arrangement with Cordell. Paid him a lot of money but never got what he paid for. He was looking to her to make it right, one way or another, if you know what I mean."

"So we were on the right track," I said. "Diana figures if she can get into her safe, she can get the pills and get rid of the threat."

"Yep, and when she heard you had the keys, she tapped in to you."

I looked over at Diana. She was sitting on the boulder with her head in her hands. She told a good story, but I was reluctant to believe it.

"Then what?" I said. "She finally finds the keys, opens the safe, and there's nothing in it but a GPS?"

Dale nodded. "That's what she claims. Said once she'd got hold of the keys, she set up a meeting with them bikers. But when she found the GPS, she didn't know what to do. But she figured if Cordell locked it up in her safe, it must be pretty important. So she gave it to them bikers and it led 'em all up here."

I couldn't help but shake my head.

"I know what you're thinking," Dale said. "She coulda known exactly what was in her safe and wanted it for herself. But the only people who know the truth are all dead."

"Skeeter's not dead," I said. "She could've asked him straight out to kill Cordell and Jeff and Becky. She could've told him to plant the evidence to frame me."

Dale filled his mouth with tobacco.

"She burnt you and you're still pissed, I get it," he said. "But if she's lying, Byrd will find out."

Floppy pulled out his multitool and started picking crud out from under his fingernails.

"So what's in them chests?" he said.

*　*　*

When Byrd finally walked across the bridge, all the deputies snapped to attention. Mike and Earl stood tall next to the bikers, while Tommy eyed Diana as if she might make a run for it at any moment. The other two deputies waited next to Skeeter. When Byrd stopped next to the two chests, Dale, Floppy, and I joined him.

"So what do we have here?" Byrd asked.

Dale gave Byrd a brief rundown of what had happened and of the story Diana had told. When he finished, Byrd shook his head and pointed to the chests.

"Let's get these open," he said. "Earl, go get the bolt cutters."

I cleared my throat. "Hold on a minute."

I walked over to Diana and held out my hand. "Give me the keys."

Diana reached in her jacket pocket, then handed me the keys that had ruled my thoughts for the past week. I took them over to Byrd, who accepted them with a frown.

Byrd cycled through the keys, selected one, and then bent down in front of the chests. It took several tries with several keys, but he finally opened all four padlocks and threw the chests open.

I was half hoping to see bars of gold. Shiny bricks looted from Germany, flown halfway across the world and dropped onto the side of Cold Mountain. Instead I saw enough pills to keep me numb for several lifetimes.

44

At one o'clock the next day, I was still in bed, trying to ignore the knocking coming from the back door. After I'd spent a couple of hours at the sheriff's department giving my official statement, Dale had driven me back to the cabin. We'd drunk beer, shot the shit, and listened to Mötley Crüe, Dokken, and Ratt until well after midnight. At which point I swallowed two pills and either went to sleep or passed out.

The knocking was relentless. I put my head under the covers, but it didn't stop. I finally gave up and threw on some clothes.

When I walked into the kitchen, I saw Byrd standing outside the door. I paused for a moment, then asked him in.

Byrd took a seat at the table while I filled the kettle with water.

"I doubt you want some coffee," I said.

Byrd chuckled.

"Actually, I'd like to try some of your beer. Deputy Johnson says it's very good."

I stared at the back of Byrd's head for a few seconds, then took a growler out of the refrigerator and two glasses out of the cabinet. I poured one full for me and one half-full for Byrd.

Byrd held the glass up to the light and examined it. Then he sniffed the beer and finally decided to take a sip.

"Citrusy," he said. "Good amount of hops but not bitter. I'd say this is very balanced."

I lowered my eyebrows. "You're not going to throw the glass against the refrigerator, are you? I've already mopped this floor more times than I care to admit."

Byrd made a noble attempt to smile.

"So what can I do for you, Sheriff?"

Byrd looked around the kitchen like he was a prospective tenant. After a few moments he finally spoke.

"I've seen a lot, son. And most of what I've seen, I've washed away, like dirt off my hands. But after a while it leaves a stain."

That comment didn't need a response, so I waited for Byrd to continue.

"But I never thought I'd see one of my own go so wrong. Louis had a promising future, but he let his demons control him."

Some beer dribbled down my chin.

"Louis? Skeeter's real name is Louis?"

Byrd nodded.

I thought about the text I'd seen on Diana's phone, the one from someone called Louis that said *Thinking about you*. The dumb asshole had it bad.

"One of those demons is named Diana Ross," I said.

Byrd's face sagged like wet laundry on a clothesline. He was exhausted. I figured that after he interviewed me and Dale, he'd spent the rest of the night talking to Diana, Skeeter, and the two bikers, trying to piece together the facts and calculate who was telling the truth and who wasn't.

I knew Byrd was also dealing with the realization that illegal pharmaceuticals were being trafficked right under his nose. It was the one thing he'd sworn would never happen in his county, and he'd helped facilitate it by renting a house to a dealer. That had to sting.

"Louis confessed to the murders," Byrd said. "He was very straightforward with me. He killed Mr. Cordell out of jealousy over the relationship with Ms. Ross. And he killed Mr. and Mrs. Ingram during an argument that transpired when Louis discovered they were bringing opioids and other pharmaceuticals into the county with intent to distribute."

He's also confessed to planting evidence here in order to implicate you. He says Ms. Ross did nothing more than ask him to help recover her property."

I laughed. "And you think he's telling the truth?"

"Son, the only time Louis lied to me was when he expressed remorse."

"All right, then. What about Ms. Ross?"

"I believe she could have made better decisions, but I understand her reasoning. She was frightened, and fear can cause people to behave like idiots. But she was brave enough to let Deputy Johnson know her location after those chests were uncovered."

I started to speak, but Byrd raised a hand.

"If you're questioning her motivation, son, then think about this. Her waiting to ask for help until those drugs were uncovered was risky, but it paid off. Those drugs, and those men, are no longer a threat to this county."

I leaned back and crossed my arms.

"You're the human lie detector," I said. "I just hope you're not losing your touch."

Byrd frowned and pointed to his empty glass. I grabbed the growler and filled both of our glasses to the brims.

Byrd took a long draw of beer, then reached into his coat pocket and pulled out a clear plastic evidence bag. The keys were inside.

"When I came here to question you, I believed you might still have these," Byrd said. "At the time I didn't know what these keys opened. But I did know they'd gotten one man killed."

Byrd tossed the bag on the table. I picked it up and manipulated the keys through the plastic. I found the one Floppy had used to open the cabin and showed it to Byrd.

"Why would Cordell have a key to this cabin?"

Byrd laughed. "I like to keep things simple, son. All of my rental homes are keyed exactly the same. That's right—every last one of them for the past thirty years. It's saved me a fortune in locks. I used to own this cabin. Same lock as all the others. I'm sure Junebug never swapped it out when I sold him the place."

"So Cordell's rental house key fits this lock?"

Byrd nodded. He wasn't trying to keep things simple; he was just cheap. I thought back to the root beer he'd made me pay for when we had lunch together and was reminded that the old man still owed me fifty cents in change.

Byrd and I drank in silence for a moment. I still couldn't figure out why he was sitting at my kitchen table. He'd already questioned me the previous night about everything that had transpired, including Perry and Greg attempting to fake my suicide. Dale had surely backed up my story. I didn't have anything more to offer.

"So did you come up here just to try my IPA?" I asked.

Byrd dragged his eyelids up to half-mast.

"You were right thinking these keys led to a fortune," he said. "Just not the kind of fortune you imagined. I hope now you'll wake up from that dream of finding lost gold."

"*There never was no fucking gold,*" I said, quoting Dale. "Is that what you want to hear from me, Sheriff?"

Byrd nodded, grabbed the evidence bag, and shoved it back into his coat pocket. He then stood up and walked to the door.

"Wait a minute," I said. "What about Perry and my brother-in-law?"

Byrd let out a long sigh. "According to Jack, they'll be transported back down to Charleston day after tomorrow."

Jack Emory, I thought. Byrd's Charleston PD buddy and the man who'd first raised Byrd's suspicions about me.

"Who is this Emory guy, anyway?" I said. "Why did he tell you to keep an eye on me?"

Byrd crossed his arms and leaned back against the door. "The first time I met Jack was at a conference over in Charlotte. That had to be, I don't know, what, '97, '98? He was with Charleston's Central Investigation Division at the time, but do you know where's he's been working for the past three years?"

Byrd was kind enough to stay silent while my foggy brain worked it out. It took a minute, but when it finally hit me, it made perfect sense.

"Internal Affairs," I said.

Byrd snickered. "That's right. When I heard Deputy Johnson had been spending a fair amount of time with a former Charleston police officer, I called Jack to see if he knew you. Jack didn't, but he told me the grapevine down there was buzzing with rumors about that storage unit robbery. Later on, when I told Jack that you'd mentioned Internal Affairs was looking into it, well, let's just say he was mighty surprised."

"Because they weren't, right?"

Byrd snickered again. "Right. But hearing that sure sparked his interest."

I leaned back and shook my head. I'd thought my sending an email to Perry about his gray Audi was what had spooked him into coming to the cabin to shut me up. But it was the living maze of the department that had sent him into a panic. The walls he was used to climbing over or digging under had begun to move in directions he couldn't outmaneuver, and Perry needed to silence me before someone found me and started asking questions. That's why he'd kept saying "things have changed."

Byrd opened the door and then looked back at me. "Those two men will be charged for what happened here. No one's above the law in this county. You'd do well to remember that."

* * *

A couple of hours later, someone in a rollback tow truck came and picked up Perry's Audi. I watched from the deck as the driver attached a winch to the car and slowly rolled it up onto the truck's bed. The whole process took less than three minutes. I was glad I'd paid cash for the Mercedes. If I'd been making payments on it, someone would have been tasked with hauling it away on a similar truck in a couple of months when my money ran dry.

When the truck was gone, I opened the laptop and sent an email to Laura. I told her Greg and Perry had been arrested and why. I told her the truth about everything and that I would call her tomorrow at noon. I asked that she please answer the call.

After that I pulled up Google and searched for attorneys in Charleston, South Carolina. A senior detective with the Charleston PD had shot me in the leg. That had to be worth something.

Epilogue

The next day was Thanksgiving. I crawled out of bed around ten, drank half a beer, and swallowed half a pill. I showered, shaved, then checked the laptop. The same spam emails and no new Facebook friends. Status quo.

* * *

At noon I pulled into El Bacaratos. I dialed Laura's number, and she picked up on the first ring. When I heard her voice, a weight fell from my shoulders. We talked for almost an hour, and by the time I hung up, I felt things were going to be okay. She'd forgiven me, and that was all I needed.

Laura was going to have a tough time. There was no way she would stay with Greg. My sister was forgiving, but she wasn't a fool. She'd been right to distrust Greg enough to suspect he was having an affair. In a way he was. He had betrayed my sister the same way Perry had betrayed me.

Laura would be alone, but she was strong; she could handle herself. For a moment I thought about packing up my stuff and heading to Folly Beach to offer my support. But she didn't need me coming back down there with all my baggage. She would be better off without someone to babysit. Plus, I had a new babysitter. And he liked beer as much as I did.

* * *

When I turned into Junebug's driveway, I pulled over next to the Johnson family graveyard. I got out of the car and stepped over the low fence that bordered the small plot of land. There were six tombstones in all. Three were so old and worn that the engravings had become practically indecipherable. I rubbed my hand over one and traced *1923* with my finger. The newest-looking tombstone belonged to Dale's mother. It was a rectangle of gray granite with a spray of red plastic carnations jutting out from its base. The etching read:

> *Margaret Ann Johnson*
> *Devoted Wife and Mother*
> *1940–1995*

It seemed strange to me for a graveyard to be sitting on private property. I wondered how Dale felt about having to drive by his mother's final resting place every day. I wondered if he even noticed it anymore or if the graveyard was just a benign patch of rocks that his conscious mind chose to ignore each time he passed by.

I'd visited my parents' burial site only once. Unlike Dale's mother, my parents were buried in a cemetery as big as a golf course. I remembered driving through the gates and getting lost along the ribbons of asphalt that snaked around hundreds of tombstones and mausoleums. When I finally found my parents' graves, I spent five minutes silently apologizing for all the grief I'd given them. I told them I was sorry for missing their funeral and promised to try to be a better man.

I haven't fulfilled that promise, but at least I haven't forgotten it. I guess there's something to be said for that.

I stepped away from Dale's mother's tombstone and over to a rounded slab of cement worn down by the elements. Its face was unmarked, and I rubbed the smooth top of the stone while wondering who was buried beneath its weight.

"Get outa there!"

I turned around to see Junebug standing by my vehicle, a single-barrel shotgun parked across his shoulder.

"Hey, Junebug. Sorry. I didn't mean any disrespect."

Junebug jerked his head.

"Get on up to the house. We's about to eat."

* * *

"I don't understand people who don't deep fry their turkey," Dale said.

We were sitting at a rickety wooden table in Junebug's kitchen. Dale had more food on his plate than anyone should eat in a single sitting. Despite that, I knew he would be having seconds.

I was drinking a cold pale ale. It was Dale's own recipe, and it was surprisingly good.

"Sorry about earlier, Junebug," I said. "I was just curious about the graveyard."

Junebug shrugged and stabbed at a piece of dark meat.

"What are you talking about?" Dale said.

"On my way in, I stopped at the family graveyard and looked at the tombstones."

Dale grinned. "Little freaky, ain't it?"

"Who's buried in that unmarked grave?" I asked.

Junebug didn't answer, and Dale looked over at him.

"That's Ol' Gerald, ain't it, Daddy?"

Junebug grunted and shoved a quarter pound of sweet potatoes in his mouth.

"You said you never got around to carving the stone."

Junebug grunted again.

"So that's Floppy's grandfather buried there?" I asked.

Junebug lifted his knife and pointed it at my chest. His eyes were full of fire.

"You stay outa that graveyard. Ain't got no reason to go messin' 'round in there. I see you in there again, I'll shoot ya, you hear me?"

Dale laughed. "Shit, Daddy, with that old shotgun, you couldn't hit a cow if you was standing next to it."

Junebug kept the knife pointed at my chest. "You hear what I said?"

As Junebug continued to glare at me, I felt as if someone had flicked a tuning fork in my chest, and the vibrations coursed through my entire body. A new dot had appeared and suddenly connected to a bunch of others. It formed a picture that was still a little fuzzy, but if I focused just right, I could make out a few clear outlines. I saw Junebug and Byrd as middle-aged men with shovels in their hands. They were making a pact. Maybe it was the same pact they'd made as kids.

"Don't worry, Junebug. I hear you loud and clear."

After a long moment Junebug lowered his knife and went back to his dinner. The conversation then turned from graveyards and threats to women.

"Got me a date with Daiquiri this Saturday," Dale said. "I told ya she'd come around."

"I'm not sure if I fully trust her," I said.

Dale scoffed. "It ain't her trust I'm after."

*　*　*

I didn't have any interest in staying to watch Thanksgiving Day football, so after the meal I tried to convince Dale to give me a growler of his pale ale to take home. It would have been easier to convince him to donate a kidney. I thanked Junebug and then limped out to my car. Dale followed me and told me to hold up when I reached the Mercedes.

"Here," he said as he dug around in his pants pocket.

"Don't say *here* to me while you fiddle with your dick."

Dale pulled a prescription bottle out of his pocket and tossed it to me. I looked at the label. It was my Xanax bottle.

"Did you take this from the bathroom?"

"Yeah, I saw it in there when I was drying my shirt after you puked all over it."

"Why'd you take it?"

Dale shrugged. "I don't know. I was so fuckin' pissed off with you that night, thinking you had something to do with that hippie up at Graveyard Fields. I figured maybe you was strung out on them pills, so I took 'em."

I couldn't help but laugh. "Aw, I think you care about me."

Dale took a step back. "The fuck I do. You're dumb as shit, and your taste in women sucks. You know what you need?"

"No. But I'm sure you're going to tell me."

"You need to get your ticket punched. That'd fix your anxiety. You oughta call Tanya; we could double date."

"Yeah, I'll give that some thought. And by the way, I'm not dumb as shit. Do I have to remind you I solved this mystery? I'm the one who realized Skeeter was involved in the whole thing."

Dale grunted and dug out his tin of tobacco.

"Yeah," he said. "But you sure let that skinny piece of ass pull one over on you."

"You mean Beth?"

"Fuck you," Dale said with a grin.

I had to admit Dale was right. Byrd seemed to think Diana was innocent, but I wasn't so sure. I was going to have to wait and see if the brewery suddenly became property of the bank. If not, then somewhere, somehow, Diana would have found $250,000. Maybe a loan from a rich relative? A refinancing agreement with the bank? A few more chests buried near the parkway?

"We'll never know what was really in her safe," I said.

Dale laughed. "Well, it weren't gold. Shit, I told you there was nothin' to that from the very beginning."

"So did Junebug and Byrd," I said. "Seems like anyone with any sense knows that gold is just another one of Ol' Gerald Johnson's lies."

I climbed in the Mercedes and shut the door. When Dale came over to the window, I rolled it down.

"You ever gonna write that book?" he said.

"Maybe. But first I'm going to write an email to an attorney in Charleston. I think there might be a settlement check on the other end of that."

Dale grinned. "Now you're talking. You get that, you can afford to rent my cabin for another six months."

"I might just do that."

"I'll have to go up on the rent, since it'll be summer, but I'm sure we can work something out."

I pushed the car's ignition button and plugged my phone into the stereo jack. Dale waited by the window to see what I was going to play. When "Flying High Again" started, Dale's face illuminated in a way that endeared him to me more than I'm comfortable admitting.

"That's your theme song, buddy."

"Indeed it is. See you around, big man."

"Hey, wait a minute," Dale said. "I'm still in the dark about something."

I turned the stereo down, and Dale leaned in close. "How does this fuckin' thing start without no key?"

I shook my head. "Haven't we had enough conversations about keys?"

*   *   *

I drove down the gravel driveway, then glanced in my rearview mirror and saw Dale walk back into the house. Dale was good people, I had to admit it. Most of the time I wanted to punch him in his pudgy face, but I knew that if I were ever in trouble, I could call him anytime, night or day, and he'd show up full of fire and fury. That's a good friend to have.

When I reached the Johnson family graveyard, I stopped and stared at the tombstones. I wasn't about to get out of the car for a closer look. I didn't doubt that Junebug was telling the truth when he'd said he'd shoot me if he found me there.

Like most graveyards, this one was full of things that were better off left undisturbed. No reason to go messin' around in there was what Junebug had said, and I knew he was right. Sheriff Byrd had been right too, when he said you never know what's out there waiting for you. For that matter, Floppy had been right when he said that a woman getting her nipple pierced was as stupid as a man putting a nail through his dick. Maybe Dale had been right too when he'd told me I needed to get my ticket punched. Maybe I'd call Tanya or Joanne. Or maybe not.

I'd encountered some pretty heavy wisdom since coming to Cruso. I wondered what else I'd learn if I decided to stick around for a while.

I looked again in my rearview mirror and saw Junebug standing just outside the front door of the house. He was watching me and I knew why. I turned back to the graveyard and stared at the unmarked tombstone, a smooth column of weathered cement. I didn't know if Ol' Gerald Johnson was buried under that stone or not, but I had a pretty good idea what was.

Acknowledgments

I'll start off the thanks with Sheriff Greg Christopher and the fine men and women of the Haywood County Sheriff's Office, because I don't want on their bad side. I took an enormous amount of creative license in regards to the descriptions and inner workings of the Sheriff's Office and I feel compelled to beg their forgiveness.

Many thanks to Ben Leroy for his support, guidance, and friendship. This book would not exist without him.

A big shout out to my agent Miriam Kriss. Thanks for having my back.

A grateful nod to author Sara J. Henry, whose instructive and sometimes brutal comments made me sit up straight and work harder.

A respectful tip of the hat to David Swinson, writer, source of inspiration, and super nice guy, for selflessly offering advice to a wannabe novelist who sent him a fan letter.

Much thanks to copyeditor Rachel Keith for her careful reading of the manuscript and tolerance for my attitude toward spelling and punctuation.

A double thumbs up to Melissa Rechter, Madeline Rathle, and the entire staff at Crooked Lane Books. Thanks for being a supportive home.

A hearty fist bump to Joe Nelms, writer and swell guy, whose comments on an early draft of this book helped light a fire under my ass.

A raise of the glass to the fine breweries of Haywood County North Carolina, including BearWaters in Canton and Boojum in Waynesville. Their output helped keep the gears lubricated.

Acknowledgments

Thanks also to the gracious and generous folks I met early on while trying to crack the publishing industry code, including Claire Dippel and Mitchell Waters.

And my deepest appreciation to the wonderful people of Cruso, North Carolina, a community I called home for nearly forty years and one that continues to be my favorite escape.

Others to whom I owe warm thanks are:

Blair Knobel, Jack Bacot, Robbin Phillips, Seth Jones, Don Koonce, Stephanie Burt, Misty Bost, Lindsey Creech, and Nichole Livengood.

And finally, to my wife Jess, who keeps me grounded, sane, and enamored.